Grave Music

An Inspector Bill Slider Mystery

CYNTHIA HARROD-EAGLES

SCRIBNER

New York London Toronto Sydney Tokyo Singapore

SCRIBNER
1230 Avenue of the Americas
New York, NY 10020

First Scribner Edition 1995
Published by arrangement with Little Brown & Co. (UK) Limited

SCRIBNER and design are trademarks of Simon & Schuster Inc.

Manufactured in the United States of America

1 3 5 7 9 10 8 6 4 2

Library of Congress Cataloging-in-Publication Data

Harrod-Eagles, Cynthia.
Grave music: an inspector Bill Slider mystery/Cynthia Harrod-Eagles
p. cm.
I. Title.
PR6058.A6945G73 1995
813'.914—dc20 94–39222 CIP

ISBN 0-684-80046-2
Previously titled *Dead End*

Grave Music

CHAPTER ONE

The Days of Woes and Rises

When Detective Superintendent 'Mad Ivan' Barrington of Shepherd's Bush nick told you he would make your life a misery unless you accepted a transfer out of his station, you defied him at your peril. As the fount of all paperwork he was in a position to pour out upon you an unending stream of department fertilizer.

Today, for instance, Detective Inspector Bill Slider had been trapped at his desk all morning with a dizzyingly uninteresting report on the connection between stress and absenteeism, which Barrington had given him to précis on a most-urgent basis. As a result, Slider went up so late to lunch that he got the last portion of the 'home-made' lasagne, which had set like crusted rubber in the corner of the oven dish. It was cool, but he dared not ask for it to be heated up again for fear of what it might do to his teeth. Still, the alternative was shepherd's pie, and he'd tried that once.

'Chips with it, love?'

'Yes please.' What other comfort was there in life for a man whose wife and lover had both left him? He sighed, and the canteen helper looked at him tenderly. He had the kind of ruffled, sad-puppy looks that made women want to cosset him.

'I'll give you extra chips, 'cause you had the last bit and it's a bit small.' She shovelled the chips on cosily. 'Gravy, dear?' she asked, already pouring, and then passed his plate over

1

with her thumb planted firmly in the brown bit; but by the time he got to a table the thumbprint had filled in so you could hardly tell. He didn't like gravy on chips – or on lasagne actually – but she had given him extra of that, too, out of compassion. Why did all the wrong people find him irresistible? And he still hadn't finished the report. Mournfully he folded it open beside his plate, speared the driest chip he could see, and continued reading.

Research suggests that disorders with psychosomatic components – headache, indigestion, constipation, diarrhoea, high blood pressure and ulcers – are more frequent among police officers than among citizens generally. What an attractive bunch they sounded, to be sure. He skipped down. *What constitutes stress?* the report asked him in a coy subheading. He was pretty sure it was going to tell him so he didn't answer, and in a minute it did, with an angst league-table two pages long. *Being Taken Hostage by Terrorists* came in at number one, followed by *Confronting a Person with a Gun.* No surprises there. Ah, here was a little light relief, though: *Being Caught Making a Mistake* was apparently more stressful than *Seeing Mutilated Bodies* or *Having to Deal with a Messy Car Accident.* Still, anyone regularly eating in a police canteen got used to dealing with messy accidents.

He pushed the report aside. Was this a fair punishment on a man for refusing to go away and play somewhere else? It wasn't even his fault that he had got so terminally up Barrington's nose. While investigating the chip-shop murder back in May, he had uncovered unsavoury facts about Barrington's former boss who was also, unfortunately for Slider, Barrington's lifelong hero. A man can forgive many things, but not being robbed of his dreams. There was nothing Barrington could do in the disciplinary way, since Slider had only been doing his job, so he had suggested, with all the menace at his command, that Slider should accept a promotion to Chief Inspector and move to Pinner station. Slider had known that he was asking for it when he refused, but that didn't mean he had to like it when he got it.

Of course, the promotion and transfer to Pinner would have meant a pay rise, and money was always an object; but he had never wanted to be a DCI anyway, and he didn't fancy going to an outer station, where life moved at a more leisurely pace. Why, at Pinner they regularly won the Metropolitan Police Beautiful Window-Box competition: they probably had time to read reports like this every day. He liked inner stations like Shepherd's Bush, where you were kept busy. A man needed a stable home-life to be able to cope with the opportunities for introspection left by a slower pace at work, and these days his home-life was about as stable as Michael Jackson's face.

He abandoned the report, sawed a section off the lasagne, and pulled out of his pocket a handbill given to him that morning by his bagman, Detective Sergeant Jim Atherton. It was a flyer for a concert that evening to be given in a local church, St Augustine's, Addison Gardens. A Mahler symphony with a seriously famous conductor, Sir Stefan Radek. Slider was not, like Atherton, a great classical music buff, though he liked some of the famous pieces – Tchaikovsky and Beethoven and The Planets, that sort of thing. The only bit of Mahler he'd ever heard he'd thought sounded like an MGM film-track, which was all right in a cinema but not what you'd want to sit through a whole concert of. But the real point here, the reason Atherton had told him about it at all, was that the Royal London Philharmonic – the orchestra which was doing the concert – was the one in which Joanna was a violinist.

Joanna, his lost love. Two and half years ago he had met her while he was on a case, and had – in the police jargon – gone overboard, with a resounding splash. He had been married then for nearly fourteen years and had never even considered being unfaithful before, believing that promises once made should not be broken and wives once chosen should not be forsaken. But he seemed not to be able to help himself, and for two years he had wrestled with guilt and responsibility, desperate to marry Joanna but unable to find a way to tell Irene, his wife, that he wanted to leave her. The worst of all possible worlds for all of them. At last, after a particularly humiliating evening, Joanna had broken it off with him, and had since steadfastly refused to re-attach it.

The really hideous irony was that it was just after Joanna had chucked him that Barrington had suggested, with more

3

than a hint of broken arms about it, that Slider should move to Pinner, which was just down the road from Ruislip and the marital home – 'So nice and handy for you,' Barrington had said menacingly; and Slider for the sake of peace and pension enhancement was on the brink of accepting it as a wise career move, when Irene had announced she was leaving him. He must have had a really horrible conjunction of his ruling planets for these blows all to have fallen together. And it was a sad fact that in his whole life he had only ever been involved with two women, and they had both dropped him in short succession. He'd been left so comprehensively he felt like the slice of cucumber in the garnish on a pub sandwich.

And now Joanna, the lost and longed-for, was playing in a concert just down the road.

'It would be a chance to see her,' Atherton had said beguilingly when he gave Slider the leaflet. 'A chance to talk to her.'

'But she doesn't want to talk to me,' Slider had replied. 'She said so.'

'You don't have to take her word for it. Anyway, Radek conducting Mahler is not to be missed. You know he's the world authority on Mahler?'

'What's he conducting in a church in Shepherd's Bush for, then?' Slider objected.

'I think it's for the restoration fund. He lives just down the road, in Holland Park Avenue. It's a beautiful church,' Atherton added coaxingly.

'Is it?' Slider said unhelpfully.

'And they're rehearsing there this afternoon. Two-thirty to five-thirty.'

Sitting over his cooling lasagne, Slider contemplated the scenario Atherton had been urging on him. The shift ended at four, and unless something came up Slider would be free then. He could stroll down to the church, quite casually, take a look in, wait until they finished rehearsing and then bump into Joanna accidentally on her way out. 'Oh, hello. Fancy a drink? They're just open.' But what if she refused? She had told him she didn't want to see him again, and inviting public humiliation was no way to run a life.

No, he thought, sighing. Better not. He had a lot to do,

anyway. There were two more survey reports on his desk for when he'd finished this one, and the car crime statistics to update. He gazed with digestive despair at the lasagne, which had withdrawn reproachfully, like a snubbed woman, under a cloak of hardening gravy. In any case, the jumbo dogknob 'n' beans he had consumed in the canteen for breakfast still lay sad and indigestible in a pool of grease somewhere under his ribs, and he didn't think he ought to add to his problems at this stage. He pushed his chair back and headed for the door, and almost ran into Mackay.

'Oh, there you are, guv.' Mackay's face was alight with pleasure: something wonderful must have happened. 'There's been a shooting in that big church in Addison Gardens, Saint Whatsisname's – one dead. It just came in from the emergency services. Some celeb's got taken out. Right on our ground, too! Luck, eh?'

Slider went cold with fright. 'Anyone else hurt?' he heard himself ask.

'All we've got is that there was a single shot fired, one body, and chummy got away.'

'All right. I'm on my way. Where's Atherton?'

'He's already gone, guv,' Mackay called after his disappearing back.

Atherton was waiting for him out in the yard. Svelte, elegant, creaseless of suit, wearer of silk socks and an aftershave you could only smell when you got close up, outwardly Atherton was nothing like a detective. He and Slider had worked together for a long time now, and Atherton was the nearest thing Slider had to a friend. He was an able man who dissipated his abilities and was far too dedicated to enjoying himself to get on in his career. If he hadn't been so intellectually lazy, he could have been Commissioner by now. If he hadn't been incurably honest, he could have been a top politician.

'We'll go in my car, shall we?' he said. 'It's hell to park up there.'

'Oh, you heard about it, then.'

'I heard.' He gave Slider a quick look and said nothing more until he had edged the car out into the stream of traffic.

5

It wasn't too bad at this time of day – not much of a challenge to a man who loved driving. Not that you could do much real driving in a Ford anyway. He'd really like an Aston Martin, but apart from the price there was the parking problem. In London there was no point in driving anything you would mind getting nicked.

Slider had not spoken, and Atherton glanced sideways at him and had little difficulty in guessing his thoughts. There was not much he didn't know about his guv'nor's home-life, and what he knew he'd never celebrated. That Slider had been married to the wrong woman for sixteen years was bad enough: Irene had no sense of humour and thought that food was something you had to have to stay alive, a combination in Atherton's eyes so unfortunate as to be bizarre. Add to that the fact that the marital home was on an estate in Ruislip, and Atherton had thought things could not get worse for his boss; but getting worse is what things notoriously specialise in. The situation at the moment was, in technical language, a right bugger.

'How are things in the green belt these days?' he asked sympathetically.

Slider didn't look at him. 'It's life, Jim, but not as we know it.'

'It was rotten luck,' Atherton said. 'Ironies of fate, and all that.'

Ironies indeed, Slider thought, running on a now-familiar track. He wouldn't have minded so much if Irene had run off with an Italian waiter or a hunky young milkman, but she had left him for her bridge partner, who was the most boring man who had ever lived. Ernie Newman had the dynamic personality of a man slipping in and out of coma: he had once been a member of Northwood Golf Club but had found the place too swinging for him.

But Irene liked him: he was retired on an enormous company pension and he moved amidst the Volvo set she so admired.

'He's always there. He can spend time with me,' Irene had said; as succinct a commentary on the loneliness of a copper's wife as Slider had ever heard. And when he had protested about Ernie's dullness: 'I've had enough of excitement,' she

6

had said. 'I want a man who thinks *I'm* exciting.' Even in their courting days Slider had never thought Irene exciting. She had always been neat, proper, unimaginative and conventional; but he had to admit that next to Ernie she was Catherine the Great.

She had taken the two children and left Slider in occupation of the house, the ranch-style, modern executive albatross which he had always hated with the pungency of a man who loved architecture forced to live with picture windows and an open-plan staircase. He had only bought it because it was the kind of thing she liked, and she, after all, would have to spend more time in it than him. That was irony for you!

Ernie Newman, a widower, had a five-bedroom detached house in Chalfont, so there was plenty of room for Irene and the children. She had always wanted to live somewhere like Chalfont. And Ernie was going to pay for Matthew and Kate to go to private school, which was something Irene had long hankered after. Ernie had never had any children of his own – Mavis couldn't, apparently – so he was looking forward to being a father-by-proxy, Irene said. All Slider's masculine instincts had got up on their hind legs at that point, but the concealed knowledge of his own guilt had made it impossible for him to attack. Irene had never found out about Joanna.

And Joanna wouldn't have him back, despite the fact that he was now free. Irony number two. He had more irony than a man with a steel plate in his head. The events of this summer had left him utterly at a loss. What on earth was he supposed to do with the rest of his life? Even work was not enough to fill the void. His sanguine temperament had previously found satisfaction even in the routine plod which made up so much of the job; but burglaries, TDAs, possession and the rest of the malarky had no power now to rouse him from his puzzled misery. He knew as a Christian he ought not to rejoice in murder, but there was nothing like a big case for 'taking you out of yourself', as his mother used to say.

'So how did you know they would be rehearsing this afternoon?' he asked as they rounded the end of Shepherd's Bush Green.

'Joanna told me, of course.'

'Oh.'

Slider resisted the urge to ask where and why Atherton had been talking to Joanna. He had no rights over either of them, and certainly had no right to feel bugged that, having given him the chuck, she continued the friendship with Atherton which only existed because she had been Slider's lover. He turned his mind resolutely away from his own problems.

'I suppose it is Sir Stefan Radek who's been shot? Mackay just said "some big celeb".'

'That's all I heard too. There isn't a soloist, so presumably it's Radek,' Atherton said.

Radek was one of the few serious musicians who had crossed over into general, man-in-the-street fame. He'd even been on tv, Slider remembered. He'd had that series last year, *Classics for Idiots* or whatever it was called, explaining the difference between a concerto and a double-bass with the help of computer graphics and a popular comedian to make it all user-friendly. And now somebody had shot him. That'd teach him to go slumming. All Slider knew about Radek came from a cheery little spoonerism Joanna had told him one night after a concert. 'What's the difference between Radek and Radox? Radox bucks up the feet.' He remembered, too, after another concert when she had been seething about the conductor's iniquities (not Radek, though, someone else), she'd said that if he were found murdered that night there'd be eighty-odd suspects in the orchestra alone. 'Half of us would put our hands up out of sheer gratitude.' She'd been joking, of course; but it made you think. Somebody evidently thought the only good conductor was a dead one, and was prepared to do something about it as well.

St Augustine's was an incongruously big church for the streets it found itself in, hinting at larger, wealthier, or at least more devout congregations in the past. It was nineteenth-century Byzantine, built of soot-smudged pale-red brick with white stone coping, like a dish of slightly burned brawn piped with mashed potato. Inside it was a miniature Westminster Cathedral, cavernous and echoing, with lofty arches lost in shadow, pierced-work lamps, gilded wall and ceiling paintings, windows stained in deep, jewel shades of red and blue and green, and dark-eyed, beardless El Greco saints with narrow hands and melancholy mouths staring from every corner. There were high, wrought-iron gates across the choir, and the orchestra had been set up in the space below them on a low platform. Chairs and music stands and the timps were all that was to be seen. The players themselves had been ushered away somewhere – presumably to whatever place had been set aside for them as dressing-rooms. Slider hoped, anyway, that they had not all disappeared. Like tea, statements were best taken freshly brewed.

He and Atherton walked down the central aisle towards the scene, which was lit by overhead spots so that it stood out from the cave of comparative darkness around, like a gruesome reverse Nativity. The body was sprawled face down on the small podium between the lectern, on which the score lay open, and the long-legged conductor's chair. He had fallen quite neatly without knocking either over, which suggested to Slider that the bullet had not struck him with great force: he had crumpled rather than reeled or been flung off his feet. And in the place of ox and ass there were two people keeping guard over the body: one Slider recognised as the orchestra's fixer, Tony Whittam; the other was a dapper, plumpish, bald man who was kneeling on the floor at the head of the corpse and weeping. Every now and then he wiped the tears from his face unselfconsciously with a large handkerchief held in his left hand; in his right he held the conductor's baton by the point, so that the bulbous end rested on the floor. It looked like the ceremonial reversing of a sword.

As soon as he saw Slider, Tony Whittam stepped towards him with a cry of relief. 'Am I glad to see a friendly face! Are you the official presence?'

'Yes,' said Slider. 'This is on my ground.'

'Well, that's a piece of luck,' Whittam said. His usually genial face was drawn into uncharacteristic lines of shock and anxiety. He was a well-fed, dapper man of fifty-two going on thirty-five, in a light biscuit suit and a tie that would have tried the credibility of a twenty-year old. The orchestra's personnel-manager-cum-agony-aunt was much given to gold jewellery, sported a deeply suspect suntan and an artificially white smile, and altogether had the air of being likely to break

9

out into a flower in the buttonhole at the slightest provocation. He looked like a spiv, but was in fact superb at his job, efficient as a machine and genuinely warm-hearted. Many a time Slider had seen him in the middle of a crowd of musicians, all clutching their diaries, all hoping to get off one date or on another; and he had always managed to spare Slider a glance and a friendly nod while coping patiently with the conflicting demands of, say, Mahler Five and the personal lives of a hundred-odd freelance and therefore temperamental artistes. Perhaps it was unkind mentally to have cast him as an ass.

'Who's this bloke?' Slider asked in an undertone with a gesture of the head towards the ox.

'It's Radek's dresser. He's a bit upset.'

Understatement of the year. 'Dresser?'

'That's what he calls himself. Sort of like his valet, personal servant, whatever. Been with him years. Everyone knows him.' He was, Slider realised, justifying the man's presence.

'Name?'

'Keaton. Arthur Keaton, but everyone calls him Buster.'

'Okay. And where's everybody else?'

'Down in the crypt – that's where the dressing-rooms are, and a sort of band room for coffee and warming-up. I thought it best to keep everyone together until someone came,' he said anxiously. 'Des is with 'em, keeping 'em quiet.' That was Des Riley, orchestral attendant, who set up the platform and loaded and unloaded the instruments – a dark, ripely handsome man dedicated to body-building and fornication. Since orchestral attendants were traditionally known as 'humpers', these would seem to be the two essential qualifications.

'You did just right,' Slider said reassuringly. 'Is everybody all right?'

'Oh yes – I mean they're shocked, as you'd expect, but nobody's hurt.' He nodded significantly, to convey to Slider that by everybody he understood him to mean Joanna.

'Who else was here apart from the musicians?'

'Well, there was Bill Fordham's wife and kid – first horn – they'd come to watch; and Martin Cutts's latest bird, of course; and the verger, he was mucking about back there with

10

some keys,' he gestured with his head towards the back of the church. 'And Georgina, my assistant, but she was through in the vestry making a phone call. They're all down there in the band room. Radek's agent was here earlier, but she'd gone before it happened. And Spaz – he'd already left as well. He's taken the van away – there's nowhere to park it here.' That was Des Riley's assistant, Garry Sparrow, usually known as Gaz the Spaz, a witticism none too subtle for him.

'All right. You've done very well,' Slider said, and crouched to take a look at the body. Radek had been lean and upright, one of those wiry old men who go on for ever and never look much different once they've passed fifty. Slider, musical tyro though he was, recognised him, as he supposed about seventy-five per cent of people would, whether they were music-lovers or not, now that he'd been on the telly. For Radek was not only hugely famous, but physically distinctive. He was very tall, gaunt, and had a great beak of a nose and bushy white eyebrows over heavy-lidded eyes, so that he looked like a half-pissed bird of prey. His shock of over-long white hair was brushed straight back like a lion's mane, but once he got going, it flew about as if it had a life of its own. It was his hallmark; and his photograph – invariably moodily-lit and against a dark background – loured, snarled and brooded famously on a million record-covers, white mane and white hands spiked against the blackness, the archetypal image of the super-maestro.

Today he was dressed in civvies of course – fawn slacks, with a black roll-neck sweater tucked into them, leather moccasins and, my God, pale yellow socks.

'He doesn't look as impressive as he does in white tie and tails,' Slider murmured to Atherton.

'Nobody looks their best dead,' Atherton reminded him.

There was no doubt he was dead, at any rate, Slider thought. Radek's face was pale grey, with a touch of blue about nose and lips, and the skin looked unpleasantly moist, like sweating cheese. His eyes were open and fixed, staring as no eyes ever stared in life, and his lips were drawn back from old-man's long yellow teeth as though he were baring them in defiance. There was a bitter smell of sweat about him, a whiff of aftershave, and underneath that a faint, unclean smell,

11

which Slider associated with mortality. Radek was lying more or less in the recovery position, one leg slightly drawn up, and both his hands were clenched – the right lying beside his head, the other, caught under him, seemingly locked onto the cloth of his roll-neck.

The entry wound was in the right lower side at the back, just above the belt of his slacks; quite a neat hole, surrounded by a blood stain. Slider examined the podium and slipped his fingers in underneath the body, but there was no blood and seemingly no hole on the other side.

'No exit wound,' he said.

'Still inside?' Atherton said.

'Presumably. He must have been hit at extreme range.'

'Or else it was deflected.'

Slider grunted agreement, and stood up, turning to Whittam. 'All right – you saw what happened?'

'Well, yes,' Whittam said unwillingly, as though it might incriminate him. 'I was standing at the side, over there, making sure everyone was in place, just waiting for Radek to start. Once they were off, I was going to join Georgina in the vestry. I'd got a lot to do, and it was a late kick-off already.'

'Why was that?' Atherton put in. 'I'd heard Radek was a stickler for punctuality.'

'He is. Woe betide the musician who's late. He won't step on the platform if anyone's missing.'

'But he's not punctual himself?' Slider asked.

'Oh he is usually. But he was in a rotten mood today. He'd had me up and down to the dressing-room half a dozen times, complaining about everything, and Des couldn't get away. He treats him like a personal servant, you know, despite –' He gestured with his head towards Keaton, who was still kneeling beside his dead master like Greyfriar's Bobby. 'Then when he finally deigned to come upstairs he stood over there by the vestry telling me the arrangements he wanted for tonight, as if we hadn't gone over them ten times already. Bloody temperamental celebrities! I tell you, dear old Norman Del Mar was never like that.'

'All right. Go on,' Slider urged. He wanted to get the general picture before the rest of the team arrived and the scene fragmented.

'Well, he got up on the podium and lifted his stick, and everyone got ready, and he just sort of stood there a minute – working himself up to start, I suppose. And then there was this bang – like a big heavy door slamming. It made my heart sink: I thought it was the verger frigging around up the back, and there's nothing a conductor hates more than someone making a noise at a moment like that. Breaks his artistic concentration, you see. I expected him to turn round and bawl me out for it, but he just crumpled up and fell. And then Martin Cutts's bird screamed, and old Buster came running past me shrieking like a hen, and it was only then I sort of put two and two together and realised he'd been shot. I ran over, but it was obvious he was dead.'

'Did you see who did it?'

'No, that was the trouble, you see – everyone was looking at Radek. By the time I even thought to look round the bloke had gone, whoever he was, and it was the same for all of us. But the verger was up the back, as I said. I think he may have seen him.'

'Doctor's just arriving, guv,' Atherton murmured, looking over his shoulder towards the door. 'And it looks like the photographer behind him.'

Slider glanced back. 'All right,' he said. 'We've got about a hundred people downstairs to interview. We're going to need the cavalry. Call home and get everyone here who can read and write.'

'And McLaren as well, sir?'

'Get on with it. And when you've done that, see if Niobe here's fit to speak yet.' He turned to Whittam. 'Can you take him somewhere and find him a cup of tea or something? The doctor will want to get to the body.'

Whittam jumped eagerly at the chance to be useful. 'Yes, of course. I'll take him in the vestry. It's nice and quiet there.'

'How do I get downstairs?' Slider asked.

'Over there, that door,' he pointed to the opposite side from the vestry. 'You can't go wrong, it doesn't go anywhere else.'

The door led onto a dank corridor which ran the length of the church. It was lined with an assortment of stacking chairs, elderly cupboards, and cardboard boxes full of mildewed

13

bunting, torn crêpe paper decorations, remnants of junior nativity play costumes, and other bits of typical church-hall junk. Looking right, he saw at the far end a door onto the street, and beside it another door leading back into the body of the church; turning his head to the left he saw stone steps leading down, and a whiff of cigarette smoke and a murmur of voices told him he was facing the right way. At the bottom was another corridor, and immediately to his left the doorway into a large room furnished with sundry chairs, trestle tables, mirrors, and a ballet barre across one end which was largely obscured by coats. A tea urn and trays of cups and saucers filled one table, and the orchestra was hanging around, making itself as comfortable as it could in the manner of people accustomed to being kept hanging around in various dismal locations all round the world. They were chatting, dozing, smoking, reading and, in the furthest corner where the trombone section lurked, playing cards on somebody's upturned instrument case. Joanna called it the airport terminal syndrome, with the emphasis on the terminal.

Joanna was sitting on the massive old-fashioned radiator right next to the door, her legs dangling, her hands knotted loosely between her knees, her head resting against the wall, her eyes closed. She seemed very pale, and the lines around her eyes and mouth looked more pronounced than he remembered. He wondered how close she had been to the podium, how shocked she had been. He was so glad to see her it took him a moment or two to find his voice.

'You shouldn't sit on radiators,' he said quietly. 'You'll get chilblains.'

Her eyes flew open. She stared at him almost blankly, and then, to his relief, there was a softening of her expression which, whatever it betokened, was on the side of pleasure rather than dismay.

'Well,' she said, 'if it isn't the mild-mannered Bill Slider.'

14

CHAPTER TWO

The Dog it was That Died

'You're looking rather pale,' Slider said.

'I've just seen someone killed,' she said. 'You think with television news reports – Bosnia, Northern Ireland and everything – that you've seen it all. But it's different in real life. One moment there's a real human being standing there, just a couple of feet away from you, and the next –' She shook her head. 'How do you ever get used to it?'

'We don't,' he answered, divining that she meant the question personally. 'If we stopped minding, we'd stop being effective. The flippant remarks are meant to fool us, you know, not you.'

'Poor Bill,' she said.

He wished he could take that as encouragement; but he had work to do. 'How close were you to the podium?'

'I was sitting at number four. Close enough, thank you.'

'You've been promoted,' he discovered with delight. The front four in the first violin section were permanent positions, while the rest of the section moved up and down on a rota system so as to share the work evenly. 'What does that make you?'

'Deputy principal,' she said shortly.

'That's wonderful. Why didn't you –?' But of course he knew why she hadn't told him. He altered course hastily. 'Well, I'm just thankful you weren't hurt. There was only one shot, is that right?'

She raised an enquiring eyebrow. 'Am I being a witness now?'

'You are a witness, like it or not. But you can be especially helpful to us – to me – because you know what we need. You know –'

'My methods, Watson,' she finished for him. 'All right, what do you want to know?'

'Start with your version of the incident.'

'Well, Radek came out from the vestry –'

'I thought he had a dressing-room down here?'

'He did, but there's another set of stairs down from the vestry. The conductor, and soloists if any, go up and down that way to avoid having to rub shoulders with the great unwashed, namely us. I've done concerts here before, you see. I know all about it.'

He smiled because she had anticipated his question. 'You see?' he said elliptically.

'I've already accepted the premise,' she said, giving him a firm look. 'You're not bright enough to put a scam by me.'

'Thanks. I understand Radek was late starting.'

'A bit.'

'Was that unusual?'

She shrugged. 'He's usually punctual, but they're a law to themselves, you know, conductors. It's our job to wait for them, not vice versa. It was only five minutes anyway. It was two thirty-five by my watch when he stepped onto the platform.'

'Did he seem as usual when he came on?'

She made an equivocal face. 'I didn't notice anything specific, but I wasn't particularly looking. He was always an ugly, bad-tempered old bastard, not the sort you gaze at rapturously. He seemed to be in a bad mood, but that was nothing unusual.'

'All right, go on.'

'Well, he crossed the platform, got up on the podium, opened the score, picked up his stick –' He could see her watching it replay in her mind.

'From where?'

'He'd put it down on the lectern while he opened the score. Oh, and he took out his handkerchief and wiped the sweat off his face. He always sweated a lot. It could be pretty nasty sitting up front. He'd flick his head to get his hair out of his eyes, and drops of sweat would fly.'

'Yuck.'

'Exactly. Anyway, he wiped his face, put his hanky away, picked up his stick and said, "Mahler".'

'Telling you which piece you were going to rehearse?'

'Of course. So he waited for everyone to find their place and get their instruments up. And then –' She hesitated.

'Go on. However it seemed to you.'

'Well, he stopped with his stick up, just staring at nothing, frowning. He might have been communing with his muse, I suppose, assuming the nasty old thing had one, but it didn't quite look like that. He looked more as if he'd remembered something bad, like he'd left the gas on or he ought to have paid his VAT yesterday or something. He put his hand up and pulled his roll-neck – like this – as if he was loosening it, like a nervous gesture.' She looked at Slider. 'I don't want to make too much of it, because it all happened so quickly, but it was something I noticed.'

'You think he was expecting something to happen?'

'God, I don't know. He looked as though he had something on his mind, that's all I can say.'

'All right. Go on.'

'Well, then everything seemed to happen at once. There was a terrific bang. I think someone out in the church shouted "No!" and someone else screamed. Radek dropped his stick and crumpled up, fell forward. It all happened in an instant. He was on the floor while the echoes were still bumping about in the roof.'

'Did you know it was a gunshot?'

'Oh yes. I don't know why, because I've never heard a gun fired in real life, but I knew it was a gun. Of course I looked that way, and I saw a man in a light brown coat and a hat with a big brim up at the back by the main door. It was too far away for me to see any detail, but he was just standing there, staring. Then he turned and ran for it. There's a small door within the large one, and he went out through that and was gone. It was all over in a second.'

'Did you see what he did with the gun?'

She frowned. 'I didn't see the gun. I think – I'm not sure – he had his hand in his pocket.'

'Did you recognise him?'

She shook her head. 'Too far away, and too dark. We were under the lights, you see. And he had a hat on.'

'So you don't even really know that it was a man?'

She thought about that. 'I assumed it was. I suppose it might have been a woman, but if it was, it was a woman hoping to pass for a man. It wasn't a female shape.'

'Okay, what happened next?'

'Old Buster came rushing over from the vestry side, screaming, almost before Radek hit the floor. Tony Whittam was behind him, and they crouched over the body, and I think Tony said "He's dead", or something like that. Des Riley came halfway, and then went back into the vestry, presumably to call the emergency services.'

'How did everyone else react?'

'Everyone was very quiet, apart from Martin Cutts's bird, who was sobbing as if it had happened to her. It's funny, in films everyone rushes about shrieking and fighting to get out, but here nobody moved or made a sound. I suppose we were all too shocked. Then Bill Fordham jumped up and went running out to his wife and kid to make sure they were all right.' She made a wry face. 'Of course Brian Tusser – the first trombone – asked in a loud voice if it meant the concert would be cancelled, and would we still get paid, but he's just a despicable scrote. I mean, I suppose we all thought it, but he had to go and actually say it aloud.'

'I suppose that means no-one in the orchestra would have reason to kill Radek? He was a benefactor to you, really.'

'I wouldn't go that far,' she said hastily.

'Wasn't he generally liked?'

'Not by musicians. He was rude, unpleasant, arrogant, conceited, and had delusions of godhead. If he'd been a good conductor we could have forgiven him, but as it was –'

'Not a good conductor? But he was famous!'

'Not synonymous terms, I'm afraid. The critics loved him, but what do they know? On the box he was erratic and his technique was non-existent, but he'd got too famous for any of us to criticise. We had to carry him and cover up for his cock-ups; and then if we managed in spite of him to give a good performance, he got all the praise *and* got paid about a hundred times what any of us got for the same concert. So what was to like?'

'Was he really that bad?'

'Are you kidding me! You've heard me complain about conductors before.'

'Yes, but everyone complains about bosses. It's a way of getting through life. Was Radek really worse than anyone else?'

'Well, just to give you an example, we rehearsed the Mahler yesterday at Morley College, and he brought the entire second fiddle section in in the wrong place *twice*. Then he was so rude to the principal second – you know, Sue Caversham? – that he reduced her to tears, and that's not easy to do, because Sue's a tough cookie – you have to be, to be a woman and get to the front desk. And then the bastard threatened that if it went wrong again today she'd lose her job. I mean, what was she supposed to do? If she hadn't followed him in, if she'd hung back and come in at the right place, he'd have bawled her out just the same.'

'Can he do that? Get one of you sacked?'

She made a face. 'Not officially. We're all self-employed, as you know. Officially we are the orchestra and the orchestra is a self-governing body, so it's *us* who hire *him*. But in reality a man as powerful as him can do what he likes, and the management won't cross him for fear of losing his favour.'

'But if he's so terrible, why do you have him at all?'

'He's got recording contracts,' she said simply. 'It's work, you see, what we exist for. The contracts go where he goes, and if he doesn't like us, he'll take them to another orchestra. So we have to kiss his boots. *Had* to, I should say,' she remembered. 'All contracts are now cancelled, by order of the Great Agent in the Sky.'

Slider was silent a moment, absorbing all this. 'So there may have been people with reason to want to kill him?'

'Almost everyone he's ever met, I should say. Old Buster must have been the only creature on the planet that loved him.'

'Well, thank you. You've been most helpful,' he said, but it came out sounding coolly official, and it broke the mood

19

between them. He looked at her, felt awkward, and saw her feeling awkward back.

'That's all right. Just doing my duty as a citizen,' she said flippantly.

He plunged, suicidally. 'Oh Jo, can't we –?'

'Now don't start that again, please. You know my feelings. Can't we leave it at that?'

'No, we can't,' he said, a little angrily, and she looked surprised. 'It's crazy to ruin both our lives like this, when –'

'My life isn't ruined, thank you very much,' she interrupted stiffly.

'Well mine is!'

'That's not my fault.'

'I never said it was. Did I ever blame anyone but me? I do understand your position, but –'

'No, I don't think you do,' she said with feeling. 'You think I'm cutting off my nose to spite my face –'

'I *don't*!'

'–but you altered the basis of our whole relationship. Look at it from my point of view: for two years you keep me dangling in limbo, and then when you find yourself all alone with no-one to come home to at the end of the day, you can't get to me quick enough.' She looked away unhappily. 'Maybe you just want a housekeeper, and any woman would do. Someone to wash your socks.'

'I don't want you for that. How can you think it?'

'Well of course *you* don't think you do,' she said, quite kindly. 'But I don't know that our being together would make us happy. And I'm not sure I want to take a chance on which of us is right.'

She said 'I'm not sure' rather than 'I don't want to', he noticed. It was little enough to pin his hopes on, but it was all he had; and besides, with a serious case to run, now was the time for consolidation rather than trail-blazing.

'All right,' he said meekly, 'but you will help me with this case, won't you? You know how helpful you can be to me, someone who knows the music scene, and knows my world; one foot in each camp so to speak –'

'If you want a native interpreter, Jim Atherton knows the music scene,' she said shortly.

20

'But I don't fancy him.'

It was probably a stupid time to risk a joke. Cancel probably: she was looking at him with narrow suspicion.

'I told you, you can't put a scam past me. I'm a witness, and I'll do my duty as a citizen, but that's all. This isn't a foot in the door, Bill. It's over between you and me.'

'Between you and me, maybe, but not between me and you,' he said painfully.

'I'm sorry,' she said, and she looked as if she meant just that. 'For it to work, I would have to have come first with you, and I didn't. You can't change that.'

The troops had arrived and were disposed about the band-room taking statements, which would later all have to be read and evaluated. Talk about making work for yourself, Atherton thought, coming back up to the vestry; but at least most of them would be short. 'I didn't see anything, can I go now?' The police doctor who had come to pronounce Radek's life extinct also pronounced Keaton unfit for further questioning, gave him a tranquilliser, and recommended he be sent home. Atherton could see for himself that the old boy was past anything at the moment: he sat pale and trembling like a vanilla blancmange, and any time he tried to speak it spilled over into helpless tears again.

'We'll get you a taxi to take you home,' Atherton said. 'Is there someone we can contact for you, who can come and be with you?'

That brought more tears. Keaton, it seemed, had lived alone with Radek, doing everything for him, and going home to the empty house was going to be painful.

'Is there somewhere else you'd prefer to go?'

But no, when he managed to get the words out, Keaton made it plain he wanted to go home. 'I just want to be alone. You're very kind, but I need to be alone.'

Atherton let it go, and Whittam went to look for a taxi. 'We'll have to come and see you, and ask you some questions,' Atherton said. Keaton raised sodden eyes. 'You must be the person who knew Sir Stefan best. You can help us understand the situation.'

'Very well,' Keaton said wearily.

'Can you tell us who his next of kin is?'

'His daughter,' Keaton said. 'Fay Coleraine. She's his only relative. Do you want her telephone number?'

Atherton took it down. 'We'll break the news to her,' he said. 'I'm sure you won't feel like doing it.'

'Thank you,' Keaton whispered. 'You're very kind.'

'I must just ask you now, before you go – did you see the man who did it?'

'I – I caught a glimpse. I was more – more concerned – with Sir Stefan.'

'I understand. But did you recognise the man?' A shake of the head. 'Have you ever seen him before?'

'No. I told you, I only caught a glimpse of him.'

'Do you know of anyone who might have wanted to harm Sir Stefan? Had he any enemies?'

Another shake of the head. 'No. How could he have? He was a wonderful man. A great artist. The nation loved him.'

The nation was not in the frame, Atherton thought; but there was evidently no point in pursuing it now. Whittam came back in. 'We've got a cab at the door. Do you want me to come with you, Buster?'

Keaton shook his head numbly. Whittam glanced at Atherton, who shrugged minutely. It was only five minutes away, and the man had said he wanted to be alone. One had to assume that adults could decide such things for themselves.

'I'll see you into the cab, anyway,' Whittam said kindly, and put his hand under Keaton's elbow to help him to his feet. The old boy did look very doddery, but that might have been the trank taking effect.

'We'll call on you tomorrow morning, Mr Keaton, if that's all right,' Atherton said. 'Just to ask you a few questions.'

Keaton turned and fixed Atherton with a red and angry eye. 'Find him,' he said in an unexpectedly strong voice. 'Find the man who did this terrible thing.'

'We will,' Atherton said, and Keaton gave him a nod and shuffled away on Whittam's motherly arm.

Atherton went downstairs to Radek's dressing-room. Some effort had been made here to soften the ecclesiastical grimness of the basement: the bare brick walls had been painted with cream gloss, and there was crimson carpet on the floor, whose sumptuousness was only marred by the number of component pieces it was in. It must have been an extremely narrow left-over – presumably a spare bit from an aisle somewhere. There was a table against one wall, with an upright chair before it and a large mirror on the wall over it, with a strip light above. A four-hook coat rail was fixed to the wall in the corner behind the door, and a dark overcoat was hanging on it – presumably Radek's. Against the wall opposite the mirror was an ancient armchair, and a smaller table on which stood a water carafe and a tumbler. Both were empty and dry, presumably put there in readiness for the evening. On the other side of the table was a minimalist two-seater sofa, upholstered in a rather loud purple and orange velours which went with the crimson carpet like sardines and blancmange. Its apparent lack of conviction as a sofa suggested it might turn into an equally unsatisfactory bed, as though performing two functions badly were the same as performing one well. On the sofa was a large, double-depth briefcase, open, and a narrow black fibreglass briefcase, closed.

A second door opposite the first led to a small, damp-smelling bathroom which contained an open-fronted shower cubicle with a fixed head and no curtain (fat lot of use, Atherton commented inwardly), a lavatory pedestal, a hand-basin fixed to the wall with a mirror above it, a thin roller-towel hanging on wooden rollers to the side of it, and a metal waste-paper basket on the floor. Still, he thought, it was luxury compared with what the orchestra had, which was two identical rooms between eighty of them, and an extra unisex loo in the passage with a wet floor and a cistern which took eighteen minutes to refill after flushing.

The light was on in Radek's bathroom; the soap and towel had been used, and in the bin there were several used tissues, a crumpled paper bag from Boots containing the outer cardboard container from a new tube of Germoloids, a smeary wad of cotton-wool, and a used baby bud. Atherton turned hastily away and went back into the dressing-room. He examined the overcoat first: navy cashmere and wool, silk lining, Austin Reed label inside. Smart but not ostentatious.

23

In the pockets were a plastic comb, not very clean, a pair of washleather gloves, old and worn comfortable, a South Bank car park ticket dated a week ago, a handkerchief, unused, and three anonymous boiled sweets in plain wrappers, the sort that hang about in cute wicker baskets round the tills of certain restaurants.

He abandoned the coat and went to look at the two cases. The small one contained two conductor's batons in a contoured velvet interior designed to hold three. Atherton lifted out one side of the contouring, and underneath found a snapshot of a young woman on a beach holding up a very fat baby to the camera. It was obviously an old photograph: judging by the unconvincing colours and the white border round the picture he'd place it in the early seventies. There was also, curiously, a paper drinks coaster bearing in curly script the name *The Ootsy-Tootsy Club* (shouldn't that be Hotsy-Totsy? he frowned) and underneath in small letters *Ningpo Street, Kowloon*. He turned it over. On the back in melting Biro was written *Beda* and *3-671111*, presumably a telephone number. He slipped it gently into his pocket.

The briefcase contained three scores, a notebook with a lot of musical scribble – notes in both senses on interpretations – and that day's *Grauniad*; an engagements diary pretty well filled in for the year; some correspondence from the agent concerning today's concert; a quantity of laudatory cuttings (did he read them before going on, to stiffen his resolve?); a clean pair of socks; a battered metal glasses case containing a pair of spectacles with gold frames; a sponge bag containing toothbrush, toothpaste, nail brush, face-cloth, dental floss and baby buds; a packet of laxative chewing-gum, opened, one stick missing; a packet of twelve Phensic, opened, two missing; a packet of twenty-four Actal, opened, six missing; and a bottle of milk of magnesia, in its box, but half empty and very crusty about the neck, as though it were regularly swigged from rather than poured into a spoon.

'A regular little pharmacopoeia,' Atherton said aloud.

'That's one word for him,' said Des, appearing at the open door at that moment. 'Des for Desirable' he sometimes introduced himself, and he wasn't quite joking; and somehow – irritatingly – his conviction that women couldn't resist him tended to be borne out by women themselves. He was tall and well-built, with glossy, insistent black eyes, and if he wasn't handsome he at least had thick dark hair and all his own teeth, which gleamed between full lips and in contrast with his year-round, gypsy-swarthy tan. He was wearing today an almost transparent cheesecloth shirt, artfully tight across his pectorals and open far enough down to reveal a glimpse of black shiny hair with a cute little solid gold ingot on a chain nestling amongst it. His trousers were also tight enough to have made further contraception unnecessary, outlining his fierce gluteal muscles behind and leaving everything to be desired at the front.

Atherton knew him by reputation from Joanna and one or two other musicians, and had met him a few times when hanging around waiting for Joanna, with or without Slider. He was friendly enough, so secure in his own irresistibility that he didn't regard other men as rivals but as also-rans.

'Hullo,' Atherton said. 'Did you want me?'

'Come for the old bugger's goods and chattels,' Des said, gesturing towards the briefcases. 'Old Buster's howling for 'em.'

'I thought he'd gone.'

'Got as far as the cab and realised he'd left 'em behind. Didn't want anyone pawing through the Holy Grail, so Tony asked me to come and get 'em.'

'I'll have to make a note of the contents first,' Atherton said. 'It looks as though he was a bit of a hypochondriac,' he added, glancing at the pills he still held in his hands. Des after all was the person in the orchestra who probably had most to do with Radek.

'Tell me about it! The ailments were as unattractive as the man: constipation, piles, bad breath!'

'By his works shall ye know him,' Atherton suggested.

'Yeah,' Des said with enthusiasm. 'That's what made him late this afternoon, you know – one of the things.'

'What, bad breath?'

Des grinned. 'He was stuck on the loo, moaning. I came in looking for him just as he was coming out with his tube of Germoloids in his hand. Old Buster was furious. He's a real vicar's daughter, Buster – doesn't like the mention of anything rude like toilets or botties, especially in connection with His Majesty. Screamed at me like a parrot when I came in – "Can't you knock?" As if I didn't know enough about his precious lord and master! I felt like telling him a few truths!'

'What sort of truths?'

Des looked sly. 'Well, it's me he comes to for his little comforts when we're on tour – Buster wouldn't approve. I always have to have a couple of cans of lager waiting for him when he comes off – and the odd spot of something stronger.'

'Like what, for instance?' Atherton asked.

The dark eyelashes fluttered down delicately. 'Well, I can't tell you, can I, you being a copper? But let's say it's white and you can smoke it, but it ain't Rothmans.'

'That's all right,' Atherton said. 'That's nothing to do with me. What else did you get for him?'

'He asked me to get him girls sometimes. Or boys, depending where we were. I didn't much care for that,' he added, giving Atherton a full stare, 'but my job wouldn't last long if I crossed the maestros, so I just shut my mouth and do my best. Of course, he tipped me well, but money doesn't make up for being used as a pimp, does it?'

Atherton agreed sincerely, while mentally recalibrating the words. He was pretty sure that Des would do anything in the world for a sufficient wad of wonga, and never turn a hair. 'So he was bisexual, was he?'

Des shrugged. 'Not really. More like indiscriminate. He was married once, you know,' he added, 'but his wife died. There was a bit of a scandal about that at the time, I don't know if you remember, because she committed suicide. Don't blame her, though. Imagine waking up married to him.'

'You didn't like him, then?'

'He was a disgusting old man. I didn't like having to hang around him saying yes sir, no sir. Treated people like dirt. He was vindictive too. There's quite a few people in the business he's ruined. He's even tried to get rid of Spaz, the poor little bleeder, but I struck at that,' he finished proudly. 'Told him Spaz was my assistant and nobody but me was going to sack him. He took it from me, because he knew I meant what I

26

said. And he knew I knew too much about him. But I've kept Spaz out of his face ever since.'

'What did Spaz do to annoy him?' Atherton asked.

'Old Radek wanted to have a little feel of the family jewels one time, and Spaz refused him,' Des said. 'Mind you, I told Spaz it was his own fault for going in there on his own. He should have come to me. I'd told him that more than once. Let me deal with the temperamental ones, I said. I suppose he got ambitious.' He suddenly remembered his errand. 'Gawd, what am I doing standing here chatting? Buster'll be foaming at the mouth. Here, give us the bags, will you.'

'I've nearly finished,' Atherton said, writing unhurriedly. 'Go on talking. I'm sure there's lots you can tell me about the late lamented. Like who wanted to kill him, for instance.'

'Can't help you there,' Des said cheerily, 'though if I meet the bastard that did it I'll buy him a pint. Anyway, you know where to find me.'

'If you think of anything, anything at all –'

'Yeah. I'll call you,' Des said. 'I've watched the cops shows on the telly. It's always the most obvious suspect that done it, but that puts me at the head of the queue, and it wasn't me.'

Atherton stared reflectively into the space left by the humper's departure. 'The world's a stage, the light is in one's eyes,' he mused, 'the auditorium is extremely dark. The more dishonest get the larger rise; the more offensive make the greater mark. Right on, Hilaire old son. Dog bites man, no story; but it seems some or other man has bitten back.' He sighed. 'I only fear we may be going to be spoilt for choice.'

CHAPTER THREE

Do Not Go, Gentle, into that Good Knight

'How did you get on with the verger?' Slider asked, placating the inner man with a cheese salad roll. Because of the call-out he'd missed lunch entirely, one of the few things to be grateful for that day.

Atherton had a smoked salmon sandwich, but that was Atherton all over. 'He's not going to be much use on the description front. He didn't really get much of a look at the bloke, what with the dim lighting, the hat and the haste.'

'Sounds like the title of a detective novel. Are we going to get a videofit out of it?'

''Fraid not. All he can tell us is that the bloke was wearing a camel-coloured duffel coat and a brown trilby-type hat with a wide brim. He was young, say between eighteen and twenty-eight, white, and slightly built.'

'Terrific.'

'Narrows the field to, say, about thirteen million people.' Atherton stretched out his legs and crossed his ankles, reaching behind him to the window-sill where he'd put his cup. 'But the duffel coat may help. Who wears a duffel coat nowadays?'

'Bird watchers?'

'Sartorial ignoramuses. Talking of which –' He broke off as the door opened and McLaren put his head around it.

'There was a phone message for you earlier, guv.' He looked at the remains of Slider's cheese roll as automatically as a construction worker looks at a passing woman's chest. 'A Mrs Hislop-Ivory, and would you phone her back.'

'I don't know any Hislop-Ivory. What was it about?'

'She didn't say.'

'Did she leave a number?'

'Er, no.'

'Are you sure of the name?'

'I wrote it down,' he said, as though that helped.

'Oh well, I suppose she'll ring again if it's important.' Hislop-Ivory sounded like fund-raising, or a complaint about neighbours' parking. 'Is Mr Barrington in?'

'Just came in, guv,' McLaren said, glad to be helpful.

'I thought I smelled the brimstone,' Atherton murmured. When McLaren had gone, he said, 'Anyway, to resume, the verger didn't see the bloke come in. He may even have been there for some time, hovering around in the back – though I doubt it. If you were going to shoot someone, you wouldn't hang around beforehand waiting to be recognised, would you?'

'Not unless you were trying to screw up your courage,' Slider suggested. 'When did the verger first see the villain?'

'He was up in the gallery checking on the seating for the concert when he suddenly remembered the door onto the street from that passage that runs down the side of the church.'

'Yes, I know it.'

'Well, he couldn't remember if he'd locked the door, and he didn't want people to be able to wander in off the street and down to the dressing-rooms without being seen. So he came down from the gallery, crossed the church – the stairway to the gallery is on the opposite side from the passage –'

'And was the villain there, then?'

'He didn't see him. So probably no. He went through into the passage, checked the street door – which was locked, by the way – and then came back out into the body of the church. That's when he first saw chummy, standing in the centre aisle, level with the last row of chairs.'

'Doing what?'

'Just standing there with his hands in his pockets, looking

29

at the orchestra. Verger goes past him, heading back towards the gallery to finish the job he was doing; so his back's to chummy now. He's just reached the door when he hears the gunshot. Verger looks round at chummy, sees him with the gun in his hand, just standing there staring, presumably at Radek. Frozen – as is the verger – with fright. Then chummy turns and legs it, stuffing the gun into his pocket as he goes, and out through the street door. Verger hesitates, wondering if he should give chase –'

'I should bloody well think not,' Slider said. 'Chasing armed killers can seriously damage your health.'

'Civilians don't always think as clearly as us,' said Atherton. 'Anyway, he decided his duty was to the living and ran the other way.'

'So the likelihood is that the killer came in during the moments when the verger was checking the passage door. Straight in and out job.' He frowned in thought.

'So what now?' Atherton said after a moment.

'As I see it,' Slider said, 'Radek was a famous man, and shootings are rare. Possibilities are that the killer was (a) a random homicidal maniac who wandered in off the street, (b) a non-random homicidal maniac like the one who killed John Lennon, (c) someone who knew Radek and had a beef against him, and (d) someone doing it on someone else's behalf. Now given that (a) and (b) are the least likely, thank God, in this country, (c) is still the most likely, by several streets.'

'But there's still a chance it could be (d).'

'A chance. But what sort of hired killer does the job in broad daylight in front of a hundred witnesses? And shooting from that distance? Hand-guns are notoriously inaccurate. From that distance he could just as easily have missed as hit the target.'

'Yes, but (d) doesn't have to be a hired killer in the professional sense. It could be someone acting on somebody's behalf without their knowledge – taking revenge for them or something.'

'Yes, it's possible. My bet is that it will turn out to be a domestic, though.'

'I'd still like to compile a list of all the people who had a grudge against him.'

'From what we've heard, it'll be a long list.' He screwed up the bag his roll had come in and potted it into the bin. 'Let's see how Anderson has got on with the computer. Then I shall have to go and see Mr Barrington.'

As he entered the Hall of the Demon King, Slider thought Barrington was looking strained and unwell. He was walking up and down the room in his usual menacing way, but there was something jerky and irritable about the movement; and when he turned and placed his hands on the desk to lean on them and glare, Slider saw that his cuticles were ragged, as though he'd been biting them. He wondered privately if Mad Ivan were cracking up at last. All that suppressed anger must eventually rot your brain.

It was Slider who had asked to see Barrington, but Barrington got in first. 'You do realise, I hope, that this station, like every other, has to run on a budget?'

'Yes, sir.'

'And that misappropriation of publicly owned resources is theft, plain and simple. You understand that?'

'Sir,' said Slider neutrally. Wisps of steam were beginning to emerge from Barrington's ears. Slider tucked his head down in anticipation of the explosion.

Barrington straightened up to his full impressive height. 'I walked into the CID room yesterday afternoon and found one of your firm – Mackay – making a private telephone call to his wife. He finished it fairly rapidly when he saw me, of course, but after he put the receiver down I waited in vain for him to offer to pay for the call. I'm still waiting. I suppose it's too much to hope that he's made the offer to you?'

Slider was put off his stroke. 'The men sometimes have to phone home to say they're going to be late, sir –'

'It's still a private call, made on the office phone.'

'I'm sure they don't abuse the privilege –'

'Privilege! Is that what you call it?' Barrington paced, and Slider watched. This had the flavour of psychosis about it, all right, full and fruity. 'I call it dishonesty. Theft is theft, and there's no difference in kind between stealing the price of a phone call and stealing from the petty cash. It's only a matter of degree.'

'It has been the custom, sir –' Slider began hopelessly, but Barrington whipped round and glared at him.

'The custom to condone theft? I think not. It has been slackness. Indiscipline. Carelessness. Officers of the law, whatever their rank, must be scrupulous in their behaviour, at all times, and at all levels. From now on, there will be *no* private telephone calls made on office telephones.'

'Sir.'

'If they want to call their wives or girlfriends or mothers or bookmakers, they can go downstairs and use the payphone. That's what it's there for. Do you understand?'

'Sir,' Slider said again. It was all very depressing. The man had clearly lost touch with reality. Once Slider told the troops, they'd dial till they puked out of sheer defiance, and he'd have to avoid catching them at it.

'This applies to all ranks,' Barrington snapped, perhaps detecting some slight lack of enthusiasm in Slider's mien.

'I understand, sir,' said Slider. 'May I talk to you about something else now? I did want to report on the Radek murder case.'

Barrington looked blank for a moment, like a man who's been smacked on the side of the head unexpectedly by a golf-ball. Then he sat down abruptly at his desk. 'I was wondering when you'd get round to that,' he said sharply. 'Well, carry on.'

Sighing inwardly, Slider carried on.

'Forensic aren't going to be able to help us on this one,' he concluded. 'There's nothing at the scene to identify the killer amongst all the hundreds of footprints and fingerprints. We've interviewed everyone who was present, but all the accounts are pretty much the same and no-one has much to contribute. Only the verger was close enough even to get a glimpse of the face under the hat, and he didn't see enough to know the man again. But we'll assemble what description we can, and we've started the door-to-door. I think this is a case where posters may help, too – someone must have seen him in the street either before or afterwards. We could be ready to go on the television for this evening's news, the local for preference, if you think it's worth it with what little we've got.'

He paused enquiringly, but Barrington only stared at him briefly as though he hadn't been listening, and then said, 'Go on.'

Slider continued. 'In case it was a random killing we've run a computer check, but nothing's come up. Description and MO don't tally with anyone on the streets at the moment – though that doesn't rule out someone with no record, of course.'

Barrington grunted.

'The post is scheduled for tomorrow afternoon. We had a bit of trouble, Freddie Cameron being away on holiday, what with the general shortage of forensic pathologists. But at least it ought to be quite straightforward – there's no mystery about the cause of death, after all. Anyway, there's a man at Thomas's, name of James: he's young but he's got some gunshot wound experience –'

'James? Yes. I know him.' Slider made a politely enquiring noise. 'I met him once or twice when I was up in Nottingham.' The Nottingham forensic lab dealt with all the specialist firearms enquiries outside the Met area. 'He's a good man. I didn't know he was at Thomas's now.'

Slider nodded and continued. 'Regarding the gun, sir, I've got two teams combing the area at the moment – front gardens, basements, rubbish bins and so on – but in view of the fact that chummy put the piece in his pocket, I'm not hopeful. In my experience either they throw it away immediately in a panic, or they hang on to it and dump it or stash it when they get home. And we don't know where home may be, of course. But my gut feeling is that this murder will probably turn out to be a domestic, and it's just a matter of finding out who wanted him dead. I think once we talk to the family we'll latch onto something fairly quickly.'

Barrington stopped at that, and turned to look at Slider thoughtfully, pulling out his lower lip with his finger and thumb in the unattractive way of someone who doesn't realise he's doing it.

'You see this as an old-fashioned police job, do you?' he asked suddenly.

Slider was puzzled. 'Sir?'

'This case. Means, motive and opportunity. Dedicated

plodding. Is that how you see it?'

Slider hadn't a clue what he was talking about, and he didn't like it. This was so unlike Barrington-talk he had an obscure sense of trouble approaching.

'I wouldn't say that exactly, sir,' he said cautiously. 'All I mean is that I don't think it was a random killing. It might be as simple as money. From what I understand of the music world, conductors earn a lot of money. Radek must have been a very wealthy man.'

'I've had a call, you see, from Bob Moston at 6 AMIP,' Barrington said.

'I see,' said Slider non-committally. The Area Major Incident Pool handled the particularly complex or high-profile cases. It remained to be seen whether this would prove to be either, but a glory-hungry AMIP boss or a responsibility-shy local boss might insist on passing the case upwards.

'Radek was rather a media honey last year,' Barrington went on, 'though he's not particularly in the news at the moment.' He will be after today, Slider thought. 'But you just never know with the press. There's a romantic side to it – the single shot fired in a dark church – which might catch their imagination. On the other hand –'

He let it hang. On the other hand, Slider filled in for himself, it might be cast into the shade by a newly discovered Soap Star's Secret Love-Nest Shock, or MP In Baby Alligator Abuse Scandal.

'Is Mr Moston anxious to take the case, sir?' Slider asked.

Barrington looked surprised. 'Oh. No. On the contrary. Two of his SIOs are *hors de combat* at the moment.' French yet, thought Slider. 'And the other three are already involved in more than one case each. He's asking whether we're likely to be sending this case up to him, because he'd probably have to tackle it himself if we did. So I want your assessment. Can you handle it here?'

If you leave me alone, I can. Slider, the brave captain, tilted his clean-cut English chin at the stern and critical general. 'I think so, sir. At the moment there's no media pressure, and we've no reason yet to think it's going to be a sticker. I've got a good team, and Atherton's pretty *au fait* with the music scene.' You're not the only one who knows French, chum.

'You – er – have a contact in the orchestra concerned, I believe?' Barrington said with unexpected delicacy. 'Is that likely to cause a problem?'

How the hell did he know that? 'Quite the contrary, sir.' He couldn't really risk *au contraire*, not so soon. 'It should be a useful source of information. Though I must point out that there's no indication the orchestra was anything but an accidental witness.'

'Very well. We'll keep the case, then. And we'll keep off the television for the time being. I think the likelihood of gain is outweighed by the disadvantage of the publicity.' Barrington got up and began pacing again. 'And I'll handle the press on this one. I want you to have a free hand.'

Free to win fame or to fuck up. 'Thank you, sir,' Slider said.

Barrington paced, and Slider began to feel restless. He had better things to do than to wait on Mad Ivan's thought processes.

'Will that be all, sir?' he prompted, Jeeves-like.

Barrington turned and stared thoughtfully at him. 'Yes. Carry on. But don't forget what I said. Discipline, and attention to detail. You can't run a successful campaign without them.'

'Yes, sir,' Slider said dutifully, and removed himself. Definitely cracking up, he thought. And who was likely to get the rubble coming down on his head?

Radek's house, now the house of sorrow, was one of those large, handsome, four-storeyed, nineteenth-century town-houses, white stone rendering over yellow London brick, porch with white pillars, steps up over a semi-basement. It was one of a terrace set back a little from Holland Park Avenue, with a private access road divided from the common pavement by iron railings, a shrubbery and a row of ancient plane trees seventy feet high. They soared with magnificent disproportion over the little cars and the little people down in the street, like members of an alien culture so advanced it did not even need to acknowledge the host infestation.

Inside the house was gracious and beautiful in a way that you simply had to be born to money to achieve. Slider

35

appreciated, but knew he could never have emulated it, even if he won the pools. It was as many light years away from the Sunday supplement, Marilyn Cripps good-taste of Irene's wistful dreams as *that* was from the Ruislip Moderne she was fleeing so hard, poor thing. And oddly enough, Buster Keaton fitted into it, and looked not nearly so odd amidst the quiet elegance as he had in the ordinary world. He was short, stout and shiningly bald, but his features held the remnants of what must once have been a remarkable beauty, and he moved among the glowing treasures with the ease of custom.

'Yes, it is a lovely house,' Keaton said, leading Slider into the first-floor drawing-room. 'I have been very happy here. I count myself fortunate to have been able to share all this, as well as the life of a great genius.' In himself he was immaculate, clean enough to have eaten off, and even indoors and at a time like this was dressed in grey flannels with a knife-edge crease, pale blue shirt, striped tie and navy blazer.

'Was Sir Stefan a genius?' Slider asked. Keaton looked at him sharply, and he smiled disarmingly. 'I'm afraid I don't know much about music.'

Keaton examined him for bona fides, and his hackles slowly lowered. 'Yes. Yes, he was a genius. It's a word that's over-used and often misapplied, but in his case it was justified. He was a man of rare and extraordinary talent. Of course like most geniuses he was misunderstood by lesser people.'

'In what way?'

'Oh, they sometimes thought him rude and intolerant. I've heard the things people say – musicians – but they didn't understand. He lived to serve Music: he didn't have the time or energy to worry about their petty feelings.' He settled himself on the end of a chaise-longue, sitting very upright, his back unsupported, and waved Slider to a chair. 'Of course his dedication took its toll of him. Not that he counted the cost: he never spared himself. But it was killing him.'

'Killing him?'

Keaton's large pale eyes seemed to widen further. 'His heart,' he said. 'He was not a well man. I've been trying for eighteen months to persuade him to do less, to go into semi-retirement, but he couldn't live without his work. "If I go tomorrow," he'd say to me, "I want to go with my stick in my hand."' Slider began to detect a very faint residual Yorkshire accent in the otherwise cultured tones. It seemed to grow with the increasing cosiness of the prose-style. 'I warned him. I said, "You're not as young as you used to be. Take it easy," I said. "Does it matter if you do one concert a week instead of two or three?" Well, he did slow down a bit, but not as much as I wanted him to. And now –' the eyes shone with tears, 'and now he's gone, even if it was the way he wanted.' He had to pause a moment to regain control. 'He could have gone at any time, I knew that,' he went on, shaking his head slowly. 'I shouldn't be surprised.'

Slider was sitting forward, hands clasped between his knees, staring at the carpet while he listened. Now he looked up. 'But it wasn't his heart that killed him, Mr Keaton.'

For a moment Keaton looked quite blank, as though he'd been spoken to in a foreign language. Then he drew out a handkerchief and slowly and carefully wiped his eyes. 'No,' he said. 'I was forgetting. You must forgive me. This has been such a dreadful shock for me, I hardly know what I'm thinking.'

'You'd been with Sir Stefan a long time,' said Slider, to get him going again.

'More than forty years,' he answered with a touch of mournful pride. 'It was June 1953 when my wife and I joined him. Of course he wasn't *Sir* Stefan in those days, but he was already world-famous. We came as a couple. My wife was cook-housekeeper and I was chauffeur-handyman.'

'Your wife?'

A gleam of something appeared in the depths of Keaton's eyes at the interjection – perhaps annoyance or even amusement that Slider had obviously been writing him down as a lifelong bachelor.

'My wife Doreen died in 1960.' He spread his hands in a little deprecatory gesture. 'I was not always as you see me now. In my youth I was thought quite handsome. Let me show you.'

He got up and went across the room to a bureau, opened a drawer, and took out a large photograph album. As he walked back, he turned the pages over and then turned it round and presented it to Slider open, holding it for him rather than entrusting it to his grasp. Alone on the page was an eleven-by-eight black-and-white print of a smiling young woman in the rolled-over hairstyle and high-shouldered print dress of the forties. Her arm was linked through that of a young man in a double-breasted suit, his thin light hair Brylcreemed down and his pale eyes almost disappearing by some trick of the light. They were standing on grass and amid shrubs, and in the background was part of a building, the sort of vast Victorian pile which usually turned out to be either a private school or a lunatic asylum – not, Slider thought, that there was always much difference. Yes, he had been good-looking. A little on the short side, perhaps, but women didn't usually mind that too much.

'What's this place?' he asked.

'Fitzpayne School,' Keaton replied. 'Not my *alma mater*, I hasten to add. I taught there after the war.'

'Classics?' Slider suggested, following the Latin clue.

Again that faint gleam. 'Biology. Botany was my subject, but I taught zoology as well. I shouldn't have liked to be known as The Bot Master.'

Slider smiled dutifully at what was obviously a well-rehearsed joke. He could just see Keaton telling it daringly over the sherry at parents' evenings, to indulgent and faintly shocked laughter.

'What did you do during the war?'

'I was at university. Cambridge. I did research there for the Ministry of Food as part of my degree – how to make two ears of wheat grow where one grew before, that sort of thing.'

It was said defensively, as though he had been accused of dodging the call-up. Slider decided to ease one sting with another. 'You're obviously an educated man. What made you give up teaching to become a chauffeur? Didn't you find it rather a come-down to go into service?'

Keaton looked away for a moment, and Slider thought he might have gone too far; but after a moment he said, without apparent offence, 'I didn't enjoy teaching. I didn't really like children, you see, especially little boys – their minds are so undisciplined. And then I decided I wanted to write. I suppose most of us feel we have a book in us somewhere,

38

don't we?' Slider assented dishonestly. He had never had the least urge to write – real life, at least in his case, being a lot stranger than fiction.

'But of course I needed some kind of employment to keep me until I made my fortune,' Keaton went on with a little self-deprecatory smile, 'and when I saw the advertisement for a couple for Sir Stefan's house, it seemed like the answer to a prayer. Accommodation was such a problem after the war, you see, with so much of the housing stock destroyed by the Blitz and no money left in the kitty to replace it. Doreen and I looked at some rooms, but the ones we could have afforded would have given me acute spiritual pain to live in.'

Slider nodded sympathetically. 'And the advertisement related to this house, did it?'

'Yes. The Radeks had just moved in here. His wife, Lady Susan, inherited it from her father.' He smiled faintly. 'When I took the job on, I looked on it as a part-time job. I thought I'd have plenty of time to myself to write. But it was impossible to live under the same roof as Sir Stefan and stay aloof, especially after his wife died. Little by little I was drawn in, and eventually – when Doreen died as well – he became my whole life.' His eyes were distant again, and shining. 'Serving him so that he could serve Music. It was a great cause. I have been part of something noble and valuable. My life has not been wasted.'

The old-fashioned ideal of service, Slider thought, half amused, half admiring. Nowadays no-one would publicly espouse it for fear of being thought a prat, though it was still what drew most of the recruits into the police service. But the fashion was to claim to be cynical and self-serving. It was quite refreshing talking to old Buster, he thought.

'Tell me about Sir Stefan,' he asked now. 'He wasn't English, was he?'

Keaton gave Slider a sharp look. 'He was a British citizen, and proud of it,' he said almost crossly. 'He was knighted for his services to music, and they don't give knighthoods to foreigners, you know.'

'I'm sorry, I didn't mean to suggest – but his name doesn't sound English. I thought I read somewhere that he was of Czech origin.'

'Polish,' Keaton corrected shortly. 'But he took nationality in 1950. He came to England with his mother after the fall of Poland, when his father was killed. Stefan joined the infantry in 1940 and fought right through the war. He finished as a major and won the MC. He had a very good war.' Keaton was obviously immensely proud of Radek's record. Slider had the feeling he'd get shown the medals if he wasn't careful. 'He didn't have to fight, you know. They wouldn't have called him up. And he risked more than most people to do it, because he was already a brilliant musician. Imagine if he'd been blinded, or deafened, or lost a hand? For him, it was a great personal sacrifice to put his career to one side for five years.'

'And why did he?'

'Duty,' said Keaton simply. 'He felt that music couldn't exist in the same world with the Nazis. To give himself to music would be pointless if they were not destroyed.'

A truly noble, selfless man, Slider thought. Can this be the same Radek I've been hearing about, or is it just a case of power corrupting absolutely?

'Did he have any family? His wife is dead, I think you said?'

'Lady Susan died in 1959. It was tragic – they were devoted, you know. He never married again. There was just one child, Fenella – but she's always called Fay. She was born in 1950. She married Alec Coleraine, the solicitor, and they've just the one son, Marcus.'

'How did Sir Stefan get on with them? Were they close?'

Keaton pursed his lips. 'Stefan adored Fay, but she was always a headstrong girl, and they often quarrelled. He didn't want her to marry Alec Coleraine – didn't think he was good enough for her – which he wasn't in my opinion. But she waited until she was twenty-one and then told her father he couldn't stop her any more. Well, Stefan put a brave face on it, and they were always very loving when they met without Alec, but if Alec was around there was friction.' He paused as though hearing himself, and added, 'It was nothing serious, though, just family bickerings.'

'It happens in the best of families,' Slider said reassuringly.

Keaton went on confidentially. 'Stefan didn't like the way they were bringing up Marcus. Between them they spoiled him, gave him everything he wanted, and when Sir Stefan tried to instil a bit of discipline in the boy, they'd take his side. So of course, he always knew he could appeal to his mother and father against his grandfather, and there's nothing spoils a child quicker. Sir Stefan did his best; he wanted Marcus to come and stay with us much more often, but Alec wouldn't let him. I'm afraid,' he added, as though forced to reveal a deeply unpalatable truth, 'that Alec Coleraine doesn't regard music as a proper thing to spend one's life on. Marcus could have been a talented soloist, but his father thought it was prissy to play the violin. He wanted him to go into a profession and make lots of money – as if that was the test of manhood, how many zeros you have in your bank balance. Well, he's only got himself to blame if the boy's turning out wild.' He sighed. 'But it all added to the strain on Stefan. It all helped wear him out.'

'Has there been any specific cause of quarrel between them recently?' Slider asked.

Keaton opened his eyes wide. 'Good lord no! This is just ordinary family tensions I'm talking about. I hope you aren't suggesting that Alec Coleraine would ever dream of –?' The tears came again quite suddenly. 'Oh dear, I'm sorry. Just for a minute I'd forgotten. I just can't believe he's – the thought of *anyone* doing such a thing is so very –'

He disappeared into his handkerchief.

'This is all so distressing for you,' Slider said kindly after a moment. 'Can I make you a cup of tea or something? If you just tell me where the kitchen is –?'

'Oh, no, no thank you,' Keaton said through the muffling folds. In a moment he re-emerged, blew his nose and straightened his shoulders and his tie, with his generation's desire always to keep up appearance. 'No, I'll do it. I should have offered you something, I'm sorry. Will you have some tea now? Or would you like something stronger?'

Slider thought it would give the old man time and privacy to compose himself, so he said, 'Thank you, tea would be very nice. Are you sure I can't make it for you?'

'No, no, that would never do. Besides, I know where everything is. I shan't be long.'

He went out, and Slider stood up and walked across to look

out of the window. Here at the back of the house was a handsome, high-walled garden with several magnificent trees, and a stretch of lawn which curved back and forth round borders and archipelagos of herbaceous plants and shrubs. From ground level, he thought, it would present an artfully simple appearance of intriguing vistas and inviting walks. He could see that the planting had been done to present blocks of sympathetic colour in the way that was fashionable nowadays: no cottage-garden riot of oranges, purples and yellows, no eye-bashing cheerfulness of vermilion muddled up with magenta. Just below him, for instance, was a long bed planted with nothing but blue flowers set amongst silvery foliage: at the back tall spires of delphinium, rocket and Mexican lupins were having their second flowering; in front of them pale flax, deep-blue cornflowers and feathery love-in-a-mist; and to the front of the bed the lower-growing blue salvia, cherry pie, cranesbill, and an edging of clumps of campanula. It was exquisite and restful, the outdoor equivalent of the cool, elegant drawing-room he was standing in.

That was the kind of gardening that he'd always wanted the time and space to do, and never had. It was the frustrated architect in him, he supposed. When he was younger, when he'd had time to spare, he'd enjoyed going to visit great houses and walking round their gardens, gathering ideas. It had bored the children rigid, though Irene had liked looking round the houses, as long as they were fully furnished and no older than eighteenth century. But she had no interest in gardening – or anything to do with the outdoors, really. She, having been born there, saw no romance in the countryside: she regarded it with suspicion and dislike as a source of mud, creepy-crawlies and rude animals. To her the modern world was the apogee of civilisation, for there was no need for a person ever to step out of doors (except from building to car and car to building again) or to encounter the inconveniently dirty habits of old mother Gaia. A centrally-heated, double-glazed conservatory was as near to God in a garden as she wanted to get.

Well, he thought, now she'd gone and the garden was his to do again. Perhaps a resuscitation of his interest in gardening would help to fill all the lonely hours ahead of him. It looked as though it would have to do it for Buster, who seemed to have nothing else.

A sound made Slider turn. He saw Keaton coming in with a large tray, and hastened over in case he needed a table cleared. But Keaton anticipated the move and said, 'I can manage quite well, thank you. I'm used to this.'

He had tidied away the evidence of his tears, but he looked frightfully old and worn – pale in cheek and blue-shadowed around the eyes. I wouldn't be surprised, Slider thought, if the old boy didn't last much longer. It was often the way when people lived closely together for a long time, that one could not outlive the other.

'I'm sorry to have to put you through this,' Slider said. 'Just a few more questions, and then I'll leave you in peace.'

'You must do your job,' Keaton said, sorting out the tray. 'We all have to do our duty. How do you like your tea?'

When they were both settled with their cups, Slider said, 'I'd like you to tell me, if you would, about Sir Stefan's friends. Who was there who was close to him?'

Keaton shook his head almost reprovingly. 'You've got the wrong idea. I told you he was dedicated to his work; it took up all his time and his spiritual energy. There was nothing left over for anything else. Friends, socialising and such, would have been a useless drain on him. He didn't have time to go to *parties*, you know.' He spoke the word witheringly. 'It was all he could do to keep up with his daughter and her family.'

'But he couldn't spend every moment of every day working?'

'Indeed he could,' Keaton said. 'You have no idea the amount of preparation that has to go into giving a concert. Studying the music, reading, learning the score, communing with his spirit, preparing himself to give *of* himself so that the great work of a man long dead might come to life again. Even the time he was forced to spend giving interviews, having his photograph taken, making speeches, attending banquets – all that sort of thing – he deeply begrudged.' He looked at Slider sternly. 'It's not just a matter of standing up and wiggling a stick, you know. That's the trouble with the world today – everything is slipshod, everything is geared to what will just

43

do. It's not "how good can I make it", it's "how little can I get away with" – even amongst professional musicians. There's no dedication to excellence any more.'

He was getting annoyed. Slider hastened to placate him. 'I know he must have been a dedicated man. But surely he must sometimes have had to relax and – recharge the batteries, so to speak.'

Keaton shrugged. 'To stay quietly here at home was enough. A simple meal, civilised conversation, a walk in the garden – they were his pleasures. He didn't hanker after the noise and racket of the modern world.'

Slider swallowed that with his tea. 'The garden is magnificent,' he said.

'Sir Stefan loved it. It was my pleasure to create a beautiful place for him to rest in.'

'Are you the gardener? I'm impressed.'

Keaton gave a modest smile. 'Gardening has always been my great love, and my relaxation. Sir Stefan generously gave me a free hand.'

'He couldn't have regretted it. It's beautiful,' Slider said, and Keaton warmed in the obvious sincerity.

'I have help,' he confessed. 'A man comes in to mow the lawn and do the heavy work. But what you see is my creation. I still plant and prune and propagate. And I do a little research work now and then, just to keep my mind active. Stefan built me a large greenhouse and shed down at the bottom. I'm trying to develop a new iris.' His mouth trembled. 'If it was accepted, I was going to name it after him. Oh dear!'

'I'm astonished you've had time to keep the garden looking so lovely, as well as looking after Sir Stefan.'

'Oh, I didn't go everywhere with him. To concerts, yes, but not always to rehearsals and recording sessions. So I have a little time for my other tasks. I do the cooking; you know, when we're at home, take care of his clothes, keep his personal correspondence – not that there's much of that. It's enough to keep me busy.' He had slipped back into the present tense. Adjustment was not going to come easily to him, Slider thought with compassion.

'Did you always go with him on tour?'

'Always. He couldn't have done without me for more than a few hours. And it was doubly important that someone who understood his delicate state of health was on hand.'

On the spur of the moment Slider decided to slip one in. 'What is the Ootsy Tootsy Club?' he asked casually.

Keaton's eyes snapped to attention. 'I don't know what you mean.'

'It's in Hong Kong. You went to Hong Kong recently, didn't you?'

'Last October. A triumphant tour – but exhausting. The heat and humidity never suited him.'

'And the Ootsy Tootsy Club?'

'I don't know any such club,' Keaton said coldly. 'Why should you think I do? It sounds ridiculous. What has it to do with anything?'

Slider said soothingly, 'It's impossible in these cases to tell what might be helpful. We often have to ask what seem like pointless questions.'

'Have to? Why do you have to?' Keaton said irritably.

'We have to find out who killed him. You want us to catch the man who did it, don't you?'

'Will it bring Stefan back to life?' Keaton said petulantly. 'Then no, I don't care about it. Leave him to his conscience and to God.'

'I'm afraid we're not allowed to do that,' Slider said gently. He stood up. 'I won't trouble you any more now, Mr Keaton, but I may have to come back another time. I hope you won't mind.'

Keaton shrugged. 'I shall be here. There's nowhere else to go now, anyway.'

On the way to the door Slider said, 'Oh, by the way, I imagine that Sir Stefan must have been a very wealthy man?'

'Yes,' said Keaton without emphasis. 'His agent dealt with the financial side of things. I suggest you talk to her about it.'

'Thank you, I will. But I wondered if you knew how his property was left. Had he made a Will?'

'Oh yes, some time ago. There was nothing complicated about it. This house and most of the contents come to me. Everything else goes to his daughter.'

*

'Bah, humbug!' Atherton said, perching himself precariously on the edge of his overflowing desk.

'Thank you, Ebenezer. Would you care to be more specific?'

'Radek, a selfless, dedicated genius? Bah, humbug!'

'Oh, that. You members of the younger generation are distressingly cynical. I've often thought it.'

'Anyone'd be cynical after what I've been hearing about Radek from various members of the orchestra. Whose version is right, I wonder, the dresser's or the musicians'?'

Slider shrugged. 'As in all things, the truth probably lies somewhere between the two.'

'Perhaps, but what about Radek's naughty habits? Do you think Keaton didn't know about them, or didn't want to know? Or was Des Riley making it all up?'

'He saw red when I mentioned the club in Hong Kong,' Slider said. 'I think he didn't want to know, because it interfered with his vision of holiness.'

'You didn't think it was all a bit too good to be true, Buster's hero-worship?' Atherton suggested.

'Oh no. I think he's genuine. But it's possible he needed to believe Radek was a saint, to make himself feel more important. Otherwise he was just a glorified domestic servant. I mean, dedicating your life to someone is a bit pointless if that person isn't something out of the ordinary.'

'I dunno,' Atherton said, 'women do it all the time. And look how I've dedicated myself to you.'

'Yes, but then I am out of the ordinary.'

'True, oh King. So, how do you fancy the son-in-law for villain?'

'He's a solicitor,' Slider mentioned.

'Case proved, then,' Atherton said simply.

'Seriously!'

'Seriously, the daughter does stand to inherit a fairish fortune – though owing to that wicked Married Woman's Property Act, it remains hers to dispose of.'

'The good old money motive,' said Slider. 'I always feel more comfortable when we get down to the *cui bono*. But the daughter's got the same motive as her husband, and a less legal mind.'

'Maybe it was the daughter then. Under a hat a slightly built young man could be a woman, and a gunning down in public does smack rather of female hysteria.'

'I don't know how you've lived to your ripe age, saying non-pc things like that. I wonder how much of a motive the money was, though,' Slider mused. 'We must find out what he was worth and exactly how he left it.'

'It makes you glad you've got nothing to leave,' Atherton said.

'I suppose so.' He looked at his watch. 'Just time for a quick bite before the post mortem.'

'Crown and Sceptre? It's on the way, more or less.'

'Okay. I don't know though,' Slider added, humpty-dumpty-like, as they started down the stairs, 'it would be nice to know you could go on being useful after you were dead.'

'We all do that.'

'We do?' Slider asked incautiously.

'Organic fertiliser. Nothing is wasted,' Atherton smirked. 'And think of all those maggots. Fishermen would pay good money for 'em.'

'Police humour is so childish,' Slider sighed reprovingly.

'At least it's *gentle* humour,' Atherton said, and it took Slider a moment or two to catch up with that one.

CHAPTER FOUR

The Late Ex Man

It was strange going to a post mortem and not seeing Freddie Cameron. He and Slider had known each other for years, and had worked together on many a case. In the natural course of things, since there were less than seven hundred murders a year altogether, there were few forensic pathologists with homicide experience, and since everyone wanted an expert, the same ones tended to be called in every time. It was bad luck, really, Freddie being away just at this moment. Forensic pathologists shouldn't have holidays. Slider hoped this new man knew his onions.

Things were already under way when Slider and Atherton arrived: the photographer had finished, the body had been undressed, and Mackay, as exhibits officer, was bagging the clothes. The body was now lying face-down on the slab, and the new man, James, was hovering over it. He was in his thirties, tall and powerful, with a rather pale and slightly alien face whose strangeness Slider eventually tracked down to the large pale-green eyes, which were slightly too shallow and too far apart to look as if he had originated on this planet. His brown hair was very long and straight, and he wore it in a pony-tail down his back tied with a leather thong. He also wore earrings, tiny gold star-shaped studs, and had a faint Birmingham accent, which may or may not have accounted for the other strangenesses. He was as different in looks from Freddie Cameron as could be, right down to the denims he

48

wore under his lab coat and rubber apron; but true to his species, he was sucking a peppermint when Slider and Atherton walked in. All corpses smell: it's only a matter of how much.

'Hullo,' he said cheerfully. 'Are you the Investigating Officer? I don't think we've met before.'

Slider introduced himself and Atherton. 'Freddie usually does my posts.'

'Oh, the ineffable Freddie! Great bloke. Where is he, then?'

'On holiday. Antigua, I think.'

'Blimey, he must be doing all right. A long weekend in Selly Oak is all I can run to.'

Slider smiled. 'This could be a turning point in your career, carving a big celeb.'

'Yeah, I do nice work. I'll give him a pretty scar.' He turned briskly to his assistant. 'Okay, let's have him over.'

With the trained strength of hill rescuers, they flipped the body over onto its back, and suddenly the likeness of Sir Stefan Radek was before Slider's eyes, the familiarity of the hawk-nosed face, but an unfamiliar colour, and unmistakably dead. Only the white hair, flying and silky, looked alive – as indeed, in a way it still was. The flesh looked not like flesh, but like some extremely realistic plastic; the old-man's body, blue-white and hairless, shamefully naked, exposed in this final humiliation, was not him, exactly, but like him, as, say, a Spitting Image puppet is meant to be. Gaunt, grotesque, veined of arm and yellow of foot, it waited for the knife and the ritual disembowelment.

James surveyed it thoughtfully. 'Funny, I saw him conduct only last year, in Birmingham. Took my mum and dad. He looked like a sort of god up there, waving his arms about.'

'Sic transit,' said Atherton.

'And then some,' James returned reverently. 'And talking of transit, come and have a look at this. I've read about 'em, but I hadn't actually seen one before. Look, it's your exit wound. See that?'

While not necessarily wanting to have it personalised, Slider had a particular interest in the exit wound. 'I didn't think there was one.' He bent closer. There seemed to be a scratch-like abrasion, v-shaped in form, in the flesh padding the waist on the right side. 'Is that it? It's just a couple of scratches.'

'Ah,' said James, as though it were a personal triumph, 'but look at this.' He took up a probe and, inserting it into the apex, gently retracted a triangular flap of skin. 'There's your exit wound, see? As I said, I've read about this in the manual, but this is the first time I've actually handled one. It happens when the bullet's lost so much velocity, it only just has the force to sort of plop out through the skin; and the skin, being naturally elastic, springs back together and hides the hole. It must have been fired at extreme range.'

'I think it was,' Slider said. 'It must have been about sixty feet. So what happened to the bullet? We thought it was still inside.'

'It was in his underpants. We found it when we stripped him. Here,' and he reached over to the side table and picked up a plastic bag, in which the nasty little object reposed. 'You'll want to send that off to ballistics. Chris Priest's your man. Tell him Laddo sends his best. We've often worked on the same shooting. We were both at Nottingham in our palmy days.'

'Laddo?' Slider queried out of a fog of thought.

James made a face. 'My mother had me christened Ladislaw. What would you have done? A cruel thing to do to a helpless little babe in arms, I always thought. And talking of arms, did you notice the left hand? Nice little example of cadaveric spasm.'

'Oh yes, he was clutching the neck of his sweater, wasn't he?' Slider remembered.

'Yeah. It was the real thing all right. Had quite a job to disentangle him.'

'Isn't cadaveric spasm a sign of great emotion or fear at the time of death?' Atherton asked.

'Or violent activity,' James answered. 'You often find it in drownings for instance, where the victim's struggling to survive – bits of weed clutched in the fingers and so on. Or in assaults, of course – scraps of torn clothing. Nothing to help you here, though, I'm afraid. No nice shred of shirt with a handy name-tag sewn in to guide you to the villain.'

'I'm never that lucky,' Slider said.

'Well, let's get started. I'll have the exit wound out first,' James said, cutting himself a neat square. 'I'm making a collection of entry and exit wounds – got nearly fifty now. It won't tell us a lot we don't know already in this case, of course, but if you can tell me exactly how far away the killer was standing, and how high off the ground the victim was, I can give you an estimate of his height.'

'Thank you,' Slider said. 'Every little helps.'

The pathologist worked in silence for a while. With a few long, powerful strokes of the scalpel he opened up the corpse as easily as Slider opened his morning mail, and examined the evidence of the bullet's path. 'Well now,' he said at last, 'you see why God gave us all love-handles. This little sucker passed through the meat of the waist without touching any vital organs. Mind you, at the speed it was travelling, if it had hit any obstruction it probably would have stopped right there, but as it was, it just slipped out the other side. Hardly did any damage at all. If he'd been a young man, he'd be sitting up in his hospital bed by now yelling for Lucozade.'

'So what killed him?' Atherton asked. 'Shock?'

'One way or another, yes, I expect so. We'll see.'

'I understand he had a heart condition,' Slider said.

'That'd help, of course,' James said. 'Though he looks a fit old boy. Not bad musculature for his age. It must be a healthy way of life, waving your arms around in public.'

'It is,' Atherton said. 'Look at Monteux: at the age of ninety-two his contract with the LSO expired, and he wouldn't accept a renewal for anything less than fifteen years. Conductors are famous for living to ripe old ages.'

'If they don't get gunned down,' said Laddo, with a grin. 'I should look for a hostile critic if I were you.' He cut out the heart, took it to the sink and sliced into it, washing out the chambers and examining them. 'Well, it all looks normal to me. No sign of any heart disease.'

'Are you sure?' Slider said. 'I was definitely told he had a weak heart.'

'Quite sure. Some normal wear and deterioration, due to age, but otherwise it looks in very good shape, considering.'

'So what killed him?'

'Tell you in a minute, when I've finished. Let's get the old loaf out, shall we?'

The removal of the brain was the part Atherton liked least, and he always kept a trivial question or remark ready so that he could turn away and engage the nearest person in conversation to drown the buzzing of the bone saw. Slider, though, watched impassively. Once the first cuts had been made the corpse lost all resemblance to a human being in his eyes; but then he'd been brought up on a farm.

Some time later James straightened up, flexed his fingers in a satisfied way, and said, 'That's it then. Syncope, caused by shock.'

'QED,' said Atherton.

'Come again?'

'Queer 'e died, isn't it?'

James's face cleared. 'Oh, there's nothing mysterious about it, especially given his age. He was – what – seventy-something?'

'Seventy-two,' Slider said.

'Well, there you are, then. At his age shock is not to be sniffed at. The physical insult together with the psychological trauma of being shot were quite enough to cause the old CNS to shut down, and Bob's your uncle. It's still down to the gunshot, even if the bullet didn't hit anything vital.'

'It's still murder then,' Atherton said. 'That's a relief. I didn't want to be wasting my talents on a mere assault.'

On the way out Slider paused by Mackay. 'Anything in his pockets?'

'A handkerchief, a pencil stub and some loose change.' He displayed the plastic bags. 'Nothing interesting, guv.'

'I thought at least he'd have the decency to be harbouring a signed blackmail demand,' Atherton complained as they stepped out into the blessed fresh traffic fumes, 'or a cassette recording of a death threat. Oh well.'

'Life is never easy.'

'You speak as one who knows. Will you drive or shall I?'

'Such exquisite grammar,' Slider marvelled. 'You drive, dear. I want to think.'

'Okay. Where to?'

'Home, James. Back to the factory.'

52

'So Radek didn't have a heart problem,' Atherton said a moment later as they took their place in the Fulham Palace Road traffic queue. 'I wonder if Keaton made it up, or if he really believed it.'

'I think he really believed it. My bet would be that Radek told him he had a weak heart in order to keep Keaton in line. Might even have pulled the old sudden spasm stunt in the middle of an argument he was afraid he was losing. Ill health can be a wonderful weapon, and heart's the best of all. From what I've heard of him so far, it's the kind of manipulative thing Radek would pull.'

McLaren called out to Slider indistinctly as they passed the door of the CID room – indistinctly because he had his face in a chicken salad bap about the size of a baby's head. It looked like one of those circus acts where a man attempts to put his head in a lion's mouth. Slider's sympathies had always been with the lion in such cases.

'Oh, guv, that woman phoned again,' he managed to say.

'What, Mrs Hislop-Ivory? Did you take her number this time?'

He looked blank. 'She said you knew it.'

Slider snarled silently. 'If I knew it, would I have asked you for it? Did she say what she wanted this time?'

'Only would you phone her back. She sounded quite shirty about it,' he added helpfully.

'If she rings again, find out what she wants, and *get the number*. Do you want me to write you instructions?'

'No, guv,' McLaren said, spraying mayonnaise-soaked shreds of lettuce over his desk. 'I'll get it next time.'

'And don't you know Mr Barrington doesn't like anyone eating in the office?' he said.

'He's gone out,' McLaren said simply.

Slider felt it was time to be stern. 'That's no excuse.'

'Sorry, guv, but it was getting so late and there's so much to do, I thought I'd better not stop. Only I've followed up that telephone number in Hong Kong –' He paused seductively.

'Where's Mr Barrington gone?' Slider asked, unseduced.

'Press conference,' said McLaren. 'This phone number –'

'Yes?'

53

'Turns out to be the central tourist information office. And Beda was a girl who used to work there, only she's moved on now. Confidentially, the office manager hinted she'd been on the game in her spare time – amateur, like – and that's what she left to do, full time. More money in it.'

'I suppose someone at the club tipped Radek off about her,' Atherton said.

'So why did he keep the number afterwards?' Slider wondered. 'Was she so important to him?'

'Probably accidental,' Atherton suggested. 'Des Riley said he was in the habit of sticking bits of paper in the back of his baton case for safe-keeping and having a periodic clear-out, so probably that one just slipped the net.'

'Anyway, guv, this bird at the tourist office knew about the club all right. A bit sniffy about it, she was – not the sort of place they recommend, she said. But it confirms what Riley said about Radek's habits. D'you want it followed up any further?'

'What else have you got on hand?' Slider asked.

'All the possible sightings of chummy. We've got the first lot of phone-ins sorted, and the most promising have got him proceeding up Addison Gardens and left into Richmond Way. So he could have been heading for the station.'

'He could.'

'He still had his hat on, and he was looking upset, according to one eye-witness,' McLaren added with satisfaction. 'So if he did go down the tube, someone'll be bound to've clocked him.'

'All right, stick with that,' said Slider. He turned to Mackay, 'Anything on the gun search?'

'Nothing, guv. He must have kept it in his pocket. When'll we get the ballistics report?'

'Tomorrow, with any luck. But it's not going to help us much until we've got a suspect. Keep plugging on.' He turned to Atherton. 'I think you'd better go and talk to Radek's agent. You speak the lingo. It's me for the daughter, I think. What do we know about her?'

'Born 1950, went to Benenden School, very posh; has her own interior design business called Fenella, office in Hampstead, charges telephone numbers to tell the rich and shameless what colour to paint their dadoes. Married to a

54

solicitor, Alec Coleraine of Coleraine and Antrobus, but uses her maiden name in business. And as you probably wouldn't know, not being a *Hello!* man, she features quite a bit in the society columns. Knows everyone; does over the houses of the glitterati and gets invited to their parties as a consequence. Very smart, and I gather reading between the lines as hard as nails in the business way.'

'Oh good,' said Slider wearily. 'She sounds just my type.'

At first Atherton took Kate Apwey, of Parker, Pool and Law, to be what he called a Victoria, meaning a good-looking, desperately smart, well-spoken but slightly daffy girl of the sort often found in publicity offices, who succeed without any particular abilities largely by getting on well with people and knowing how to behave at promotional parties. She was certainly easy on the eye, well groomed, and talked in the obligatory rapid, lightly slurred, upper-class falsetto, full of ums and sorts-ofs and other aids to well-bred inarticulacy. Atherton, who loved language, wanted to strangle her within ten seconds of meeting her, and wondered what she was doing working in an agency at all, unless it be a branch of Jackson-Stops; but ramming his fists into his pockets and sticking it out, he discovered that there was more to her than met the eye, and supposed belatedly that there would have to be if she had been Radek's agent for the last five years.

'He's a tremendous loss to us,' she said brightly. 'We've had him on our books for nearly eleven years now, ever since he sort of quarrelled with Holton and Watson, and he's been um, very, very lucrative indeed. We handle everything for him – concerts, recordings, personal appearances, everything really. His workload is phenomenal. But I could book him ten times over for every date. Everyone wants him. He's very big box-office.'

'So tell me, why was he doing a concert at St Augustine's Church? That's a bit down-market for him, isn't it? Surely they couldn't have been paying him his usual fee?'

'No, he wasn't getting a fee at all – though I'm not supposed to tell anyone that. He didn't want anyone to know. He said if anyone found out he'd be swamped with begging letters.'

'He didn't like doing charity work, then?'

'Not at all. He hated it. He said no-one helped him when he had nothing, he had to look after himself, so everyone else could do the same.'

'So why was he doing this concert, then?'

'It was for his daughter,' she said. The notion seemed to puzzle her. 'She asked him to do it for the restoration fund, and he agreed. He said it was a once-only thing. It surprised me quite a bit, because it wasn't really his style, if you know what I mean; but I suppose he wanted to please her. He did care about her, I suppose.'

'That can't be bad, can it? Did you like him?'

She hesitated over the answer to that. 'Oh, well – he earns us so much money he's entitled to be sort of particular. He makes his own conditions, sort of thing.'

'Which are?'

She hesitated again. 'He wanted me to um handle him personally. To be available all the time, you know? No substitutes allowed and no excuses.' She reflected glumly for a moment. 'It made it difficult for me to have any private life of my own. I mean, men friends are not sort of understanding when you're called out at short notice at night to hold someone's hand for them.'

'But it was worth it to you?'

'It was my job,' she said snippily.

'And you were glad to serve the cause of music?' Atherton suggested smoothly. 'To be handmaid to the great genius of the podium was enough reward for giving up your private life?'

She looked at him askance, and rather pink. 'Um, not really.'

'You did it for the money, then?'

Now she blushed. 'Look, it's my job, all right? He wanted me, and if I'd refused he'd have got me sacked, and I'd never have got another job as good as this one. And it wasn't going to be for ever anyway.'

'He wanted you, did he?' Atherton said with bland interest. 'I'm sorry, I didn't realise when you said he wanted you to handle him personally that you meant it literally. Lots of evening work, was it? Organ recitals, that sort of thing?' He thought she would get angry, but though her colour remained high, she looked at him steadily.

'What business is it of yours?' she asked.

He reassessed her rapidly. 'I apologise. But I have to know exactly how the land lay. And it's better if I hear all about you *from* you, isn't it? That way you can be sure I hear the truth.'

She stared at him, her brain evidently working behind her impassive eyes. 'Did he ask you to sleep with him?'

'Yes,' she said after a pause.

'And did you?'

A longer pause. 'Yes,' she said at last. It was difficult to tell what she felt about that.

'For the money? Or to keep your job?'

She seemed to make up her mind about something. 'Look, whatever he was in ordinary life, he was a great conductor, a world-class celebrity, and there's something about a man like that. At the end of a concert, especially on a tour, when he's just come down off the platform and the audience is going mad out there, there's a sort of atmosphere. I mean there's a sort of, like, electricity about him.'

'He was on a high, and the excitement transmitted itself to you. So when he asked you back to his hotel room you felt honoured to be asked.'

She looked at him doubtfully. 'Sort of. How do you know?'

'I love music. I go to concerts,' he said. 'I can understand that you might go willingly, at least the first time. Where was that, by the way?'

'Frankfurt.'

'And you went to bed with him.'

There was a long silence. He thought she might not answer, but suddenly it burst out. 'It was horrible! He was so old, and he smelled, and the things he wanted me to do –! It was like you said at first, I was sort of excited, he was a celebrity. But it wore off, and then there I was in this hotel room with this horrible old man.' She put her hands to her face, pulling the skin of her cheeks back with her knuckles. 'Afterwards,' she went on, 'he gave me a lot of money, and said how good I was, and he'd tell my boss I was terrific at my job. Well, I wanted to get on. And anyway, I knew – I mean, it was obvious what he meant. He said he'd say I was so good he wanted me to look after him all the time –'

'You thought he was hinting that if you refused him next time he'd tell them you were no good and get rid of you.'

'It was no hint. He'd have done it all right,' she said almost indignantly.

'So you went on sleeping with him to order, to keep your job.'

'It wasn't often,' she said in self-justification; and then, the horror returning to her eyes: 'It was just – having it hanging over me. Not knowing when. But I was saving the money. And when I had enough –' She stopped abruptly.

He waited to see if she'd go on, and when she didn't, he said, 'You said it wasn't going to be for ever. What did you mean by that?'

She flicked an alarmed glance at him, and then looked away. 'Nothing really. Well, I mean, he was an old man, wasn't he? He couldn't live for ever.'

'You were hoping he'd die?'

'No, not hoping. But sooner or later he'd have to, wouldn't he? Or retire.'

'You have a boyfriend?' She nodded, either doubtfully or reluctantly. 'Did he know about your relations with Radek?'

'I never actually told him about – he knew I had to be with him at concerts and things – but he sort of guessed, or assumed. So I didn't deny it. I mean, I wouldn't have lied to him.'

'He didn't like it?'

'No, of course not.'

'You had rows about it?'

'Sometimes. Steve loses his temper, but it doesn't mean anything. I mean, he's soon over it.'

'Did he know Radek gave you money?'

'We were saving up for a house,' she said with wonderful inconsequence.

'You and Steve were going to get married?'

'Eventually. But I wanted to carry on working. I told Steve that. He understood that. My career is important to me.'

'But you couldn't go on sleeping with Radek once you were married, could you? And if you refused him, you'd lose your job.' She didn't answer, looking away from him, biting her lips. 'Bit of a dilemma for you,' he said warmly.

'He was a hateful old man,' she said suddenly, fiercely. 'He knew how I felt, but he liked tormenting people. I'm glad he's dead. Whoever killed him did a public service.'

Back in his car, Atherton consulted a copy of the orchestra's schedule which Tony Whittam had given him and reckoned there was just time to catch one of the orchestra members before she left for an evening session at Abbey Road. He drove to Joanna's flat in Turnham Green, and found her in, but not alone.

'I'm giving Sue a lift to the studio. You know Sue Caversham, don't you?'

'We have met,' Atherton said, accepting the offered hand of the principal second violin. She was a nice-looking, strongly built woman in her forties with very shiny brown hair and a wide mouth and an air of being secretly amused by everything, which some might have found daunting, but which Atherton found inviting.

'Briefly,' she said. 'It wasn't you who took my statement, more's the pity.'

'We've just finished a late lunch,' Joanna said, 'but I can get you some cheese and biscuits if you're hungry. Policemen are always hungry,' she added to Sue. 'It's all that brain activity.'

'No thanks,' Atherton said, and then, 'What sort of cheese?'

'Dolcelatte.'

'And Carr's water biscuits? Yes please, then.'

'Not another foodie!' Sue laughed as Joanna departed to get the cheese. 'I'm always so impressed with Jo, all the cooking she does. We just had the most marvellous pasta, and the sauce wasn't even ready-made. Me, I have difficulty opening a tin.'

'Don't you *like* food?' Atherton boggled in horror.

'Love it, but when I get home from work, if it doesn't get on the plate of its own accord, it's too much effort. I get a piece of bread out of the fridge, or if I'm in unexpectedly good shape I pour out a bowl of cereal.'

'Is playing the violin really so exhausting?' Atherton asked disapprovingly.

'No, I'm just bone lazy,' Sue said comfortably. 'Also it depends what you're playing and who for. Some conductors make life harder than others.'

'Like the late unlamented?' Atherton asked. 'Can a conductor make that much difference?'

'He can if he's a nasty, self-obsessed, vindictive old sod, and I use the word advisedly, like Radek,' Sue said. Joanna, returning, looked amused.

Atherton caught her eye and said, '*De mortuis?*'

'*Non est disputandum*,' she finished for him. 'Here we are. Cheese, biscuits, and I've even found you a glass of wine. Left over from last night, so it's not too old.'

'Ah, Château Hot Tin Roof,' Atherton said, holding it up to the light. 'Were you going to use it for cooking?'

'Snob,' said Joanna. 'You don't have to drink it.'

'I'm sure it's delightful,' he said hastily. 'Reverting to the subject, are all conductors hated?'

'Oh no,' Sue said quickly. 'Barbirolli, for instance, was a lovely old geezer. He used to share his sandwiches on the coach. And Pritchard *never* forgot to thank you, or to stand you up if you'd had something tricky to do.'

'But then there are those like Lupton – when he gets lost he just bottles out and stops conducting. Gets you into a mess and expects you to get him out of it,' Joanna offered. 'And Farnese, who's so convinced he's a genius he takes the parts home and *rewrites* them. I mean, actually changes notes, never mind annotations.'

Sue put in, 'You know the old saying, don't you: what's the difference between a bull and an orchestra?'

'Tell me.'

'A bull has the horns at the front and the arse at the back.'

Atherton snorted crumbs. 'You're my sort of woman. Tell me, didn't you have a blow-up recently with the arse in question?'

'Yes, and very nasty it was.' She made a face. 'Six point six on the Sphincter scale. I thought I'd had it, actually. Our management is as wet as a fortnight in Cardiff, they never stick up for us – as poor old Bob Preston found out.'

'Who's he?'

Sue and Joanna exchanged glances, and Joanna shrugged

and took up the story. 'He's – or he was – our co-principal trumpet. We did a Messiah with Radek a couple of months ago, and Bob always does the solo in "The Trumpet Shall Sound" because the principal, Les, doesn't like playing D trumpet parts. Everyone who conducts us knows that, and Bob's very good – Messiah's his specialty. But that wouldn't do for bloody old Radek. He said he wasn't having any mere *co*-principal doing a solo under his magnificent direction.'

'The fact was that he wanted to promote one of his little protégés,' Sue put in. 'He's always got some wunderkind he's discovered tucked up his sleeve, and when they get famous, he's there hovering in the background taking half the glory. Anyway, there was this boy-wonder trumpeter, Lev Polowski –'

'Polish, or Russian of Polish extraction, so he felt entitled,' Joanna explained.

'So he said Bob was off the case. There was a big row, and Bob stood up to Radek, the twonk.'

'Brave but foolish,' Atherton commented.

'The upshot was that Radek said he wouldn't have Bob in the orchestra any more,' Sue finished. 'He told the management if they didn't chuck Bob he'd take his contracts elsewhere, so poor old Bob got the big E.'

'Do you think Radek would have carried out his threat?' Atherton asked.

Joanna looked at him. 'Nice point. I think he just might have – he was megalomaniac enough. And besides, he'd never want for work. He could command any fees he liked, and any orchestra in the world would fight to have him. So the management had no leverage. Couldn't take the chance.'

'What's happened to Bob now?' Atherton asked.

Sue shrugged. 'He's freelancing when he can get work, but it's hard for trumpeters. You don't need many of them per orchestra, and there's hardly any solo work. I've seen him once or twice. He's very depressed.'

'So he has a real grudge against Radek?' Atherton said.

The two women gave the impression of suddenly sitting bolt upright. 'Oh hang on,' Sue protested, 'you can't think Bob would murder the old bastard because of that?'

'I'm not thinking it, I'm canvassing possibilities,' Atherton said blandly.

61

'It's not a possibility. If I'd thought you'd suspect him, I'd never have told you about it,' Sue said angrily.

Joanna was watching her with faint amusement, having gone down this path herself long before. 'I should have known these questions weren't all random,' she said. 'It doesn't matter, Sue. They'd find out anyway. Better he hears it from someone who can give them a balanced picture.'

'All the same –'

'And if Bob had murdered Radek, you wouldn't want him to get away with it, would you?'

'Yes, but Bob –'

'I know. The idea's ludicrous. He wouldn't hurt a fly.'

'You might as well suspect me,' Sue said, looking defiantly at Atherton. 'After all, I had a row with Radek just the day before he was killed.'

'I have taken that into account,' Atherton said smoothly. Sue went scarlet, and Joanna stepped in.

'What he means is he doesn't think that would be enough motive for you to actually want to kill Radek,' she said firmly. 'Isn't that right, Jim?'

'Oh, I think I can eliminate you,' Atherton said generously. 'After all, you wouldn't have had time to hire the killer.'

Sue stared for a moment, and then burst into laughter.

'You rotten sod. I'm keeping score now. You'll pay for that.'

'I do hope so,' Atherton said warmly. 'You must let me cook for you some time. Joanna will tell you I'm a noted cook.'

'That sounds good to me,' Sue said. 'What about tonight, after the session?'

'Brilliant idea! If I can get off early enough, I could do you a *boeuf en croûte*. It's what I call casing the joint.'

'Oh God!' Sue groaned in protest. 'What am I getting myself into?'

Joanna looked from her face to his and back, and suddenly felt rather left out of things.

CHAPTER FIVE

How Green was my Volvo

Slider finally ran Radek's daughter to earth in Hampstead, in a house she was redecorating. Her little van, painted ecology green with a nice curly Fenella in crimson lettering edged with black on the side, was parked on the paved hardstanding (what had once been the front garden) behind a Volvo estate and a dark blue Jaguar XJ which made Slider whimper. He'd always wanted one. He parked his own shabby Vauxhall across the front, blocking them all in, since there wasn't anywhere else to put it: the streets here were only about one car wide. The tall, narrow, eighteenth-century house would have made him whimper too, if it had been anywhere else, but Hampstead was one of those places, like Greenwich Village, you either adored or didn't.

The door was opened to him by a maid, and that was something you couldn't often say nowadays. She was foreign, of course – something east of Clacton, he surmised – and, smiling as if she hadn't understood a word he said, she invited him to wait in the hall with a gesture as graceful as part of a temple dance, and disappeared upstairs. The house was very quiet: all he could hear was the measured sound of a long-case clock ticking somewhere out of sight, and once a creak of a floorboard from upstairs. It gave him the feeling that he had sometimes had as a child, when he had been ill in bed on a schoolday: that everyone in the whole world had gone away somewhere, to another planet, perhaps, leaving him absolutely alone.

To distract himself he examined the letters on the hall table and discovered that the house belonged to a Famous Writer (of the Booker as opposed to the Airport type), so famous even he had heard of her. A quick poke about in the mental files suggested that she was married to an almost equally famous Historian who was now Arts Editor of one of the serious newspapers. That accounted for the money, at least. What they could want with redecorating he couldn't imagine – everything looked immaculate – unless it was somehow deductible.

At last the maid came downstairs again, and with another uncomprehending smile and lovely gesture said, 'Please,' and led him upstairs. She showed him into a beautiful double drawing-room, where Mrs Coleraine and the Famous Writer were standing at the window examining fabric samples. The writer was tall and rangey with big teeth and big hair and a large, jolly voice which left her eyes untouched by humour or humanity. Slider had been abused, insulted and even spat at by many a potential interviewee, but it was a long time since he had been made to feel that he ought to have gone round by the tradesman's entrance.

'Ah yes, Inspector,' she said witheringly, like a heart surgeon looking down at the nit nurse, 'come in. You want to see Mrs Coleraine, I understand. I can't imagine why you couldn't have waited until this evening when she's at home, but I dare say you have your reasons. Something tremendously urgent, I suppose?'

Slider declined to be drawn, and merely gave her a humble smile. She turned to her companion.

'Fay, my dear, I suppose I had better leave you to it, but I shall only be upstairs in my bedroom.' In case I attack her, Slider thought. 'I am beginning to incline towards the green. The raw silk is so lovely I can't resist it. Can we think along those lines? What I'm looking for is a sort of *underwater* feeling. We can talk about textures later.' When this horrid little man has gone, said her glance, and she bestowed a gigantic smile on Mrs Coleraine, large enough to last her till she came back, and went out of the room.

Fay Coleraine turned to Slider. She was a tall woman, but being much more lightly made than the Famous Writer had

64

appeared small in her company. She had a sweet, worn face in which he could find no likeness to Radek except for the height of the cheekbones and the heaviness of the eyelids; on her they looked beautiful rather than menacing. Her hair was strawberry blonde, short and set in the sweeping waves that women of a certain age always seem to adopt, revealing her ear-lobes in which small pearls were set. She was wearing black slacks and a black silk blouse, with a black and white scarf in the neckline which was twisted in and under a string of very good pearls. Slider couldn't tell if it were a uniform for her work, a concession to mourning, or merely a random choice of clothes, but she looked smart, attractive and expensive.

'I'm sorry to interrupt you at your work,' he said, and she smiled a kind smile that made him want to take her out to tea and tell her not to worry about anything.

'Don't mind Maggie. She doesn't mean to trample. Was it something urgent?'

'Not urgent, in that sense, but trails do get cold, and the sooner we ask our questions the better. I did call your house, but they told me you were working today.'

She almost shrugged. 'I thought it better to keep busy. There didn't seem any reason to stay at home; and Maggie's hard to pin down.'

'I won't keep you long,' Slider said, and she gestured towards a brocaded chaise longue.

'Oh, don't worry, take whatever time you need. Shall we sit down? Though I'm not sure what help I can be. I simply can't imagine who would do such a dreadful thing. I've racked my brains, but I can't think of anyone who hated my father that badly. You're sure it wasn't just one of those random things, like the Hungerford massacre?'

'We don't think so. It doesn't look like it. The symptoms are wrong.'

She sighed. 'Well, you must know, of course.'

'I'm very sorry. It must have been a terrible shock for you.'

She sat forward a little, folding her hands together and trapping them between her knees in a rather girlish gesture. 'It was, of course, but I must be absolutely frank with you and say that I didn't like my father very much. I don't think anyone did, except Buster. But then I don't think my father wanted to be liked. Worshipped was good enough for him.'

'Your mother must have liked him,' he suggested.

'Oh, I don't think so. Swept off her feet by him, more like.' She looked at him from under her eyelids. 'He wasn't a nice man, you know. He was mean and spiteful. He liked tormenting people and playing them off against each other. He used to do it with Mummy and me, and with Mummy and Dodo –'

'Dodo?'

'That was Mrs Keaton – Doreen Keaton. I called her Dodo. She was our cook-housekeeper when I was little.'

'You were – what – three years old when the Keatons came to work for your parents?'

She nodded. 'We'd just moved into the Holland Park house. It's the first home I remember – we were in a flat before, in Kensington. My grandfather died and left everything to Mummy, including the house. She was the only child, and my grandparents were only-children too, so I was very short of relatives. And then Mummy died when I was only nine.'

'That's very sad. I'm so sorry.'

She looked at him as if to see whether he really was, and then nodded, accepting his interest. 'I loved her so much, and that's when I really started to hate my father. Because he drove her to it, you know.'

'No, I don't know. What did she die of?'

'It was an overdose of sleeping pills. Well, of course, she wouldn't have had any sleeping pills if my father hadn't been such a beast to her. They brought it in as an accident at the inquest, but I believe – I still believe – it was suicide. And Dodo did as well.'

'Did she say so to you?'

'Not in so many words, but she told me that it wasn't an accident. And on her deathbed she said to me that "things were not as they seemed". Those were her words.'

'Did she look after you when your mother died?'

'Yes, she was very good to me. I don't know how I would have coped if she hadn't been there. But she died less than a year after Mummy. It wasn't really surprising, she was such a pale, wispy sort of creature, always full of aches and pains – though she never complained. She just soldiered on, cooking and cleaning and looking after me. Do you know, I have no memory of her laughing? Smiling, yes, but not laughing. Isn't that sad?'

'What did she die of?'

'Gastroenteritis. It just got worse and worse over a couple of days, and then they took her into hospital, but it was too late. Nowadays I suppose they would have been able to save her. It amazes me to think how far medical science has advanced in just thirty years.'

'You must have missed her very much. Who looked after you then?'

'Oh, well, after that my father wanted to get rid of me, of course – I would have got in the way of his career – so he sent me off to boarding school. Do you really want to hear all this? It hasn't anything to do with this awful business,' she said abruptly.

'If you don't mind,' he said. 'It helps if I have the whole picture. Sometimes something can have a completely different meaning if you can put it in context.'

'Well, if you're sure. Where was I?'

'You went to boarding school. Who looked after you in the holidays – or did you spend them at school too?'

'Oh no, I came home in the holidays. Buster looked after me. He didn't trot round after my father quite as much in those days.'

'Did you like him?'

'Buster? Oh yes, he was all right. He was very kind to me, really. I always remember he used to make me Shrewsbury biscuits, because I'd once said I liked them. I'd got them mixed up with Garibaldis, and every school hols he'd have a batch of them ready for me when I got home, so I had to eat them, even though I didn't like them much, rather than hurt his feelings.'

She smiled, and Slider smiled back. 'Your father didn't marry again?'

'No. To tell you the truth, I don't think he'd have married the first time if Mummy hadn't had money. He didn't really want any competition, you know.'

'With whom?'

'With anyone. If he was married people would always say, "Oh, and how is your wife?" Divided attention, you see.'

'Yes, I see.'

'He had Buster to take care of him, and Buster was better than a wife. He didn't have to remember Buster's birthday or buy him flowers.'

'He does seem very devoted.'

'Oh, he is. Poor old thing. He'll be so lost without Daddy.' It was the first time, Slider noticed, that she had said 'Daddy' instead of 'my father'. 'He's like a faithful old dog. A bit creepy almost, I sometimes used to think, the way he dedicated himself to him. But now they've grown old together they're a bit more on equal terms. They fight like cat and dog, you know. It's quite funny sometimes, as long as you're out of range. They sling plates at each other like a married couple.'

Slider inched in a delicate question. 'The relationship between them – was it ever – was Buster more than –?'

She cut him off, looking genuinely shocked, and even a little annoyed. 'Good God no! Oh, I know nowadays it's the first thing anyone thinks, and it does make me cross. There was nothing like that between them. My father may have been a swine, but he was perfectly normal.'

'I was really asking more from Buster's side.'

'He was married too, you seem to forget. Of course he was normal.'

'It doesn't always follow.'

She looked at him, and then sniffed. 'I suppose not. But I assure you Buster wasn't – isn't – like that. He thinks my father's a genius, that's all.'

'And was he?'

She noticed the change of tense. 'I keep forgetting. He was always such a larger-than-life figure, it's hard to remember he's gone. Well, I don't know – a genius? Yes, I suppose he was. If I hadn't been his daughter I probably would have worshipped him too. I do love music, you know. But by the time I was old enough to leave home, I'd had enough of the world of music, if you follow.' Slider nodded. 'That's why I married Alec.' She smiled. 'Alec's a musical ignoramus. He wouldn't know Schubert from Schoenberg. It was so refreshing! And it drove my father mad, of course. He absolutely forbade me to marry, so I waited until I was twenty-one and then thumbed my nose at him. He never really forgave me.'

He couldn't tell how she felt about that. He asked, 'What were relations like between you and your father? Recently, I mean.'

'He didn't really care about me, not as a person. But I was *his* child, you know, so he wanted me to do well so that he could bathe in reflected glory. He was very into all that. Buster said a clever thing once – that my father never discarded, he only added to his hand. If he'd ever talent-spotted anyone or helped them in their career, they were his for life, and he expected them to go on being grateful and referring to his influence in all future interviews. He didn't much care for my business – he thought it was frivolous – but when I did well at it and made lots of money and became famous in my own small way, he liked to claim the credit.'

'How did he do that?'

'He brought me up to have good taste, of course, and taught me to stand on my own two feet and be tough, which made me a good businesswoman. And his fame rubbed off on me, so that people used me because they wanted to say their house was done over by Sir Stefan Radek's daughter.' She smiled tautly. 'All nonsense, of course, but I stopped arguing with him. If it made him happy.'

'Did you see much of him?'

'No, not really. I suppose it averaged out at about once a month. Family occasions, and the odd invitation if he felt we would do him credit. I didn't pop in. For one thing he was hardly ever at home – although he had slowed down a bit in the last year or two. Buster's influence, I think. And for another, we always ended up quarrelling, and it wore me out.'

'What did you quarrel about?'

She hesitated just perceptibly. 'Alec, usually. He thought he wasn't good enough for me. He always wanted me to admit I'd made a mistake and that he'd been right, that I should have listened to Daddy's advice, that sort of thing. I know I oughtn't to have risen to it, but my father had ways of getting to you. He had a vicious tongue.'

'How did your husband get on with him?'

'He didn't mind him so much. Well, he hadn't had to put up with him all his life, had he? He didn't like my father criticising the way we brought Marcus up – that's our son – but he was better at holding his tongue than I was.'

'You have only the one child?'

'Yes. We'd have liked more, but –' She shrugged. 'We're very short of family altogether. It's like a chronic condition. Alec always wanted a large family, but all he has is me and Marcus, and a godson he's rather fond of. I suppose that's why he's tended to spoil Marcus. He gives in to him much too easily. He's so soft with him he would never even let me punish him, and of course a child soon learns he can play one parent off against the other.' She stopped, and stared thoughtfully at the carpet, pursuing a private thought.

After a moment Slider said, 'When was the last time you saw your father? Can you remember?'

'Oh yes. It was three weeks ago, on my birthday. We went there for dinner. I did speak to him on the phone last week about the concert – it's a pet cause of mine, the St Augustine's Restoration Fund. I was rather surprised he agreed to do it. To be frank, I think Buster persuaded him in the hope that it would bring us closer together. He always cherished the hope that we'd be reconciled into one big happy family.'

'But it was kind of your father to do it. It shows he cared for you.'

'Does it? I expect he just wanted people to think what a wonderful person he was, to do it for charity.'

Slider felt a first twinge of indignation on Radek's behalf, that his gesture was being so undervalued. But perhaps it was a case of too little, too late. After all, he didn't know how Radek had treated his daughter all his life. 'And your husband?' he asked. 'When was the last time he saw your father?'

'It would be the same time, of course. Alec didn't go visiting without me. What a funny question.'

'Oh, I thought they might meet in town or something. Your husband's office is in town, isn't it?'

'Yes, in Bedford Street, just off the Strand. But Alec and my father weren't friendly like that. I've told you, Alec doesn't like music. They had nothing to say to each other.'

'I understand,' Slider said. 'Now, you've said you have no idea of anyone who might want to kill your father?'

'None at all. The idea's ludicrous. Oh, lots of people disliked him, but it takes more than that, doesn't it?'

'Yes, usually,' Slider said. 'Did he have any interests or activities outside of music?'

'Never, to my knowledge. Music was his whole life. It left no time for anything else.'

'Did he have any close friends that you knew of?'

'He didn't have any friends of any sort.'

'What about the people he'd helped? You said he liked them to keep up with him.'

'Yes, but that wasn't friendship. He liked them to keep telling everyone he had been a forming influence on them. Sometimes he got invited to their special concerts, or to the parties afterwards, and sometimes he went. Sometimes he invited them in the same way, if they were hot enough property. But he didn't entertain at home, and I've never known him go to a private dinner or party. He always said he hadn't time to waste on purely social events.'

The Famous Writer appeared in the door. 'I say, I wonder could you move your car?' she said to Slider, in the sort of way she might have asked him to take his boots off the sofa. 'It's rather blocking us all in.'

'Yes, of course,' Slider said meekly, standing up. Mrs Coleraine stood too, and gave the writer a slightly puzzled look, by which Slider understood that the interruption was contrived, his welcome having been deemed to have been outstayed. 'I've more or less finished now, anyway.'

'I'm afraid it hasn't got you anywhere,' Mrs Coleraine said contritely. 'I wish I could help you more, but I really can't.'

'That's all right,' Slider said. 'It all helps to build up the picture. And if anything should occur to you, please give me a ring. The smallest thing may be of help, so don't think you'll be wasting our time.'

'I'm sure she wouldn't think that,' the writer said, baring her teeth. 'Would you, Fay darling?'

71

Fay darling seemed to think that was on the verge of being rude, and she put out her hand to Slider and said, 'If you need to speak to me again, I'll be glad to give you all the time you want.'

Slider took the hand. It was warm and dry and firm. 'Thank you,' he said. He really didn't think he could suspect her. She had hated her father, blamed him for her mother's death, resented his criticism of her husband, but Slider just couldn't imagine her shooting him in that silly, half-arsed way. On the other hand, in a silly, half-arsed way was the only way she would be likely to be able to do it, given she was an honourable citizen and Radek was her father. And she had stood to gain a vast amount of money by his death. Well, she'd have got it anyway, eventually, so there was no need to hurry him along. Unless he'd threatened to change his Will. Or unless she had some absolutely urgent need that couldn't wait. Hadn't old Buster said the son was a bit of a wild thing? Maybe he'd got himself into some trouble that needed a large sum of money to sort out. He must find out. And, sadly, find out where she'd been on Wednesday. But he'd be glad to discover she had a watertight alibi.

The maid was waiting outside the drawing-room door to show him out, proving it had not been a random interruption. He followed her downstairs and she opened the door for him and held it, making a graceful gesture with the other, an exquisite temple-maiden's version of the good old A & C.

'Lovely technique,' he said, bowing to her as he passed.

She smiled a smile of complete incomprehension. 'Please,' she said.

Slider pulled up on the hardstanding outside his house and let himself in, shoving the front door against an interesting-looking heap. It turned out, however, to consist of two local freebie newspapers, an envelope for postal film-developing, a coupon for a free half-bottle of wine with any two adult meals ordered at the Ruislip Harvester ('for a limited period only, not to be used in conjunction with any other promotional offer' – did that mean that after the limited period it could be used in conjunction with another promotional offer? You simply couldn't trust people's punctuation these days) and the spectacular offer of a free watch and inclusion in the *Reader's Digest* prize draw. Open now! You may already have won £100,000! You never know your luck! I bloody do, Slider thought, gathering the ex-rainforest together and heading for the kitchen. As they say in the Job, I'm so unlucky I could fall in a barrel of tits and come out sucking my thumb.

The house smelled strange, a marginally sub-pleasant odour which he could not pin down, somewhere between margarine and Shake'n'Vac, with a hint of cold plimsolls thrown in. There was a chill echo about it, too: it was strange to come home and find the television not on – as if, like a fifth member of the family, it had left him too. The house was still fully furnished – Irene had taken nothing except her and the children's personal belongings, and the new wicker conservatory furniture she loved so much – but that only made it worse. Chairs and carpets without personal clutter gave it the feeling of an institution; a sort of kindly brutality designed to wipe out your inconvenient personality traits. Strange how the word 'home' could have two such opposite connotations.

He had only come to change his clothes and have an urgent reunion with his deodorant stick. He dumped the papers on the kitchen table and debated making a quick cup of tea, but the inhospitality of the kitchen daunted him. The dishcloth draped over the tap had dried into a hoop, and the last footmark he had made on the lino-tiled floor (Monday, putting the dustbin out – it hadn't rained since) reproached him mutely where it had dried. Sherlock of the Homes could have deduced a thing or two about him from that: this man is five-foot-eight, weighs ten stone, wears rubber soles, and his wife is away.

It had never really been *his* home, he reflected; but, oddly, was much less so now that Irene and the children were gone. He hadn't spent much time here in the weeks since it happened. He stayed long at work, ate out, and once or twice had managed to sleep out, too. He hated waking up in the morning to find himself curled up on 'his' side of the otherwise empty bed. It made him feel like a prat, but even when he deliberately started off in the middle he migrated in his sleep out of obedience to habit.

O'Flaherty, uniformed sergeant at Shepherd's Bush and

one of Slider's oldest friends, knew his circumstances and had several times invited Slider back to supper. His wife was a noted cook of the steak-and-kidney pie, Irish stew and jammy pud school; aided by the Guinness intake, it accounted for O'Flaherty's shape and his nickname of Flatulent Fergus. But they both made Slider welcome, and after one particularly indulgent evening, Fergus had pressed him to stay the night.

'I don't like to think of you sittin' around like an unde-scended testicle in that empty house o' yours. We got loads a room, now the kids are gone. You can have Brendan's room – less clutter than in the girls'.' And when Slider had argued politely, 'Ah sure God, would you sit down and have another drink? It won't take Margery a minute to put some sheets on.'

So Slider had stayed the night in a sagging single bed, which had a hollow in the middle you could have parked a Mini in (the effect of years of having been used as a trampoline, as the father in him rather than the detective recognised) in a tiny room with Superman wallpaper and Muppet bedlinen. It was a night of crowded dreams peopled with caped crusaders and woolly monsters, amongst whom he searched in vain for someone without ever knowing who it was. He woke late and unrefreshed, and had felt both ashamed and comforted when he found that Margery had washed and ironed his shirt for him while he slept. She refused to be thanked, as if it were the most natural thing in the world for her to do. The kindness of strangers got him where he was most vulnerable. He felt like Blanche.

Drifting back from the memories to the present, Slider suddenly wanted to be out of here. The place was like a corpse waiting for the post mortem to begin. He went upstairs, had a quick shower, and changed his work suit for cords and a sweater, and then went into the familiar annoying routine of trying to find a pair of socks that matched and didn't have holes in them. What did they make socks out of nowadays, anyway? In a fit of fury he pulled the drawer out and up-ended it on the bed. As he rummaged he heard Joanna in his memory saying, 'You only want a housekeeper. Someone to wash your socks.' She was right in a way, but it

74

was not really the sock-washing, it was more a case of needing something solid somewhere in a life that was otherwise fraught with peril and uncertainty. When the house was sold he would really have to accept that his marriage was over, and that there was nowhere he belonged and no-one who wanted him. It was not a prospect he relished.

There were enough coppers who lived bachelor lives, and got by very well in their own individual ways. Atherton for one. He lived in the part of Kilburn so extensively done up it dared to call itself West Hampstead, in a Victorian terraced cottage which he shared with a former tomcat called Oedipus. Atherton was an archetypal bachelor, Slider thought: being otherwise alone in the world, he dedicated his leisure and disposable income to putting his body into nice things and nice things into his body. Bathing, dressing, eating, drinking and mating – not necessarily in that order of preference – were his pleasures, and he took them very seriously. Slider remembered that Joanna had once said Atherton was in danger of becoming a caricature of himself. Precise, almost dilettantish in his enjoyments, he had already probably gone past the point where he was likely to be able to make the transition from bachelorhood into marriage, even if he wanted to. That he wanted to was moot: his reputation was envied amongst the younger coppers. Awap – Anything With A Pulse – they called him behind his back.

It was a pity, given Atherton's freedom from domestic cares, that he wasn't a career man, Slider thought, rolling over-ventilated socks together and throwing them back in the drawer, whence they would return to haunt him one day. Dickson had once told Atherton that as a policeman he suffered from the disadvantage of too much education – an insult rated very differently by insulter and insultee. Too much of a smartarse, was the general opinion. But Slider believed it was more a spiritual malaise that held Atherton back: an inability to take things seriously, which itself was a function of the chronic outsiderism they all suffered from. Grown like callus to protect the tender places of the soul, it performed a useful function in keeping them sane while dealing with the world's worst madness; but excessive growth could deform. There were lame coppers in plenty; Slider was sometimes afraid his friend was becoming one of them.

Or, to put it another way, if all coppers were odd, those who lived alone were easily the oddest. And he, Slider, was going to join them. He saw himself in years to come living in a small place of his own (it would have to be small, after Irene had had her share of the dead albatross) with his own few, well-liked things around him. Pottering about in his off-duty hours. Cooking for himself. Gardening maybe. Taking up his architectural drawing again, perhaps. Growing more idiosyncratically himself year by year, as people do who have no-one to rub the nobbly bits smooth against. He could see himself ten years on, greyer and more leathery, spreading a little in shapeless sweaters and half-moon glasses, full of annoying little habits of speech and gesture. But probably in the end not discontented – not absolutely.

That was the worst part. He didn't want it that way. He had not been built with that in mind. He abandoned the sock quest, feeling useless and helpless, mourning the awful waste of the situation. How had it come to this? All those years of dull faithfulness, for Irene's sake, for the children's sake, and now they'd all fled like wet nestlings under Ernie's protective wing. It was as though the gods were playing some elaborate practical joke on him. His life was falling apart. He wandered out into the passage and looked down at the stairs – narrow, low-ceilinged, joining the top to the bottom of a house built out of margarine boxes and spit. Everything had been designed in a spirit of meanness, with no consideration but to push back a little further the limits of human tolerance. He had only bought it for Irene's sake, and now she was gone, and he was left with the house. Ha ha, good one, Life.

He walked two steps and pushed open the door of Matthew's room. The furniture was all there, but the room was stripped of his personality, except for the paler patches on the walls where he had taken down his posters of state-of-the-art jet fighters. He must have done it in some haste, because on one wall there was a drawing-pin left in, holding a small triangle of dark shiny paper. Absently, Slider removed it and sat down on the bed with it in his hand.

He had no-one to blame but himself, he thought – as though that made anything better. He had married Irene, knowing what she was like. He had remained a policeman, knowing what it did to home lives. He had followed his career while his children grew distant from him and his wife grew first bored and then resentful. And if she had run off with another man, well, hadn't he been unfaithful to her first, even if she didn't know about it? And hadn't he neglected her until – what an indictment! – even Ernie Newman looked attractive? What kind of a rôle model would Ernie provide for his teenage son, he wondered? Better than his own father, probably: Ernie would always be there, boring, pedantic, costive, but indisputably *there*, and Matthew would forget the Dad who had taught him to bowl overarm and take a fish off a hook without damaging it. And Kate –

He had forgotten he was holding the drawing–in, and fiddling with it, he accidentally drove it into his thumb. He looked down in surprise and hurt. The dark triangle of paper came from Matthew's absolutely favourite poster, the moodily lit, seriously brill picture of a Stealth jet: he'd be really upset that he'd torn it getting it off the wall.

Suddenly, and with shocking vividness, Slider remembered a moment from his own childhood. It was not long after his grandmother, Dad's mother, had died. He was standing in the kitchen of their dank little cottage: winter and summer it always smelled of water, standing or running, mossy or soapy. In the dresser drawer he'd found the picture Gran had given him at Christmas, printed on card in soft, Walt Disney colours: Jesus the Good Shepherd, in a blue robe, with a crook, surrounded by sheep, children, and a brown-and-white collie. He'd loved it when she gave it to him, had thought it lost, and found it again: a moment of joy. But then he remembered she was dead, and suddenly the picture seemed unimportant, stupid, hatefully trivial. In a violent gesture, instantly regretted, he had torn it in two and flung it on the floor. Then Dad came in. He didn't immediately say anything, just picked up the two pieces and held them against each other, looking at them in a silence that made Slider suddenly terrified that he might be going to cry. But Dads never cry. At last he said, 'Never mind, son. We can put it together again with sticky-tape. It won't show from the front.' And suddenly the boy Slider had found himself weeping, his face pressed to Dad's rough, hairy, horse-smelling jacket, his arms round Dad's stringy waist; weeping as though he'd never stop, because then he knew for the first time, really knew, that nothing could make life the way it had been again.

It had been the beginning of the loneliness of growing up. In every life there comes a moment when the individual realises for the first time how separate and untouchable they are, alone in sin and alone in sadness; after that a wholeness is gone, and pleasures, though they may be many, can never be taken for granted. In his mind's eye he could see Matthew taking down his posters, and, in spite of all his care, tearing the corner off his favourite one. Sitting alone on his son's bed, Slider felt his loss as though it were his own. He would have cried, except that Dads don't.

CHAPTER SIX

Turner Blind Eye

It's a human habit which persists in the face of any amount of disappointed experience to imagine, on first hearing a person's name, what they are going to look like. Slider saw Alec Coleraine as a tall, lean, thick-blond-haired sort of name; distinguishedly handsome, perhaps going just a little romantically grey at the temples – silver threads among the gold, tra-la. One thing he wasn't expecting, and it turned out to be the one thing you simply couldn't help noticing on meeting him, was that Alec Coleraine was short. Slider was not a tall man, but as Coleraine advanced hospitably across the carpet of his office to greet him, Slider overtopped him by a good two inches.

'Inspector Slider? How do you do?'

'I'm grateful to you for seeing me at short notice,' Slider said, shaking hands. The hand was small, too: he was built in proportion. 'I hope I haven't kept you here inconveniently.'

'No, no, I had plenty to do. I don't usually leave the office until sixish, anyway. Besides, my convenience is hardly important in a matter as grave as this, is it?'

'I wish everyone I had to speak to thought like that,' Slider said with a smile. While all this making nice was going on, he was studying the face. Coleraine was one of those men who by dint of a small-featured, boyish face and a good head of hair (brown, with a coppery glint) managed to look a good ten years younger than they really were. It was when you came to the eyes that you found the age, but as long as they were crinkled up in a pleasant smile, it was easy to miss it. But on further examination there was something about these eyes that Slider associated with disability or long childhood illness. It was hard to pin it down – it was something to do with the skin around them, a faintly freckled pallor, the unexpected deepness of the fine lines – but he would not have been surprised to learn that Coleraine had suffered from polio or had had a bad accident which had resulted in years of plaster casts and traction. There was nothing visibly wrong with him, however. He was good-looking, with regular, Grecian features, powerful about the chest and shoulders, and he moved and spoke with the sparky briskness that often lumbered short men with the Napoleon-syndrome label.

As they went through their preliminary chatting, Slider could see that he had considerable charm, and could understand why Fay Coleraine had wanted him. Probably a great many women would want him, he thought – that combination of boyishness and power could be intoxicating. But as Coleraine talked, Slider detected a harshness about the shapes the mouth and eyes made; charm and dynamism overlaid a brittleness, as if he had spent his life defending a vulnerable place by keeping it hidden. There was an edge to the voice, too, which Slider found almost unpleasant. But he knew Coleraine didn't like music: perhaps it was simply that he was tone deaf.

Eventually they got on to the subject of Radek. 'What did you think of your father-in-law?' Slider asked. He was seated in an antiqued leather chair, buttoned to within an inch of its life, on one side of the vast reproduction Georgian desk. Coleraine, on the other side, sat well back in an executive swivel that pivoted through so many planes it could have done service as a flight simulator. Slider had accepted the offer of whisky, and was nursing a dangerously large measure of Glenmorangie in a vast cut-glass tumbler so heavy it was going to take both hands to get it up to his mouth. Everything in the office seemed to have been chosen to declare that if money was no object, good taste certainly wasn't either.

'I don't really care for that kind of music,' Coleraine answered, 'so I don't know whether he was a genius or only fabulously successful. He was certainly the latter. But the *cognoscenti* seem to think he was one of the world's all-time greats, too, so who am I to argue?'

'I meant, what did you think of him as a person,' Slider said patiently, aware that Coleraine knew perfectly well what he had meant. Was this just another game of bait-the-policeman – a favoured pastime amongst some members of the middle classes, who cherished the Father-Christmas belief that all coppers were thick – or was he putting off an evil moment?

'Oh, I see.' Coleraine seemed to consider for a moment. 'Well, he wasn't an easy person to like,' he said at last. 'Not that he cared whether he was or not. He liked to play power games with people, as long as the odds were stacked for him to win – and let's face it, when a man is as rich and important as Stefan, they usually are.' He had put rich first, Slider noted. Was that accidental or a significant psychological marker – what they called in more technical police language, a bit of a dead give-away? Coleraine went on, 'It was sad, really: being who he was, he could have done so much good; but he was arrogant and selfish and mean. It seemed such a waste.'

'I suppose he was a very wealthy man?'

'Oh, I didn't mean "mean" in that sense,' Coleraine said hastily – too hastily to avoid the clumsiness of the sentence. 'Fay and I have plenty of our own. We both have successful businesses which we built up entirely ourselves, without any help from Stefan.'

'You think he ought to have helped you?'

Coleraine looked confused, as Slider meant him to be, by the near-sequitur, and hesitated over the possible paths out of the apparent misunderstanding. 'Look, I wasn't interested in my father-in-law's money. I want you to realise that. I've done all right for myself,' he said, with a vague wave of the glass at his surroundings. 'It was the way he treated Fay that I didn't like,' he went on with an air of being absolutely fair. 'I mean, when we were first married. That's all in the past now, of course.'

'How did he treat your wife?'

Coleraine frowned at the question. 'I don't want you thinking this is some festering sore. It's ancient history now.

81

And in fact, I got on pretty well with the old boy at the end. He wasn't half so bad if you stood up to him and let him know you didn't give a damn what he thought of you.'

'You were on friendly terms with him, then?'

'Yes, he wasn't such an ogre really.'

'You visited him quite a lot, I suppose?'

'No, not a great deal. Just now and then. From time to time,' he said with diminishing eagerness. 'He wasn't the sort of man you'd drop in on out of pleasure.' Slider was interested that Coleraine seemed to think it mattered what he thought of his relationship with Radek. He was trying to create an impression, or perhaps trying not to create another impression. Now why was that?

'So what did you drop in on him out of?' he asked.

'Oh, for God's sake,' Coleraine said impatiently, lifting one hand towards his brow in an uncompleted gesture. 'I wasn't in the habit of dropping in on him. All I'm trying to say is that I got on all right with the old boy, but we weren't great chums, all right?'

Slider smiled enigmatically. 'How did he treat your wife when you were first married?' he reverted. Coleraine didn't answer for a moment, looking annoyed, or perhaps rattled, and Slider went on, 'I understand he didn't approve of the marriage? Or didn't approve of you?'

'Who told you that? Oh, never mind. The fact is Stefan wouldn't have approved of Fay marrying anyone. He wanted to keep her to himself.'

'But he'd sent her away to school, hadn't he, to be rid of her?'

'He could hardly keep her at home once his wife died,' Coleraine objected. 'With no-one to look after her, he had to send her to school. But that didn't mean he didn't want her. She was one of his possessions, and he liked to keep hold of them. And he certainly didn't want anyone else to have her, particularly a nobody like me. So he forbade the marriage, and when Fay went ahead and defied him, he told her she could stew in her own juice from then on, and cut her off without a penny. He was rolling in money, but he enjoyed watching us struggle. And it was a struggle at first, I can tell you. But we made it. I think it riled him that we showed him we didn't need him. I think that's why he offered to pay Marcus's school fees later on. But Marcus got a scholarship, so that wiped the old devil's eye for him.' He paused, perhaps listening to himself critically, for he went on, 'I felt almost sorry for him in the end. It must be sad to have to keep proving to yourself that people need you, and then finding out they don't.'

'Your son is how old now?'

'Twenty-one.'

'And what does he do?'

Coleraine frowned. 'What has all this got to do with Stefan's murder? Why are you asking about me and my family?'

'I'm just trying to get a picture of Sir Stefan's life,' Slider said innocently. 'You see, no-one seems to know of anyone who might want to kill him. So I have to collect every scrap of information I can, to put the whole jigsaw puzzle together. You never know which piece might prove crucial.'

'It all sounds a bit unscientific,' Coleraine said patronisingly. 'We aren't living in the nineteenth century, you know.'

'Oh, we've got people out doing all the high-tech things as well,' Slider said kindly. 'I have my own area of expertise.'

Coleraine, to do him justice, recognised fifteen-all when he saw it. 'Well, I don't know that I can tell you anything,' he said more helpfully. 'I can't think who might want to kill Stefan either.'

'When did you last see him?' Slider asked.

A slight hesitation. 'Actually, it was on Tuesday – Tuesday morning.' His voice had changed. He was trying to slip it out as lightly and unimportantly as possible, and his eyes were watchful. Presumably he thought it was a damaging admission, and that might mean something or nothing: people had the oddest ideas of what was damaging, and often lied about something of no importance at all. It was one of the major frustrations of police work.

'Where did you see him?' Slider asked.

'Oh, at home. At his home, I mean. I – just popped in.'

'Why?'

'No reason in particular. I was just passing, saw his place, wondered how he was.' He shrugged and smiled. 'Passing

83

fancy, you might say.' Something visibly occurred to him. 'I think he'd been having a flaming row with Buster. They were glaring daggers at each other, so it was a good job I did turn up. Poor old Buster looked fit to burst into tears.'

Odd how everyone referred to Keaton as 'poor old Buster', Slider reflected. He seemed to have been very comfortably placed and quite content in his lot. 'What were they quarrelling about?'

'Oh, I don't know. They stopped when I arrived of course. But I don't suppose it was important. They often had barnies. It didn't mean anything.'

Slider smiled. 'Like a married couple.'

Coleraine shook his head. 'It wasn't like that, if that's what you were thinking. And for God's sake, don't suggest anything of the sort to Fay. It makes her mad as hell. She hates the way people always assume that every friendship has to be that way.'

'I wasn't thinking that. I was only suggesting that people quarrelling doesn't mean they don't love each other or aren't happy together.'

'Yes, well, I'll pass over your use of the word love,' Coleraine said with a tight smile. 'Basically you're right.'

Slider switch-hit. 'Do you know how your father-in-law's estate was left?'

Coleraine opened his eyes wide and frank, to show this was not a problem question. 'The bulk of it goes to Fay. I think Buster was to have the house for his lifetime, which is only fair, considering the years he's put in with the old boy; but it did belong to Fay's grandfather, after all, so it's right it should go to her when Buster dies. He hasn't any family to worry about it anyway. But everything else goes to Fay.'

'It's a considerable fortune, I understand,' Slider said.

'Is it?' he said with enormous indifference. 'I don't know exactly how much. But Fay and I have all we need anyway.'

'Oh, a little extra money never comes amiss,' Slider said genially. 'Perhaps you could put it in trust for your son.'

That touched a nerve. Coleraine offered only a terse and forbidding, 'Perhaps.'

Slider changed direction again. 'Where were you on Wednesday afternoon?'

84

Something quickened in Coleraine's face. He was suddenly alert and wary. 'Why are you asking me that? Surely I'm not a suspect?'

Slider smiled. 'Telling me where you were doesn't make you a suspect.'

'Why else would you ask that?'

'I can think of lots of reasons. Supposing someone who was a suspect was naming you as their alibi? I'd need to check it out, wouldn't I?'

He had spoken more or less at random, but he seemed to have struck something. Coleraine's face was taut, his mouth ugly with tension. 'Has someone done that?'

'Have you some reason not to tell me where you were on Wednesday afternoon?' Slider countered smoothly.

'No. Not at all. I – er – I was at home,' Coleraine said with some reluctance. 'I was supposed to be lunching with a client that day, but I didn't feel well, so I cancelled it and went home. Mrs Goodwin, my secretary, will confirm that.'

'What time did you get home?'

'About a quarter to two, I suppose. I didn't go out again.'

'Were you alone?'

'Of course I was alone. What sort of question is that?'

'I meant, is there anyone who can confirm that you were there?'

He shook his head. 'Fay was at work. She came home about seven.'

'And your son?'

'He doesn't live with us. He has his own flat in Bayswater.' He tried a smile. 'I'm afraid it's not much of an alibi, is it?'

'Well,' Slider said innocently, 'as long as you don't need one, it doesn't matter, does it?'

'No, of course not,' Coleraine said, looking at Slider thoughtfully. 'You wouldn't, by any chance, be taking the piss, would you?'

'Not by any chance,' Slider said, returning the look. 'A man is dead, Mr Coleraine. What's dead can't come to life, I think.'

'Browning,' he said rather blankly. 'Not a very popular poet.'

'But then mine is not a very popular job. Except with the victims. We're the only ones who actually have to see the victims. The lawyers, the judges, the juries, the social workers, the journalists – they only see the accused, looking very small and put-upon in the dock, or being hustled into a police car.' He drained his whisky and stood up. 'I'm very grateful to you for your time. If I have any more questions, I'll be in touch, and I hope you'll be patient with me. We will find out who killed your father-in-law,' he promised.

'Yes,' said Coleraine, as if that was the only safe word he could think of for the moment.

In the outer office the secretary was rattling away on a word-processor. She looked up and smiled hesitantly at Slider, and he paused by her desk.

'Mrs Goodwin, isn't it?'

'Yes,' she said. 'Helena.' She was a striking-looking woman in her mid-thirties, with large brown eyes and high cheek-bones, dark, fine hair escaping from an Edwardian cottage-loaf, the legal secretary's uniform garb of blue-and-white striped shirt and navy skirt. She looked as though she hadn't been getting much sleep lately: she was pale and there were dark shadows under her eyes, and the smile on her rather lovely mouth was troubled.

'You've been with Mr Coleraine for some time now, haven't you?'

'Four years, and two with Mr Antrobus before that. I don't know if you'd call that a long time.'

Slider nodded encouragingly. 'It's an upsetting business, this.' She watched him carefully, committing herself to nothing. 'A murder in the family,' he expanded, 'even if the victim wasn't particularly popular.'

'I didn't really know Sir Stefan,' she said. 'Only as an ordinary member of the public. He never came to this office.'

'Do you like classical music?'

'Some,' she said circumspectly.

'You've been to concerts when he's been conducting, I suppose?'

For some reason the question bothered her. A faint pinkness appeared. 'One or two. I – I don't really go out much. I have a little boy. Babysitters aren't always easy to find.'

'What does your husband do?'

'I'm divorced,' she said abruptly, the pink deepening. She stood up. 'May I show you out? I have rather a lot of work to catch up on.'

'I'm sorry, I don't want to put you behind,' he said with his most engaging smile, and she softened a little.

'No, it's all right, really,' she said, coming round the desk and crossing to the door. He waited until her hand was on the doorknob.

'Can you tell me what time Mr Coleraine left on Wednesday?'

The hand remained steady, but she said, 'I should have thought you could have asked him that.'

'What an evasive answer,' he said lightly. 'Is there something I ought to know about Wednesday?'

She turned and looked at him steadily. 'No, nothing at all. He left at twelve-thirty.' He waited in silence, looking pleasantly expectant, until she felt obliged to add more. 'He had a luncheon appointment for twelve forty-five, but he came out of his office at half past and said that he wasn't feeling well and was going home, and asked me to cancel it for him.'

'That was rather short notice, wasn't it?'

'Yes, but it wasn't a client, it was a colleague, Peter Gethers. His office is only round the corner in King Street, and they were going to a local restaurant, so I was able to catch him before he left. Mr Coleraine looked very unwell. I wasn't surprised he had to go home.'

She was defending him. Loyalty – or something to cover up?

'Did anything happen that morning to upset him? Anything out of the ordinary?'

'I don't think so.'

'Did he have any visitors?'

'Not that morning.'

'Phone calls.'

'Of course. Lots of them.'

'What was the last one you put through? Do you remember?'

'It was Marcus, his son,' she said with faint reluctance. 'He telephoned at about a quarter to twelve. Then Mr Coleraine buzzed me and asked me to hold all calls for half an hour. And at half past twelve he came out from his office and said he was going home.'

'Do you think those things had anything to do with each other?' Slider asked pleasantly, as though it were a matter of no importance.

She was not wooed. 'I don't know. How could I know that? You must ask Mr Coleraine.'

'Of course. I just thought he might have said something to you about it.'

'Well he didn't. Is there anything else now? Because I really do have a lot of work to catch up.'

'Nothing else at present. Thank you very much, Mrs Goodwin. You've been a great help.'

She opened the door for him, looking faintly puzzled about what she could have said that was so helpful. There was never any harm in leaving people slightly off balance.

Slider walked in to his office and found Atherton lounging like a tame Viking against the cold radiator talking to WDC Kathleen Swilley – always called Norma for her sins which, since she led a social life of well-guarded privacy, had to be largely imagined by her colleagues, and were. She was blonde and bronzed and mighty like the heroine of a Halls of Valhalla SF mag, and she exuded a degree of sexual vitality you could light a campfire with if you only had a magnifying glass handy – the sort of woman who her colleagues told each other, with varying degrees of wistfulness, must be a lesbian.

'Oh don't be such a stiff,' she was saying sternly. 'You know exactly what I'm talking about. Your idea of safe sex is not telling the girl where you live.'

'Wearing a condom is avoiding the issue,' Atherton said, at his most maddening.

'It's not a joking matter, Jim, not any more. These days you –'

They both saw Slider at the same moment, and Norma sprang off the edge of his desk where she had been warming a neglected circulation file with her delectable and (Slider could only assume) peachlike bottom. She brushed her skirt down, turning to face him with a slight and extremely fetching blush; Atherton declined to be caught wrong-footed, and continued to decorate the radiator with a catlike smile, his weight on his hands and his legs crossed at the ankle, like a third-year student at a tutorial.

'Am I interrupting?' Slider enquired pleasantly. 'Don't stop on my account. I know my office is a public place within the meaning of the Act.'

'The ballistics report has come in, sir,' Norma said. She held out the sheaf of paper, trying to look like a civil servant and failing.

'Tell me,' he said, taking it and passing round his desk to sit down. 'I assume you've read it.'

'Yes, sir. The bullet was a .38, and it was fired from a Webley and Scott Mark IV revolver. Priest thinks given the range it was likely it was the model with the five-inch barrel.'

Chris Priest was the top firearms guru at the Home Office lab at Huntingdon. One glance at the striations on a spent bullet, and he could tell you the gunmaker's sock size. Nothing, unfortunately, about the gun owner.

'A .38 Webley?'

'It was a popular handgun for British officers during the Second World War,' Norma said, 'which would make it bad luck for us, because if it was a World War Two trophy it won't have been registered.'

'Why should you assume that?' Atherton said. He was looking faintly annoyed, perhaps at Swilley's display of expert knowledge in a subject in which he had no interest – or perhaps it was a residue from their interrupted conversation.

'Because, brain, all weapons issued during the Second World War are Government property and cannot lawfully be retained. Don't you know your firearms law?'

'All right, but it doesn't have to be a World War Two gun, does it?' Atherton objected. 'Presumably they've been used at other times.'

'Priest thinks the gun was pretty old; and besides,' she turned to Slider again, 'the actual bullet turns out to be quite interesting. It's marked DC 43, which stands for Dominion Cartridge 1943. It was a brand made in Canada and shipped over towards the end of the war. Apparently we couldn't make enough over here to keep up with demand.'

'Nice and specific,' Slider said, 'but unfortunately not much use to us unless we have a suspect.'

'I quite fancy the agent's boyfriend,' Atherton said. 'Stephen or Steve Murray. I've done a bit of work on him. He's a stage-hand at the Royal Opera House – sweat and singlet type – more brawn than brain. Apparently Kate Apwey likes a bit of rough trade.' He glanced at Norma but she refused to be provoked. 'I ran a make on him, and he's got a little bit of form: possession, a couple of cautions for drunk and disorderly – pub fights – and, here's the juicy one, a suspended for assault and ABH. Bloke on the management team of one of the big orchestras – Murray thought Kate was having an affair with him; waited for him outside the Festival Hall, caught him coming out of the artists' entrance and broke two of his ribs.'

'It's too much to hope that Murray's known for carrying weapons?' Slider asked.

'Much too much,' Atherton said. 'But he jumped this bloke in full daylight with people walking past, and then ran away – which is the same sort of MO as Radek's murderer – and also he had good reason to suppose Radek was humping Apwey – which is the same motive as the assault.'

Norma looked unimpressed. 'You think sex is at the bottom of everything.'

'Unfortunate turn of phrase, Norm.'

'But look,' she went on, ignoring him, 'the person who shot Radek was small, not a hulking great scenery-humper.'

'Ah, that's the beauty of it. I said Murray was brawny, not a hulk. He's more your small, wiry type. Kate Apwey reckons he's five-nine, but you can take an inch off for adoration. *And* he wasn't at work on Wednesday afternoon. He phoned in sick.' He looked appealingly at Slider.

'It sounds promising. You'd better check up on the alibi, and go round and have a look at his drum. Does he live with Apwey?'

'Surprisingly, not yet. She shares a flat with two other professional girls – sorry, Norma, women – and he has a flat in Covent Garden, handy for work. I don't get the impression he earns much.'

Slider nodded. 'That would tend to put him in a dilemma. On the one hand jealousy of his girlfriend's relationship with Radek, and on the other hand, knowing she needed both the job and the tips for them to be able to get a place together.'

'Jealousy, deep frustration, ambivalence of mind – boom!' said Atherton happily.

'On the other hand,' Slider said, 'we mustn't lose sight of the other possibles. It won't hurt to take a look at this sacked musician, what was his name? Preston, Bob Preston. At least find out where he was so we can eliminate him. And then there are the Coleraines.'

'Not Mrs, guv,' Swilley said. 'Polish checked her alibi and it's tight. She was at her shop until two o'clock, and then she drove to Peter Jones's to buy fabrics. They know her there, and the manageress of the department says she served her before she went off for her tea at three, and she was about fifteen to twenty minutes buying stuff. There's no way she could have been at Shepherd's Bush shooting Radek at two thirty-five and got to Sloane Square by two forty-five.'

'Good,' said Slider. 'I didn't really think it was her. Her husband, now, he's another matter. He struck me as nervous and evasive, and his alibi is unprovable. He says he was at home alone all afternoon.'

'Wait a minute, guv,' Norma said. 'He can't have been at home all afternoon, because we tried to phone Mrs Coleraine there and got no answer. That must have been about four-ish. We eventually caught her at the shop, after she got back from Peter Jones. That's when we told her about Radek being shot.'

'Coleraine says he got home at a quarter to two. Let's find out everything we can about him. Maybe his business was in trouble. Maybe his son's in trouble. He knew his wife would inherit Radek's estate, and a good dutiful wife wouldn't fail to share the loot with him.'

'It was quite a loot, too,' Atherton said. 'I checked with the solicitor that Parker, Pool and Law put me on to. Radek was worth about three million pounds.'

There was a brief silence. 'Just for waving your arms about,' Norma said wistfully.

'Now that's what I call a motive,' Slider said. 'I'm glad I

91

didn't know how much before I talked to Mrs Coleraine.'

Slider put his head into the CID room, looking for Atherton, and Beevers looked up from his desk.

'Sir, over here,' he called.

'No, sir over here,' Slider corrected.

Beevers looked at him with grave Nonconformist reproof. 'Have you got a minute, guv? Only it's something a bit odd.'

Slider went meekly and looked over Beevers' shoulder at some printed lists. 'What's this, stolen property?'

'It's something that came in this morning, that I was working on before. You know that load of stolen antiques and stuff we found in that big house in Paddenswick Road?'

'We took Lenny Picket up for it.' Slider shook his head. 'I can never get over that name – Picket the Fence. What other line of work could he possibly have taken up?'

Beevers thought about it. 'I suppose he could have been a landscape gardener.'

Slider was thrown into confusion. Was the Pillar of the Chapel making a joke? Normally Beevers disapproved of humour, believing that lightness of mind was an infallible indicator of lightness of morals – and with the example of Atherton before them, who could argue with him? 'What about it, anyway?' Slider said hastily.

'Well, guv, there were some paintings in the haul, so we sent a description round all the dealers to see if they could place them. This letter came in this morning from Christie's. I was going to pass it on to one of the TDs when the name caught my eye. Look –' He squared the letter before Slider. 'They identify the three paintings as stuff they sold to Alec Coleraine only five months ago, paid for with a bank draft drawn on his personal account. Important paintings, too.'

Slider read, and let out a soundless whistle. 'You're not kidding.' A Turner, a minor Constable and an Italian painter Slider hadn't heard of – religious and Italian, sixteenth-century. The three together had been bought for a total of one million, two hundred and fifty thousand pounds. 'And Coleraine wasn't kidding when he said he was doing all right. One and a quarter million on piccies? I wonder if Lenny knew what he was getting into. Pictures like that are a bit out of his league.'

92

Beevers scratched his woolly head thoughtfully. 'The funny thing is, guv, Coleraine never reported 'em missing. You know McLaren used to be at Kensington, where Coleraine's gaff is? Well, he got a mate of his over there to look up the records. There was a break-in at the house on the fifth of June, three weeks after he bought the paintings. It looked like a professional job – burglar alarm bypassed and a window taken right out, nice as pie, not kid's stuff. This mate of McLaren's faxed us the report, and there's a list of stolen gear – small antiques, silver and some figurines – but no mention of these paintings. But,' he added the word weightily as he drew another sheet forward and turned it for Slider's scrutiny, tapping with his forefinger, 'if you look here, on this list of the gear we got from Lenny's, this occasional table sounds very like the one Coleraine says he lost; and these figurines, here, they've got to be the same, haven't they?'

Slider read. 'They sound like it,' he admitted.

'Staffordshire glazed figures, 1840s, Victoria and Albert, Admiral Nelson, Sir Robert Peel, George Washington, they're all on the list. George Hudson – who was he, anyway?'

'The Railway King. Pioneering railway builder. Didn't you want to drive a steam train when you were a kid?'

'I'm not old enough,' Beevers said with unconscious cruelty. 'Anyway, guv, here we've got gear from Coleraine's break-in turning up at Lenny's, plus paintings we know Coleraine bought, but he never reports 'em stolen.' He shook his head with dark reproof. 'It's a bit queer.'

After consulting with the duty sergeant, Paxman, whose specialist subject on *Mastermind* could have been Drinking Habits of Shepherd's Bush Lowlife, 1960 to 1990, Slider ran Lenny Picket to earth in The George in Hammersmith Broadway, a vast Edwardian pub of mahogany panels and acid-embossed glass screens, in whose womblike darkness the few daytime drinkers sat at a respectful distance from each other and politely never looked up when anyone came in or went out. As if out of a sense of artistic coherence, everything about Lenny was as narrow as his name – narrow face, narrow shoulders, narrow chest. He smoked very thin roll-ups and during the brief period they stayed alight narrowed his eyes against the rising smoke. He was a squirrel of a man, small, neat, quick and adaptable; a player of many rôles, who at the drop of a hat could switch speech modes from Parkhurst to Park Lane.

He was reading up the forthcoming antique sales in the *Telegraph*, and folded the paper hastily when Slider arrived alongside his table.

'Oh, Mr Slider, you gave me a start,' he said. He had a curiously husky voice which made him sound a bit like Lauren Bacall. Perhaps that was why Slider had always liked him.

'Hullo, Lenny. I wanted to have a word with you. Mind if I sit down?'

'Can I stop you?' Lenny shrugged. 'I'm on bail, my life isn't my own any more.'

'Drink?'

'Might as well take one off you. Gold watch – make it a double – no ice.'

When Slider returned with the drinks he settled down on the other side of the table, and Lenny abandoned the dismal remains of his last roll-up, brought out a packet of Rizla and a tin of Old Horrible, and started anew. 'What's the beef, then?'

'It's about that last haul we nicked you for.'

'Come on now, Mr Slider, I put me hand up for that like a good boy,' he protested. 'End of story. *Finito*.'

'All right, Len, it's not grief for you. I just want some information,' Slider reassured him. 'About those three oil paintings.'

Lenny looked gloomy. 'I wishter God I'd never touched 'em. I don't know what came over me. I've been in this business all my life, and rule number one is never touch nothing there's only one of. I mean, what the 'ell was I going to do with 'em? A nice bit of furniture, a nice garden stachoo, who'd to say where it came from? But an oil painting, and a ruddy Gainsborough into the bargain –'

'It was a Constable, actually.'

'Don't say that word, please,' Lenny shuddered delicately. 'I'll never forget when that PC D'Arblay came bursting in.

94

The irony was not lost on me, I promise you.'

'Does it never bother you that what you're doing is completely immoral?' Slider asked in wonder. 'You seem such a nice bloke otherwise.'

'Come on now, Mr Slider, be fair. I'm a businessman,' he said in wounded tones. 'I pay an honest price for what I buy, and sell it again at an honest profit. I've got thousands of satisfied customers who'd give me a testimony. I don't ask where the stuff comes from or where it goes to, but then who does? It's not my fault if other people break the law, is it?'

'A fascinating rationale,' Slider said. 'I like you, Lenny. It's such a pity you're bent.'

'Bent? Listen,' he leaned forward earnestly, 'I had a young bloke in my place a couple of weeks ago, posh accent, posh clothes, all the education money could buy: he comes in to look at some lead allegorical figures for his garden, argues about the price, finally writes me a cheque – and has it away with my fountain pen. Now *that's* bent. Young people today! They got no standards.'

Slider smiled. 'Well, I'm not interested in statues. It's those oil paintings I want to know about. I want to know where they came from. D'you want to give me a name, Len, and save me a lot of trouble?'

Lenny lifted a hand. 'Now then, now then, you know me better than that. I may not be lily-white in your eyes, but I don't grass up a business associate. Where'd I be if I got meself a reputation? I'd be finished. No-one'd ever do business with me again if they knew I was going to put Plod on their tail.'

'And you know me well enough to know I wouldn't ask you unless it was important,' Slider said. 'I suppose I didn't really expect you to tell me, though I could make a fair guess – within three names.' He looked deep into Lenny's eyes, or as deep as you can look into the slit in a pillar box, but Lenny faced him out unmoved. 'Look,' Slider went on, 'at this stage you don't have to tell me who you got the pictures from, I just want to know where they were stolen from. The address, that's all.'

'What d'you mean, at this stage?' Lenny asked suspiciously.

'It may or it may not prove important. If it doesn't, you won't hear any more about it, my word on it. If it is important, I'll try to keep you out of it and establish the information from another direction.'

'Try?' Lenny sounded peevish. 'And I'll be inside *trying* not to get my boat altered during association period.'

'It's a murder case I'm investigating,' Slider said impatiently. 'Don't mess me about, Lenny. I'm asking you nicely now, and ten to one you'll hear nothing more about it. But we can do it the hard way if you like, and you can have all the publicity you want.'

'That's blackmail. I'm surprised at you, Mr Slider. I always though you was a decent bloke.' He shook his head over the unreliability of humankind. 'Look, I tell you straight, I don't know where the pictures came from. That's not something I ever ask. I can go back to my supplier and ask him, but whether he'll tell me or not –' He shook his head again.

'He'll tell you. You'll make him. You'll find a way, Lenny. I have confidence in you.'

'It might take me a bit of time.'

Slider smiled. For such a kind-faced man he could look surprisingly menacing when he wanted to, Lenny thought.

'Oh, you'll have the information by Monday, I'm sure of it. An anonymous phone call is all I want. Just an address. Got me?'

'Got you,' Lenny sighed. He pushed his roll-up into the corner of his mouth and fumbled in his pocket for his lighter. 'Tell me, does anybody ever make the mistake of thinking you're soft?'

'Only my wife,' Slider said sadly.

CHAPTER SEVEN

Humming and Erring

On the whole Atherton liked what had happened to Covent Garden. Some of the shops might be a bit poncey, and it seemed to be impossible to cross the piazza without having to avoid someone in black tights and a striped jumper miming his way round a sheet of glass; but at least the place was vital now. Empty upstairs rooms were being turned into flats and bedsitters, the reversal of the usual trend in Central London, and it had the comfortingly Manhattan feeling of a place where people lived, shopped, ate and sat out on sunny evenings on their doorsteps and window-sills watching the world go by.

It had always been rich in restaurants, and he decided to fortify himself with lunch before seeking out Kate Apwey's lover. In a state of pleasant anticipation he strolled into what had been his favourite tatty tratt, a place of check tablecloths and heartwarming Italian vulgarity, only to find it had changed hands since his last visit. Atherton knew he was in trouble when he saw sun-dried tomatoes and balsamic vinegar on the menu: life at the Casa Angelo had suddenly got serious. Gone were the tight-trousered boys with priapic pepper mills, the vast mamma in black wedged behind the till, the clusters of strawed Chianti bottles hanging about in corners like evil funghi, the loop tape of *Volare* and *O Sole Mio*. Now there was rubber music played almost but not quite sub-aurally, the tablecloths were white and the light fittings chrome, and the pictures on the walls were numbingly abstract. Gone were the familiar comforts of avocado vinaigrette, spag bol and pollo sorpreso, the mountain of profiteroles on the sweet trolley overshadowing an untouched bowl of oranges in somethingorother. Now the food made sparse patterns on the oversize plates; olive oil seemed to get drizzled over most things, and the owner actually came out in a grey silk suit and supervised the drizzling. Atherton ate and left a sadder but not much wider man; nobody, in his opinion, ought ever to come out of an Italian restaurant still able to do up all their buttons.

Chastened, he sought Murray's address – a flat above a former warehouse – and found it with some difficulty, for the door was not where it might be expected to be, but round an apparently unrelated corner. He was prepared for there to be no answer to his ring, but after a few moments there was a thunder of feet and the door was opened by a young man, dark-haired and olive-skinned, small and powerful as an Etruscan warrior, standing on the bare wooden stairs onto which the door opened directly. He was wearing grey flannel trousers and braces over a bare chest, his bare feet were very dirty, his chin was unshaven, his eyes were bloodshot, and his hair looked as though he had slept in it. He looked about mid-twenties, though there were lines in his face which suggested a hard life – or perhaps merely chronic bad-temper. He looked at Atherton with an expression of suspicion if not hostility: this was not the man to give anyone the benefit of the doubt.

'Are you Steve Murray?' Atherton asked mildly.

'Who wants to know?' he barked.

Atherton showed his brief. 'Can I come in? I want to talk to you.'

'What about?'

The memory of the sad meal sapped Atherton's patience. 'Oh, don't get funny with me,' he said. 'What do you think I want to talk about? The Arts budget?'

'How the hell should I know?' Murray said. 'Have you got a warrant?'

Atherton sighed inwardly. They all watched too many tv cop shows these days. 'Should I need one?' he asked pointedly.

Murray stared a moment and then backed off, turning himself with some delicacy on the stairs, and Atherton followed him up. At the top was another door, letting onto a long dark corridor running the width of the building, fragrant with the ghost of a thousand cabbages and sounding hollow underfoot. At the far end a rectangle of light was the doorway into the main room: large, lofty and lit with a range of old-fashioned metal-framed windows all along one wall. An upstairs storeroom, he thought, and imagined it stacked with wooden crates of bananas from the Windward Isles, oranges from Cape Town, pineapples from the Gold Coast – ah, the romance of greengrocery! It had probably been a very good storeroom and was now, with the perverse fashion for housing humans in structures designed for inanimate objects, a comfortless living-room. It was bare-floored and sparsely furnished – some of the pieces giving the impression of having been made from those same crates – and one corner accommodated the kitchen, divided off by a breakfast bar. The air was heavy with the smell of joss-sticks not quite masking the smell of pot. Atherton was glad it was none of his business: he wouldn't have wagered a dead cat on there not being little plastic bags of forbidden substances lying about.

Without a glance at Atherton, Murray walked straight across the room, swung himself up onto a bar-stool at the kitchen counter, picked up the newspaper lying there and began to read it.

'Nice place,' Atherton said. 'Do you live here alone?' Murray continued to ignore him, turning a page with ostentatious concentration. 'I know you're not reading that,' Atherton said pleasantly, 'it's *The Sun*. You might as well talk to me and get it over with.'

Murray flung the paper down petulantly. 'You people never leave me alone, just because I got into a bit of trouble once. What do you want, anyway? I've got to go to work in half an hour, so you'll have to make it quick.'

'I want to talk to you about Radek – Sir Stefan Radek.'

Murray's face darkened. 'He's dead,' he said. 'Good thing too.'

'Did you kill him?'

The question didn't seem to surprise Murray. 'I wish I had.

I hate his sort. They think money's everything. If you're poor you're nothing. Scumbag!'

'Did you know he was having your girlfriend?' Atherton enquired sympathetically.

Murray stared at him. 'What do you think, I'm stupid?'

'Is that a yes?'

'Of course I bloody knew. I'd have broken both his arms, but *she* wouldn't have it. Told me she was milking him. Huh! Piddling amounts he gave her; I knew who was screwing who.'

'How piddling were the amounts?'

'Couple of hundred. Tarts in Soho get that. Five hundred once, when she went to Hong Kong. For having that filthy old goat slobbering over her – I told her she was mad.'

'I'm amazed you let her do it.'

Murray's face darkened. 'What are you talking about, man, *let* her? A woman's got the right to do what she wants with her own body, right? She's entitled to her own space, rules her own destiny. What are you, one of these chauvinist scumbags, think you can own a woman?'

Ah, evidently a *Guardian* reader, Atherton thought. 'No, not at all,' he replied mildly. 'You seemed so angry about it I thought perhaps you were.'

'You didn't expect me to like it, did you, sharing her with that capitalist filth-bag? But it was her choice. No-one's got the right to tell her what to do and who to go with.'

'Very liberal of you,' Atherton said. It was a sound position for Murray to adopt: there must have been a few people urging Kate not to go with him, after all – Mr and Mrs Apwey, for a bet.

'She's too soft, Kate,' Murray said more reflectively. 'Lets people push her around. He blackmailed her, you know, told her she'd lose her job if she didn't do what he wanted. I told her to stuff the job, but she said no. It paid well, and she was saving up for us to get married and buy a house.' He sniffed and wiped his nose on the back of his hand.

Atherton was entranced by him. 'You were happy about marrying her and living in a house, were you?'

'Why not?' he said. 'Marriage is okay, and you gotta live somewhere. She doesn't like it here. I said, baby, you're

100

paying for it, you got the right to live where you want. She wants furniture and stuff. Me, I can fuck on a bed or I can fuck on the floor, it's all the same to me.' He paused. 'What're you asking me all this shit for, anyway? Is this a bust?'

Far too much tv, Atherton thought. 'Does it look like a bust?'

'You people never leave me alone,' he muttered.

'You didn't go in to work on Wednesday,' Atherton said. 'Why was that?'

'Last Wednesday? I was sick. What's it to you?'

'What kinda sick? You see a doctor?' Atherton gave in and adopted the local style.

Murray glared at him. 'Sick like you get when you've had too much the night before, all right?' He jumped down off the stool and kicked at the newspaper, his voice rising. 'I had a few beers, did a few lines, I was canned, I felt lousy, so I didn't get up, okay? I called in and told them I was taking the day off. I stayed in bed all day. Okay?'

At that moment the door in the long wall opposite the windows opened, and a fair young man came out, tousled, gummy-eyed, wearing a grubby red towel over an expensive tan and a St Christopher on a gold chain round his neck. His nose was running, and if he was not now he had certainly recently been in an illegal state of mind. 'What's the matter, what's all the shouting?' he mumbled, and broke into a huge open-mouthed yawn revealing fine teeth and a regrettable tongue. Closing his mouth he looked at Atherton. 'Who's this bloke, Steve?'

The voice was blurred but the accent was unmistakably upper class. Steve Murray evidently believed in sinning above his station.

'Never mind. Just go back to sleep, dickhead,' Murray snarled.

'I'm Detective Sergeant Atherton,' Atherton said. 'Just having a chat with your friend. Who are you?'

The young man looked wary. 'Does it matter?'

Atherton smiled. 'I wouldn't have asked if I hadn't wanted to know, son. What's your name?'

The eyes flickered across to Murray and back, and he gave

101

a tiny shrug. 'Marcus Coleraine, if it's any of your business,' he said sulkily.

'Oh, I think it is,' Atherton said smoothly, hiding the lift of his heart at the scent of a lead. 'I'm just asking your friend here what he knows about the death of your grandpa.'

Marcus's eyes widened. 'Oh shit!' he breathed.

Slider was just about to leave his office when the phone rang. He hesitated a moment, and then thought that it might possibly be Joanna and answered it.

'Bill!' Wrong. It was Irene, annoyed. 'Why didn't you call me back?'

'I didn't know you were trying to reach me,' he said stupidly.

'I rang you twice. Didn't you get the messages?'

Belatedly he identified Mrs Hislop-Ivory. He imagined the exchange: 'Who's calling?' 'It's his wife, Irene.' McLaren must have been doing X-rays without his lead hat again. Or was he just deaf?

'Now I come to think of it, yes,' Slider said. 'Is something wrong?'

'Not wrong exactly, but we have to talk, you know. About the house, for one thing.'

'I can't talk now, I'm just going out.'

'Oh yes, it's lunchtime, isn't it? Don't let me spoil your pleasure!'

'It's not that. We've got a big case on. I've got a lot to do.'

'There's always some excuse. Well you can spare me a few minutes of your precious time. There are things we have to sort out.'

'Can't it wait until tonight?'

'Who's to say whether I'll be able to catch you tonight? You can't put it off for ever, Bill. I know you. You always think things will go away if you ignore them, but they won't.'

No he didn't. That annoyed him. He knew they wouldn't. 'Ernie Newman didn't go away. I tried ignoring him.'

'Maybe that was the trouble,' she said sharply. 'Any normal man would have felt jealous about another man hanging around his wife. Any normal man would have done something about it.'

'Like what?'

'Like taken a little interest in me.'

Ouch, that smarted. He turned the attack. 'No normal man could have felt jealous of Ernie Newman. You can't tell the size of his house and pension just from looking at him.'

'Do you really think I'm that shallow?' Irene asked, hurt.

Now Slider felt ashamed, and in his shame hit out again. 'Well, let's face it, you're not after him for his body, are you?'

'How dare you say that?' she retorted. 'Do you think because you don't please me that no-one can?'

Slider reeled, on the ropes. By God, that got him where he lived! On a scale of chauvinism he ranked pretty low amongst his peers, but still he had always assumed that Irene was not interested in sex. It was shocking to be told suddenly, after all these years, that *au contraire* she was simply not interested in him; the more so because of the unpleasant revelations it made about him to himself – not so much about his sexual technique, but about his conceit, of which he had believed he was fairly free. Perhaps the greatest conceit of all was to think you were not conceited? He'd have to run that one past Atherton's giant brain. In the meantime he wasn't doing too well, conversationally, and especially not in the office. He groped belatedly after a shred of dignity.

'I'm sorry,' he said. 'I shouldn't have said that. I didn't mean it.'

'It's all right. I know you didn't,' she said after a moment, but she still sounded hurt.

'What was it you wanted, anyway?' he asked, trying to be helpful. 'Something about the house, you said?'

'Yes. Well, it will have to be sold, you know, so that we can split the proceeds. Have you done anything about finding somewhere to live yet?'

'I haven't had time.'

'You must *make* time,' she said impatiently. 'Do you want me to sell it out from under you? I could, you know.'

'What are you in such a hurry about? You're comfortable, aren't you? It's not as if you're living on the street.'

'It's not the point,' she said, and something in her voice made him think that what *was* the point embarrassed her. Maybe Ernie was pressing her to get her share of the money.

But no, not Ernie, he corrected himself. To be fair to old fart-face, Ernie wouldn't do that. More likely it was Irene's friend and mentor, Marilyn Cripps, in whose distressed pine kitchen he was pretty sure Irene would have poured out everything over the herb tea and rough-baked oat cookies. The she-Cripps had never liked him. She'd tell Irene exactly what she was entitled to and urge her to extract every last cent, if it meant squeezing him till his socks squeaked. And Irene, the cluck, was always fatally impressed by anyone with a detached house and a Labrador.

'The point is you're always prevaricating,' Irene went on. 'You've always been like it, and you're no better now. Look, I know what you're thinking,' she added more gently, 'but it's no good delaying things in the hope that I'll change my mind. I'm not coming back, and you might as well accept it, and get on and sort things out. You'll be happier in the long run. Start a new life of your own.'

'It's nice of you to care,' he said. There was a silence while she tried to work out if he was being ironic or not.

'Well, what are you going to do? Either we have to talk and agree a settlement between us, or my solicitor will have to talk to yours. You wouldn't want that, would you?'

This was such big talk from little Irene – 'my solicitor', forsooth! She was moving upmarket in a big way, leaving him far behind. 'How are the children?' he asked suddenly.

'Fine,' she said briefly; and there was a silence in which painful thoughts, memories and regrets surged about like bacterial activity. A great hopelessness swept over Slider. What had brought him to this pass, homeless, loveless, childless, and short of socks? As a punishment for sin it was pretty effective; the sin not so much of adultery but of vacillation.

'I'd like to see them,' he said, a statement of fact rather than a request, but she said cunningly, 'You'll see them if you make a date to come round here and talk things through.'

He panicked at the idea of going to Ernie's house and seeing his children nesting amongst the late Mavis Newman's furnishings. Too bizarre. He'd end up like Barrington. Anyway, there was the case – oh case, oh sweet oh lovely case! 'I just don't know what I'll be doing for the next few days,' he said desperately. 'I'll call you tomorrow about it.'

He could feel her doubting. 'Well, what about the house? Are you going to put it on the market?'

'You do it,' he said, 'I really haven't got time to talk to estate agents.'

'But what about the furniture?'

'I don't care about it. I don't want any of it. Get in a firm of house-clearers. Just let me know when they're coming so I can get my own things out.'

This clearly made Irene unhappy. 'But what are you going to *do*? You have to have somewhere to go.' He didn't volunteer anything, and she went on, 'You don't sound like yourself at all. I'm worried about you. Are you all right?'

'I'm deliriously happy, what do you think?' Then he regretted it. 'No, I'm all right, really. Just do whatever you want, and I'll make my own arrangements. Don't worry about me.'

'But are you sure you want me to sell the furniture? Won't you need it for wherever you go?'

'Quite sure,' he said firmly. He hated that three-piece suite, the reproduction mahogany dinette set, the Dreamland bed with the Dralon velvet headboard (which frankly he'd always thought rather unhygienic apart from anything else), the Jacobethan glazed oak corner cupboard in which were displayed the Birds of Britain limited edition decorative plates set. He'd always hated them. This was not life, it was a Home Shopping Experience.

'It'll be a load off my mind,' he said sincerely. 'Look, I must go. I'll call you tomorrow.'

'Well, see you do,' she said doubtfully, and rang off.

The Coleraines lived in one of those large Edwardian service flats at the back of Kensington High Street. Slider rang the bell, and the door was opened almost before his finger had left the button. Mrs Coleraine was standing there in the hall, half in and half out of her overcoat.

'Oh, Inspector,' she said with a smile and a hint of apology. 'Do come in. Did you want me? I was just going out.'

'No, as a matter of fact it was your husband I wanted a word with.'

The smile widened with relief. 'It's work, you see – well, half work, half pleasure. I'm doing up a little flat for Henry – Alec's godson Henry Russell. He's getting married and it's going to be my wedding-present to him. I want to have it all ready for them to move into straight away, but I've got so behind, and I expect – I imagine –' She paused, an anxious frown bending her fair brows. 'I was wondering about the funeral. I don't mean to sound callous, but I suppose I will lose some more time over it. Have you any idea when we're likely to be allowed to go ahead with it?'

'Well, we have to wait for the inquest, of course. In cases like this that's a brief formality. We tell the Coroner that an investigation is going on and ask for an adjournment, and unless there's any reason not to, he then issues a certificate allowing the body to be released for burial.'

'And is there,' she said carefully, 'any reason not to?'

'Not as far as I know,' Slider said. 'There was nothing mysterious about the death, except for who did it. I can't see any reason why the body shouldn't be released. The inquest will be on Monday, so I should say you could safely arrange the funeral for the middle of next week.'

'Thank you, Inspector. That's very helpful. I'll work on Wednesday, then, though the arrangements may be –' She sighed, and then straightened her shoulders. 'Well, I mustn't bother you with my worries. My husband is in the drawing-room. I'll take you to him, and then I shall have to go, if you'll forgive me.'

Slider got the impression Alec Coleraine had assumed his wife had gone, for he seemed startled when she appeared in the doorway, and was noticeably put out when he saw Slider behind her. He was sitting in an armchair with a book in his lap, a glass of whisky on the table beside him, and Barbra Streisand barely contained by the hi-fi. The room was large and almost aggressively comfortable, capacious chairs and sofas bloated with stuffing, a carpet so thick it looked as if it needed regular mowing, and heavy curtains at the window that would have muffled Armageddon. Every perching place had its little table to elbow, and there was a large drinks cabinet in one corner and a range of bookshelves along one wall filled with books in bright dust-jackets. This was not a room for impressing intellectuals, this was a room to slob out in, and Coleraine was slobbing out in leather house-slippers and the sort of cords and sweater Slider would have kept for best.

'Mr Slider's called in for a word with you, darling,' Fay was saying as she ushered him in. 'I must dash, though – you don't mind?'

Coleraine had stood up, courteously lowering Barbra's blood-pressure with the remote, but he hadn't time to assemble any words before his wife had disappeared again. Slider thought he was looking unwell, as though he was under considerable strain, which boded well for the investigation, though the human in Slider would have liked to hold back, even to leave well alone. These domestics were the devil, he thought. That nice woman would be the victim of anything that happened to Coleraine, and Radek had been an unpleasant man according to most sources, no loss to the world. If Coleraine had been driven by desperation to hurry him on his way, why should society care? It was not as if Coleraine was dangerous; he was unlikely ever to murder anyone else.

Ah, the comfort of sloppy thinking! But being an unpleasant old gink did not cancel your right to live, and every person's life was precious to them, whether they were universally sympatico or Noel Edmonds.

'Won't you sit down, Inspector,' Coleraine said with an obvious effort. 'Can I get you a drink?'

'No thank you, nothing for me,' Slider said. Coleraine resumed his seat and Slider perched on the edge of the sofa nearest him. The vast upholstered spaces behind him were clamouring for his body, but he was afraid he'd be sucked down and sink without trace if he leaned back. 'There's a little matter I wanted to talk to you about. I have here –' He produced from his inside pocket the paper Christie's had faxed through that afternoon. 'I have here a copy of a bill for three pictures you bought back in May from Christie's. Three oil paintings. I wonder if you could tell me what happened to them?'

Coleraine took the paper from him with a stringless hand. It was obviously something he hadn't expected to be asked, but there was a sick and confused look rather than honest

107

puzzlement in his face. Whatever the story was, the pictures were part of it, Slider thought. Coleraine examined the bill for a long time, as though wondering whether he could doubt its authenticity.

'Why do you want to know about these?' he asked at last. 'Is there something wrong?'

'Just answer the question, please. Have you got the paintings here? Can I see them?'

'No. No. I – I don't keep them here,' Coleraine said. He put a hand up to his brow as though shielding his face, like a character in an old ham movie trying to get past the patrolman without being recognised.

'Oh? That's a pity. They must be lovely paintings,' Slider said warmly. 'I'm very fond of Turner myself. You didn't buy them for pleasure, then?'

Coleraine tried to smile and thought better of it. 'No, not really. They aren't my kind of art. I prefer something more modern, abstract.' There were pictures on the walls around them, all richly old-fashioned and representational. Seeing Slider looking, Coleraine hurried on, 'No, I bought them for an investment, actually.'

'A very sound investment, too,' Slider said approvingly. 'The chap I spoke to at Christie's said that you got them at a very good price on a rising market. He said that you could expect to sell them again in a year's time at quite a profit.'

'Yes. Yes, I hope so. Of course. But you haven't told me why you're asking about the paintings.'

'You haven't told me where they are,' Slider countered pleasantly. 'You don't keep them here, you said. So where?'

'At the office.' It sounded as if he'd spoken at random, and presumably hearing the same thing himself, he hurried to justify it. 'They're safer there. There's a better alarm system. I wouldn't want them to get stolen.'

'At the office? So if I come up tomorrow you can show them to me?'

Coleraine took a desperate gulp of whisky. 'Oh – er – no, I remember now. I sent them to be cleaned.'

'So, not at the office,' Slider said, like one questioning a very young child.

'No. They're still at the restorer's.'

'And which restorer's would that be?'

'I don't remember.'

'You don't remember?'

Coleraine flashed him a look of pure hatred, like a cornered cat. 'I didn't mean – of course I've got the address somewhere.'

'It would be on the receipt, I expect,' said Slider helpfully.

'Yes,' said Coleraine defiantly. He met Slider's eyes in the full knowledge that Slider knew he was lying.

'So perhaps you'd like to show me the receipt, then?'

'I – I'm not sure I still have it. I might have lost it.'

Slider stood up abruptly. 'Oh, come on, Mr Coleraine. This is getting silly. One and a quarter million pounds' worth of paintings, and you can't remember where you sent them and you're not sure if you still have the receipt?' He walked over to the mantelpiece and leaned an elbow on it, looking down at his wriggling victim. 'I may as well put you out of your misery and tell you that I know where those paintings are.'

'I doubt that you do,' Coleraine said, with a resurgence of spirit.

Slider smiled. 'I've got them.'

The whisky lapped up the side of his glass, and Coleraine put it down carefully. 'You've got them?'

'Yup.' Slider nodded. 'We recovered them as part of a burglary haul, including some other items stolen from your house, here, during a break-in in June. You reported the break-in to the police, but you didn't mention the pictures. Why?'

Coleraine looked as though he was not going to answer, but at last, licking his lips, he said, 'I had my reasons.'

'Well, do share them with me. Because if you didn't report the pictures stolen, you couldn't claim for them on the insurance, or hope to get them back. Now money may not be everything, but I've never met a man so willing to chuck away one and a quarter million for want of a few words to the police.'

'I don't have to tell you anything,' Coleraine said sulkily.

'Not yet you don't. This is just a friendly chat we're having. But I do advise you to confide in me now rather than later.'

Coleraine thought for some time, staring into the middle distance. He looked very unwell. At last he lifted his eyes to Slider and said with almost childish defiance, 'They weren't insured. The premiums would have been astronomical. So I couldn't have claimed on the insurance anyway.'

'Why didn't you tell the police they'd been stolen? How did you hope to get them back otherwise?' Coleraine didn't answer, only shook his head in a hopeless sort of way, looking down at the carpet. 'Where did you get the money to buy them in the first place? That's a lot of spare money to have lying around. Is there something you ought to be telling me about that?'

He glanced up. 'I've nothing more to say to you,' he said, setting his mouth into a hard line. 'My money is my private business.'

Prevarication is the thief of time. Slider looked at him wearily for a moment, and then looked away, fiddling idly with the things on the mantelpiece – an eclectic assemblage, fit for one of those Sunday supplement articles. *The View from My Mantelpiece.* 'Mr Coleraine, I'm bound to say that you haven't said anything to satisfy my curiosity about this business. In fact, rather the opposite. When people behave in an uncharacteristic way, there's usually a good reason, or perhaps I should say a bad reason, especially where large sums of money are involved –' He broke off. One of the things on the mantelpiece, which now came to his exploring fingers, was a length of black silk line wound around a brass spool. The presence beside it of a clear-plastic topped case of fishing-flies told him what it was doing there, but the interesting thing to Slider was that the brass spool was a spent .38 cartridge case. He picked it up.

'What's this?' he asked.

Coleraine looked up. 'It's fly-line.' He seemed surprised at the question. 'I go trout fishing. It's a hobby of mine.'

'No, I meant, what's this it's wound onto?' Slider asked.

Coleraine frowned. 'Well, what does it look like? It's a cartridge case. I've had it for years. I've always kept my spare line on it. I make my own flies, you see.'

'Where did you get it from?' Slider asked quietly. Why didn't detectives carry magnifying glasses? Come back, Lord

Peter, all is forgiven! But there was a pair of reading glasses lying on the table by Coleraine's chair, and he stepped across and picked them up, and took them, with the cartridge, to the light.

'You do ask the most peculiar questions,' Coleraine was saying, sounding half peevish, half relieved. Evidently he liked this line of questioning better than the last, anyway. 'My father-in-law gave it to me, as a matter of fact, years and years ago. We were in his study talking about fishing, and the subject of making flies came up, and he took it out of his drawer and gave it to me. He said he always kept his line wound on one.'

'Did he have a gun, then?' Slider asked, angling the glasses to get the best magnification.

'Only his old war-time revolver. Souvenir. He fought on our side, you know. I don't know if he's still got it. The last time I saw it was when Marcus was a boy, and the old man showed it to him. That's got to be ten, twelve years ago.'

Ah yes, there it was, just above the rim: little stamped letters, DC 43. If it was a coincidence, it was going to make the *Guinness Book of Records*.

'Do you mind if I borrow this?' he asked politely.

CHAPTER EIGHT

I could have been a Judge,
only I never had the Latin

'Hello, Bill?'

Slider's heart, and sundry adjacent organs, lifted at the sound of the voice. 'My dreams come true,' he said. 'How often I've picked up the phone hoping to hear those very words.'

'Stop messing around,' Joanna said sternly. 'You won't be so happy when you know what I've phoned about.'

'I'll get used to it,' he promised eagerly.

'Oh shut up. Look, I've had a phone call from Bob Preston. He was terribly upset. Apparently some of your blokes went round to his house, asking him and his family questions about Radek. Poor old Bob was in pieces, thinking you suspect him. He phoned me up to ask if I knew anything. What's going on?'

'It's just routine questioning,' Slider said warily. She sounded really annoyed. 'You know the form.'

'But you can't really be suspecting Bob,' she said wildly. 'He's a trumpet player, for God's sake!'

'That makes him immune from suspicion, does it?'

'Yes. And trombone players,' she said defiantly. 'You can't suspect the brass section. It's ridiculous.'

'Oh look, you know the form. We have to ask everyone, even if it's just to eliminate them.'

'You didn't ask me.'

'You didn't have a motive.'

'You think being sacked is a motive for murder?'

'Look, it's just routine –'

'It isn't routine to him or his wife or his daughters. They're really upset. And they're worried that it's going to get about to the neighbours and the other kids in their kids' school, and people are going to start saying there's no smoke without fire. Did you have to go trampling over his life like that? Haven't your people got anything better to do?'

He heard her hear herself say it, so he didn't follow it up. Instead he said, 'They won't be bothered any more. You know that we had nothing physical to go on. All we could do was look at motive. A man's been killed, you know. We have to be thorough.'

There was a pause, and when she spoke again her voice was defiant with contrition. 'Well I tell you one thing, Bill Slider, you were on the wrong track with Bob. No person who spends their entire life playing a musical instrument would ever commit murder – not even an oboist.'

It was an attempt at a joke, and he felt a surge of tenderness fit to melt his buttons. 'Jo –'

'I'm *telling* you,' she said as if he had argued the point, 'it wasn't a musician who killed Radek. You mark my words. You'll see I'm right.'

'I hope you are,' he said.

'You've definitely cleared Bob?' she asked after a pause.

'Yes. He won't be bothered again.'

'Because you don't realise how frightened ordinary people are by the law. Most ordinary people never open their door to find a copper standing there. It's like being invaded by aliens from Mars.'

'Of course I realise. Don't you think I know how I'm looked at? Do you think I like being a Martian?'

He spoke more warmly than he meant, and she said, 'I'm sorry.'

'No, it's all right.' There was an awkward silence. The real issue came thrusting upwards again. He had to say something. 'Jo, can we meet? I need to talk to you.'

'What about?'

'If I could answer that on the phone I wouldn't need to meet you, would I?'

'I suppose not. Oh, Bill, I don't know. It won't do any good, you know. It's over between us.'

'It isn't. If it were, you wouldn't be on the phone now, getting mad at me.'

'You were my friend once. I could get mad at you,' she said.

'I still am your friend. Whatever happens, you can't say there's nothing between us. Let me see you and talk to you, just that at least.'

There was a long silence, and he had no idea whether she was going to say yes or no. He thought probably she didn't know either. Then at last she said reluctantly, 'I'm off tomorrow night, as it happens.'

Relief rushed straight to his trousers. 'All right. Good. Wonderful. Look, I should be able to get away around six, half past six. I'll come round to your place, shall I?'

'Yes, all right,' she said, but on a dying cadence, as if the idea didn't exactly thrill her. But she'd said she'd see him. It was a start.

Slider was astonished by the change in Poor Old Buster. When he had first seen him he had been dapper, spry, with the alertness and movements of a man in his fifties; now, only a few days later, he had shuffled to answer the door like an octogenarian, and climbed the stairs ahead of Slider slowly, pulling himself up by the banisters. Here in the drawing-room he sat in the armchair with his hands in his lap, utterly immobile, like an old man in a home waiting to die, his eyes blank, his muscles slack, his clothes crumpled, his previously firm face seeming somehow untidy with grief. Here, if anywhere, was the justification for Radek's life. If even one person mourned him as deeply as Keaton, he could not have been without worth.

'Mr Keaton, I'm sorry to bother you again,' Slider began.

Keaton sighed and said with an obvious effort, 'It doesn't matter. I've nothing else to do.'

'Are you managing all right?' Slider enquired gently.

'Managing?'

'Cooking and shopping and so on.'

'Oh – that.' He shook his head. 'There's nothing I want. I have nothing to live for now.'

'Oh, you mustn't say that,' Slider protested, and Keaton lifted dull eyes to him.

'It's a statement of fact. How can I help you?'

'I understand from Mr Coleraine that Sir Stefan had a gun – a revolver, in fact.'

'Yes,' Keaton said, without any particular emphasis. 'It was the one he used during the war. He kept it as a souvenir.'

'Do you know where he kept it?'

'In the drawer of his desk, in his study.'

'May I see it, please?'

Keaton got up with an effort, pushing himself with his hands on the chair arms. The study was across the hall from the drawing-room, a large and handsome room furnished with desk, chair, map-table, a large leather sofa, and a handsome range of bookshelves, several shelves of which were dedicated to leather-bound music scores. There was also a baby-grand piano, and over by the window a magnificent mahogany and brass music stand. Seeing Slider notice it, Keaton said, 'He used to work here. People don't understand how many hours of preparation and practice went into his performances.'

Slider nodded sympathetically. Performances seemed an odd choice of word, until he noticed that opposite the music stand, fixed to the wall, was a full-length mirror. He actually practised his arm-waving then, Slider thought with wry amusement; watched himself in the mirror. He would love to tell Joanna that.

Keaton had shuffled over to the desk, and now opened the top left-hand drawer. 'He kept it in here,' he said.

Slider moved to his side. 'Wasn't the drawer usually kept locked?'

'Oh no. It wouldn't have been any use against burglars if he'd had to unlock a drawer to get at it,' Keaton said, as though it were obvious logic.

'Did he keep it loaded as well?'

'Of course. What use is an unloaded gun?' He pulled the drawer further out and bent to peer in. 'That's funny. He must have moved it.'

'The gun isn't there?'

'No. Here's the ammunition, all right, but –' He pulled out

a box, old, softened, grimed with time, the lettering rubbed and faded: DC 43. Slowly, painstakingly, he searched every drawer. 'I can't find it. He must have put it somewhere else. I wonder why?' He straightened up, frowning at Slider. 'Is it important? Will we have to search the house?'

'No, I don't think so,' Slider said. 'Do you remember when you last saw it?'

A sort of bleak dawn suffused Buster's face, and his mouth sagged like a baby's who had just been given a spoonful of spinach. 'Oh my goodness, you don't mean –? Are you saying that it was his own gun? That someone shot him with his own gun?'

'I don't know for sure, but it looks that way.'

'Oh, but that's terrible!' He gaped with dismay. 'What a mean, awful thing to do! I had no idea! It never occurred to me that –' He shook his head agitated by the enormity of it. Humankind is so strange, Slider thought. Amid all the butchery of war, the fact that someone was shot on Christmas Day will be held up as the nadir of depravity. Forty-eight hours later it would be ho-hum just another body.

'If someone did steal Sir Stefan's revolver,' Slider prompted him, 'it would be useful if you could remember when you last saw it in its usual drawer.'

'To give you a *terminus a quo*, yes, I see,' Buster said helpfully. Blimey, the education you get on this job, Slider marvelled. Better than going to grammar school. 'But we haven't been burgled, you know. And Sir Stefan can't have missed it, or he'd certainly have mentioned it to me.'

'So it must have been taken by a visitor to the house – unless he lent it to someone?'

'Oh, I'm sure he wouldn't do that. He was very careful with it. He would never let Marcus touch it, for instance, however much he begged. You know how fascinated little boys are with guns.'

'Unfortunately, as it wasn't kept locked away, anyone who came to the house and was left alone for a few moments could have taken it. Do you remember when you last saw it?'

'Wait, wait, let me think. I'm sure it was –' Keaton folded one arm across his chest, rested the other elbow on it, and cradled his jaw in deep thought. At last his face brightened.

'Yes, of course, I knew there was something! It was on Sunday afternoon when I brought him his tea. He usually has it in here, and when I came in with the tray he was sitting at his desk cleaning it – the gun, I mean. I remember because I don't like the smell of the oil, and I was going to say something to him about being careful not to spill any on the carpet, but in the end I didn't because he'd been a bit on edge and I didn't want to start a quarrel.' He looked at Slider hopefully, as though for praise. 'Sunday afternoon, definitely.'

'Very good,' Slider said. 'Now if you could think very carefully and tell me everyone who called at the house between then and Wednesday.'

'Oh, but no-one came,' he said quickly. 'We don't have callers of that sort.'

'Of what sort?' Slider asked in private amusement. Was he visualising swarthy villains in masks ringing the doorbell and saying, 'Burglar, sir, come to nick your gun. All right if I go up?'

'Well, of any sort really. Nobody comes here – or at least, no-one gets let in, because we have people collecting and that sort of thing.'

'Mr Coleraine told me that he called on Tuesday to see his father-in-law.'

Enlightenment transformed Keaton's face. For a moment he looked almost happy. 'Oh, family, you mean? Naturally I didn't think you meant anyone we knew. Certainly Alec was here on Tuesday morning.'

'At what time?'

'It would be about half past nine. I was annoyed that he called so early, but he said he was on his way to work.'

'You let him in?'

'Of course.'

'And then what?'

'I don't understand.'

'Did you show him upstairs, or did he go up alone, what?'

'I accompanied him to the drawing-room, and then went to fetch Sir Stefan. He was still in his bedroom. He doesn't get up early unless he has an engagement.'

'So Mr Coleraine was left alone down here for some minutes?'

Buster's eyes widened. 'You surely aren't suggesting –!'

'I'm not suggesting anything. I have to make a note of every possibility, even if only to eliminate it.'

'But Alec wouldn't – you can't think he or Marcus –'

'Marcus? Was Marcus with him?'

'No, no, but he called on his grandfather on the Tuesday afternoon. It was inconvenient – we were just going out. But Sir Stefan saw him for a few moments in here.'

'Did he leave Marcus alone for any of the time?'

'I don't know. I was downstairs. I was really annoyed because it was making us late for rehearsal, and we dislike very much to be unpunctual. Young people are so thoughtless. I told him when he arrived we were on the point of leaving, but still he kept Sir Stefan a quarter of an hour, and put him in a temper.'

'In a temper? About what?'

'I don't know. I told you. I was downstairs. It was just some nonsense, I expect. Marcus can be very annoying.'

Slider nodded. 'And who else called between Sunday teatime and Wednesday lunchtime?'

'No-one else. No-one at all.'

'You're quite sure? Not friend or relative, however well trusted? Not meter-reader, plumber, double-glazing salesman, or wandering faith-healer?'

Keaton frowned. 'No-one. I'm quite sure. And I don't think this is a matter for levity.'

'I'm sorry. Do you know what Alec Coleraine called for? Did you hear his conversation with Sir Stefan?'

'I wasn't in the room. I went to make coffee. Sir Stefan wanted his coffee – Alec refused any. When I brought the tray in, things seemed rather heated. Sir Stefan was quite angry, and Alec was pleading with him.'

'Do you know what about?'

'I think he'd been asking for money.' Buster's lips folded in disapproval. 'It wasn't the first time. There's always some people willing to spend what they haven't earned.'

Money again, Slider thought. It was coming together nicely now. 'You think Sir Stefan refused?'

'Certainly. He believed people should stand on their own feet, as he always did.'

'I see. And you're quite sure no-one else came to see Sir Stefan?'

'Yes. But I'm also quite sure neither Alec nor Marcus had anything to do with his death. I know them, I've known them for many, many years. It is simply not in them to do such a thing. In fact –' He hesitated, something visibly working through his mind.

'Yes?' Slider prompted. 'You've thought of something else?'

'No,' he said, and then again, more surely, 'no. I was just going to say that in their own ways they were probably all very fond of each other. It doesn't do to judge by appearances. People often quarrel with those they love best.'

'Mr Coleraine said just the same thing to me the other day.'

'Yes, yes, so you see?' Keaton said eagerly.

Slider smiled comfortingly. 'I assure you I never judge by appearances. I always turn over every stone. It's astonishing what can be under them.'

'Quite so,' Keaton said. The animation drained from his face, and he returned abruptly to the listlessness of grief.

The drawback to being a human, Slider thought as he took his leave, was that pleasure tended to be over quite quickly, while unhappiness went on for great big indigestible lumps of time.

Nutty Nicholls was in the front shop when Slider went through. Nutty, a burly Scot from the rain-lashed shores of the far north west, had once at a fund-raising concert sung the *Queen of the Night* aria from *The Magic Flute*, and was known in consequence as the copper with the *coloratura*, or occasionally Noballs Nicholls. The latter was manifestly unjustified, but Nicholls only smiled and took it in his stride. It was a performance practised and polished to perfection, he told Slider, in a part of the world where there was nothing else to do, and no airborne pollution to damage the vocal chords.

He called to Slider as he passed through. 'I've got a message for you, Bill. An anonymous caller, no less, leaving you an address. I'd congratulate you on a secret assignation, but by the voice it was either a bloke or the bearded lady from the fairground on the Scrubs.'

'It was a bloke, and not my sort,' Slider said, coming across

119

for the piece of paper. On it, in Paxman's bullish hand-writing, was Coleraine's address.

'Is this to do with your murder?' Nicholls asked, rolling his r's superbly. 'Is that not the son-in-law's address?'

'How did you know that?' Slider asked in amusement. Not much got past Nicholls.

'I was at the fax machine when McLaren got his burglary report through. Is the son-in-law in the frame, then?'

'Like a Gainsborough,' Slider answered, and thought of Lenny Picket. But not like a Constable. 'Is Barrington in?'

Nutty shook his head. 'Not back yet. That man is developing a dangerously high tolerance of lunch.'

'Do you think it's lunch? It strikes me he's not firing on all cylinders these days.'

Nicholls cocked an eye at him. 'You think he's heading for a breakdown? I've been wondering myself. D'you know he was down here this morning looking through the waste-paper baskets?'

'Did he find what he was looking for?'

'He found a couple of paper clips in the charge room, and went straight into circuit overload. Paxman told me about it. Result is we've got a new ukase wet from the press.' He gestured towards a memo lying in the in-basket. 'To all departments: paper clips are not to be thrown away but must be kept and re-used. Department supervisors must make regular checks of the waste-paper baskets to see that this instruction is being followed.'

Slider shook his head sadly. 'He's just playing for pop-ularity. Taking the easy course.'

'It doesn't surprise me,' Nutty went on. 'All that business over the chip-shop murders – Home Office, Foreign Office and everyone else asking him searching questions – and then you not taking your transfer. Every time he comes in to the office the sight of you rubs his face in it.'

'You think it's my fault, do you?' Slider protested.

'If you mean to sup with the devil, you need a long spoon,' Nicholls said with Highland inscrutability. 'You had troubles enough, but he'd four times as many. He'd yours times his.'

'That's what bosses are for.'

'Oh, I know,' said Nutty tranquilly. 'I'm just mentioning.'

The last thing in the world Slider wanted at the moment was to be induced to feel sorry for Mad Ivan Barrington: it came in even behind being trapped in a lift with a man who'd done his own conveyancing. He turned away, and then turned back to say, 'Oh, and I have got an assignation, as it happens. I'm having tea with a lady.'

Nutty grinned. 'You English!'

'The trouble with revolvers is that the cartridge cases are carried away in the chamber, so until we find the gun we can't be absolutely sure of a match,' said Swilley.

'This obsession with guns is just penis envy you know, Norma,' Atherton pointed out.

'Bollocks,' she replied.

'If you've got 'em, clang 'em,' said Anderson.

'You're all morons,' Norma said kindly.

She was perched on her desk resting her weight on her hands like a 1950s Coca-Cola girl. Normally this would have had Mackay dribbling at her feet, but in emulation of his old oppo, Hunt, he had recently bought a Golf GTI, and his lusts had all been diverted into motor-mechanical channels. Now all that passed through his mind was the extra pair of Bosch halogen superspots he'd set his heart on. 'It's a pretty fair bet we're onto the right gun, though,' he said. 'The same sort of ammo, and not your everyday brand either. Radek's shooter was kept loaded and in an unlocked drawer, where Coleraine knew where it was, and he was in the house and left alone for long enough to nick it.'

'It's a good start,' Slider said, 'but it's not proof. Norma's right, we've got to find that gun – and that means we've got to find where the killer went after the shooting. What's the latest on that?'

'We've got various reports to follow up,' Beevers said, referring to his papers. 'A woman saw a man in a duffel coat looking very nervous coming out of Queensway tube at about three o'clock. He turned left and went on up Queensway. She said he was youngish and medium height with light-coloured hair. But he didn't have a hat on.'

'All the better to recognise him without,' Atherton said, 'supposing it's our man.'

121

'Supposing,' said Beevers. 'Then there's a man with a hat and light brown coat who came running out of Bond Street tube at about twenty past three, but the witness doesn't know if it was a duffel coat or not. He ran across the road – almost getting himself knocked down, according to witness – and up James Street. And there was a fair-haired man acting suspiciously at White City outside the BBC centre –'

'Isn't there always?' Slider said.

'Probably Jimmy Saville,' said Anderson.

'– again at about three o'clock, but not wearing a coat or hat, though he was carrying a large carrier bag, so they could have been inside it. He was sweating and looked nervous. Hung around for a bit and then jumped on a seventy-two bus heading north when it stopped at the crossing.' He turned the pages back. 'The Anti-terrorist Squad got that report as well. Those three are the most promising. There's dozens of others, of course – men, women, hats, coats, parcels, and every tube station on the Underground.'

'Well, keep at it,' Slider said. 'Something will come up. Let's have videofits from those three to start with. And try them with a photograph of Coleraine, see if it tweaks any hairs.'

'But guv,' Anderson said, 'if Coleraine did want to off the old man, surely he wouldn't be so daft as to use Radek's own gun, when it could be proved he knew about it and had the opportunity to nick it? And when he's got a cartridge case from it stuck on his mantelpiece for all to see?'

'He probably never thought twice about the cartridge case,' Norma said. 'It'd been there so long it was –'

'Part of the furniture,' Atherton supplied.

'Well, it's not that easy for your average law-abiding citizen to get hold of a gun,' Slider said. 'He'd have to make do with what was to hand – and it must have been tempting, lying there loaded and ready and available.'

'Maybe he meant to put it back at some later stage,' Norma suggested, 'hoping no-one would make the connection. Not everybody knows that you can tell which gun a bullet's been fired from.'

'Let's not forget the son in all this,' Atherton said. 'He knew the gun was there as well, and had just as much opportunity to steal it.'

'You don't know that,' Norma objected. 'You don't know he was left alone.'

'You don't know he wasn't.'

'What's his motive then?' Mackay asked.

'The same – money,' said Atherton. 'From the little I know about Marcus so far, he's an immoral, selfish little tart who'd sell his granny for the gold in her teeth.'

'You've been looking into his background, haven't you?' Slider intervened to impose a bit of structure on the talk. 'Let's hear it.'

'Our Marcus is a naughty boy,' Atherton obliged. 'His prep school had him "could do better" – clever but lazy, not amenable to discipline and inclined to think too well of himself. The head I spoke to came over rather puzzled and a little wary: liked the boy in spite of everything but was afraid I was going to tell him he'd gone to the bad.'

'Prophetic,' Slider nodded.

'After prep school he went to Harrow by the skin of his teeth. They weren't too keen to take him, but he'd got a scholarship; and besides, Coleraine's mother was a Russell, and her family's men have gone there for a hundred and fifty years or something.'

'Coleraine's godson, Henry Russell –?' Slider remembered.

'Is a second cousin, yes. He was at Harrow at the same time and presented an unhappy contrast with Marcus, which probably helped to reinforce the bad behaviour. Anyway, Marcus got sent down in the end for running an adolescent version of long firm fraud: offering to get hold of tickets for popular events – student balls and pop concerts and the like – taking the money up front and then not delivering the tickets. One of the boys complained to his father, and the balloon went up. Coleraine managed to hush it up by paying back all the boys out of his own money – Marcus had spent the lot, of course – so the school didn't call in the police, but still insisted Marcus left. So he went to a crammer for two terms, got his A levels, just, and went to university.'

'What did he study?' Mackay asked.

'Economics. I spoke to his tutor, who said that the father had wanted Marcus to read Law, but he didn't have the grades – another source of friction. And from the first Marcus

123

didn't make any attempt to do the work and obey the rules. It was all gigs and girls and drunken parties – the tutor thought he'd got interested in recreational drugs too – and he was frequently in minor trouble. Nobody was surprised when he dropped out. Since then he's set up to live in the flat in Bayswater and spend money – presumably his father's, since he's never done a day's work in his life.'

'Sounds like an absolute sweetie,' Norma said sourly.

'What's his connection with Steve Murray?' Anderson asked.

'Met him at a Radek concert at the Festival Hall. Marcus was hanging around backstage hoping to tap his grandad for a few bucks; Murray was hanging round hoping Kate Apwey wouldn't have to go off horizontal jogging with the old bugger. The two lonely lads took to each other and became friends. Reading between the lines, Murray had a supplier and Marcus was free with his money, so they were obviously made for each other.'

'Just a moment, are you saying that Marcus is an addict?' Slider asked.

'No, strictly a recreational user. You could almost like him better if he was – there'd be some excuse for him then. But he's just a self-indulgent little parasite.'

'I'm getting a sort of feeling here that you don't like him,' Slider said tentatively.

'He disgusts me,' Atherton said.

'He may be a spoiled brat but it doesn't make him a murderer. From what you've said his father keeps him supplied with money. Why should he take the risk of killing his grandfather when he can have anything he wants for the asking? Radek's money goes to Fay, anyway, not to Marcus.'

'Far more likely Coleraine's feeling the pinch, if he's funding his son's delightful habits,' Norma agreed.

'It'd come to the same thing, wouldn't it?' McLaren said as best he could. He had just finished eating a packet of McVitie's Chocolate Homewheat and was hooking squashy chocolatey bits from the corners of his gums with his little finger. 'I mean, if his old man was up the swannee, and his old lady came in for the wonga, it'd come to him anyway. She'd wedge him up all right.'

'English is such a beautiful language when spoken by an

expert,' Atherton said admiringly. 'Why shouldn't Marcus and Murray have dreamed up the whole scheme in an idle moment – of which, let's face it, they have an unlimited supply – just for the fun of it? The idea of diverting the money from tight-fisted grandpa to soppily generous mamma would just be an added incentive.'

'You take a large size in assumptions,' Slider reproved. 'What about Marcus's movements that day?'

'Ah, now, there's the really interesting bit,' Atherton said. 'He says he was mooching about at home all morning, which rings true; left home at noon and went to see Murray, got there at half past one and stayed the rest of the evening. Murray confirms it all like a paid-up member. So for the crucial period they are each other's alibi.'

'How convenient,' Slider said wearily.

'Damnable, isn't it? Covent Garden being what it is, there must have been hundreds of people around, any one of whom might have seen Marcus arrive. The problem will be finding them.'

'But hang on,' Anderson said, 'how did Marcus know Murray would be there? Murray called in sick that morning. He should have been at work. Marcus would've known that, surely?'

'Right. But if Murray wasn't in, Marcus was going to pop into the Opera House and get his key to let himself in. Murray was a friendly soul, not above giving his mates the run of his gaff.' Atherton shrugged. 'As an alibi it's like a string vest – it fits all right, but it's full of holes.'

'It's a better alibi than Coleraine's got,' Norma pointed out.

'Which is not saying a whole hell of a lot,' Atherton retorted.

Slider cut through the witty badinage. 'Now here's something. Marcus left home at twelve and got to Murray's at one-thirty – an hour and a half for a half-hour journey. Coleraine left the office at twelve-thirty and says he got home at a quarter to two – an hour and a quarter for a half-hour journey. Where's the missing time? Suppose he met Marcus at twelve-thirty somewhere near the office?'

'You said Marcus phoned him at a quarter to twelve and rang

125

off at about twelve,' Norma said. 'They could have arranged to meet. It fits all right. But what's it got to do with us?'

'Do you think they were both in on the job, guv?' Atherton said. 'That they met to arrange the murder?'

He shook his head. 'No, I can't see that. But suppose Marcus were in some worse than usual financial crisis, and after meeting him and hearing about it Coleraine went home in despair and decided the only way out was to kill Radek?'

'But he'd taken the gun the day before,' Mackay pointed out.

'There's no reason he couldn't have planned it earlier,' Atherton said. 'The meeting with Marcus might have been incidental.'

Norma said, 'If it was planned in advance why didn't Coleraine sort himself an alibi while he was at it?'

'Typical amateur. All right, maybe it wasn't planned. He might not have taken the gun for that: Radek might have lent it to him for some reason, and the fact that he had it gave him the idea of the murder.'

'At all events, there was something going on there, and it's a probable twelve to seven that it has something to do with the murder,' Slider said. 'And I'm sure the paintings are in it too. Christie's say they were a very good investment, likely to turn a good profit in as short a time as a year. Why did he buy them? Why didn't he insure them? Why didn't he report the theft?'

There was a generous silence in answer to all these questions.

'All right, action,' Slider said. 'I want to find out what state Coleraine's business was in. Norma, you've got a good head for figures. Find out who the auditors are, talk to them, and to the bank – the firm's and his own private one. Any irregularities, unusual transactions, change of pattern – you know the form.'

'Yes, sir.'

'Then I want to find out if Coleraine did meet Marcus that day. Restaurants, cafés, pubs in the area – probably they would have sat down somewhere to talk.'

'That sounds like a job for Superman,' Norma murmured, looking at Atherton.

'Yes, all right,' Slider nodded. 'But if you don't get a bite – sorry – try street traders, newspaper vendors, everything. If they walked about the streets talking, probably heatedly, someone must have seen them. Take Anderson with you. He'll help you resist temptation. And I want the home end of Coleraine's alibi checked out. Mackay, McLaren, try the tube station, try the neighbours, find if anyone saw him arrive or go out again.'

'And you, guv?' Atherton enquired.

'Following up an idea. I'm going to see a lady about a bit of a dog.'

CHAPTER NINE

It's a Game of Two Halves

It was quite obvious that Helena Goodwin had been crying over her keyboard: her eyelids were swollen and the wings of her nostrils were red, though she had repaired her make-up and seemed composed when she let Slider in.

'Alec – Mr Coleraine – isn't in today,' she said apologetically. 'I only came in to try to catch up with some work while it's quiet.'

'That's all right,' Slider said. 'It was really you I wanted to speak to.' He glanced at his watch, although he knew perfectly well what the time was. 'Look, I don't know what time you were thinking of knocking off, but would it be too early for me to buy you a drink? If you don't mind my saying so, you look as though you could do with one.'

She turned her head. 'I'm sorry. I must look a wreck.'

'Not at all, but my compassion circuits keep switching in and it plays havoc with my logic. How about a large gin and tonic? I've got a nice line in shoulders to cry on.'

She looked at him cautiously as if unsure how much of anything he was offering her, and then gave a slightly tremulous smile. 'You're very persuasive. All right, I'll give it up for today. Can you wait while I lock everything up?'

A little while later they were seated in a comfortable corner of a dimly lit pub in St Martin's Lane. Around them was the usual early evening clientele of a few anonymously tweedy men reading the papers, two reps with baggy suits and baggier eyes standing at the bar with two packs of Embassy, two gold lighters and two double Scotches in front of them, and some suburban couples done up regardless with time to kill before their pre-theatre meal. Mrs Goodwin had evidently been doing some thinking during Slider's lengthy absence at the bar trying to get served by a kohl-eyed blonde so laid back she was almost comatose; for when he had slid onto the plush banquette beside her, she said, 'I think there are some things you ought to know about Alec Coleraine and me.'

The sentence together with the red eyes told him everything in a nutshell, but he lifted his glass to her encouragingly, and while she took a therapeutic slug he said, 'I should be glad if you would tell me everything you can. I promise you I am very discreet.'

'Yes, you look as though you were,' she said, eyeing him judiciously. 'Tell me, do people often feel compelled to pour their hearts out to you? You look like the kind of man who has children who adore him.'

'Well, you're half right,' he said with a rueful smile. 'Policemen get home so little it's hard to sustain a home life without a great deal of patience from the rest of the family. Who's looking after your little boy today?'

'He's with my mother. She's always asking to have him, but she lives in Sussex so getting him to her is sometimes a problem.' She took another drink. 'She doesn't think I'm a very good mother. I sometimes think it might be better to leave him with her permanently. He seems to like her better than me anyway. "Grandma's more fun than you," he says.'

'You have the stresses of work to contend with,' Slider said. 'It's never a fair comparison.'

'No.'

'What does your ex-husband do?'

'He's a management consultant.' She met his eyes. 'So there were lots of opportunities for comparison, fair and otherwise, as he travelled around the country. My mother warned me not to marry him. Said he wasn't steady enough. Isn't it funny how it's only good advice no-one listens to? But when he left she said it was my fault for not staying at home and being a housewife.'

'Have you been on your own for long?'

'Almost four years,' she said. 'Nick left me just after Mr Antrobus retired and I transferred to Alec. I suppose that's why it all happened – with him and me. I was in a vulnerable state, you see.'

'And he was there. Nothing propinks like propinquity.'

She smiled. 'True. But he has a great deal of charm, you know. You probably haven't seen him at his best.'

'I wasn't criticising,' he said quickly. 'So how did it come about, exactly?'

'Oh, the usual corny way. Hackneyed as hell, only when it happens to you it all seems fresh and original, of course. We worked late together a few times, started going for drinks on the way home now and then. Then it was going for meals and working at weekends. Then one Saturday night we went for a meal and sat so long at the restaurant talking and laughing that the tubes had stopped, so he insisted on taking me home in a taxi. I invited him in. Ben was in Sussex and Fay was at some textile exhibition in Brussels –' She shrugged eloquently. 'Crescendo of music, soft-focus lens, montage of limbs, firelight and ecstatic expressions. It's been done to death on the screen.'

'But you loved him.'

'Madly. But why are you talking in the past tense?'

'I assumed from the fact that you'd been crying and having sleepless nights that it was over between you. Forgive me if I was wrong.'

'No, you're not wrong. It's been coming for a long time, but I've tried to pretend, even though it was only myself I was cheating. I've had to come to the conclusion that whatever he says, he's never going to leave his wife for me. In fact. I'm not even sure any more whether he ever meant it, or whether it was just what he said to string me along. I haven't said anything to him yet – I suppose that's cowardice, or hoping it will still come out right somehow.' She sighed and was silent a moment. 'Funny how you go on and on doing something you know is bad for you in the hope that it will turn out not to be. And most of the time it isn't even pleasurable – hanging around, pretending, being disappointed, feeling humiliated. The nice bit, being with him and actually

130

enjoying it, works out at about ten per cent and the bad bit ninety per cent. Why do we do it?' She drained her glass and put it down. 'Do you think I could have another one of these?' Catching his very slight hesitation she met his eyes and said, 'Don't worry, I won't get drunk.'

'It wasn't that,' he said quickly. 'I just didn't want to interrupt your flow.'

'You're very frank, aren't you?' she said curiously.

'There wouldn't be any point in being anything else with a woman as intelligent as you.'

'You overestimate me.' Her eyes filled suddenly with tears which she tried to blink back. 'I want to be lied to as much as the next woman. It's more comfortable than the truth. But your professional interest is better than nothing.'

'My interest is both professional and personal,' Slider said, holding her gaze, 'and that's the truth. Otherwise I could have sent someone else to talk to you.'

'Thank you,' she said, a little unevenly. 'I believe you. Now if you'd be so very kind as to get me another gin. I'll blow my nose and pull myself together. Then I'll tell you the rest.'

Slider padded off to the bar feeling both hopeful and glum. A good secretary must know a great deal both about the business and the boss's private life, and a mistress gets told things that are kept from a wife. And if she had a beef against Coleraine, she'd be more likely to spill the beans. The glumness stemmed from her recital of the old, old story, and the recollection of his own ignoble part in the same play on a different stage. 'The nice bit works out at ten per cent and the bad bit ninety per cent.' Oh Joanna! Had she felt like that all that time? Surely not – he hoped not. He had really meant it – he hadn't been stringing her along. But the sad fact was that it must have felt just the same, whether he meant it or not. Without in the least meaning to he had treated her badly, and if she now made him suffer it was no more than he deserved, the bus fare to hell being paid with good intentions. Had Alec Coleraine been tortured by guilt while he romped, or had he merely felt like laddo-me-buck; rich and shameless, fingers stuck in the jelly bowl, getting his just desserts?

When he returned, she smiled at him more comfortably, as if they had long been friends. 'Thanks. I feel better now.

You'd better ask me the questions you want, or I shall maunder on self-indulgently for hours.'

'I'm in no hurry. You talk. Tell me about when it was good between you. It can't always have been nine to one against.'

'No, of course not. For about the first two years it was wonderful. The only difficulty was how to see enough of each other. And then it was up and down for about a year, wonderful when I believed we had a future and terrible when I doubted it. And this last year it's been getting worse all the time. He's been moody, depressed, irritable. I've seen he's has something on his mind, and sometimes I hoped it was us, but mostly I knew it wasn't, which made it worse when he took his tempers out on me. And finally I discovered –' She stopped and her expression hardened.

'Yes?' Slider prompted gently, though he'd guessed, of course.

'He's been seeing someone else,' she said, fixing her eyes on the stem of her glass as she revolved it in her fingers. 'I think it's only recent, but even so it's hard to believe. He still says he loves me, that he can't live without me; but for the last few weeks he's made excuses every time I've wanted to see him outside work. And I can't do a thing right any more, and he flares up at me over the least thing. I think he's been hoping to provoke me into breaking off with him, so as to save him the trouble. Bastard!' A silence. 'The difficulty now is what do I do about my job?' She flicked him a stormy glance. 'Oh, I know, I should have thought of that before getting involved with my boss. My own fault. Doesn't make it any easier though.'

'You've been worried about your job for other reasons lately, haven't you?'

The fingers stopped their restless twisting. 'Why do you ask that?'

'It wasn't just sexual infidelity that was making Alec tense and withdrawn. There's something else wrong – probably financial. You've had suspicions and they've made you feel disloyal, but you can't entirely suppress them. Am I right?'

'Quite a clairvoyant,' she said, trying to sound flippant and only managing nervous. 'Do you do this at parties?'

'You've no reason not to tell me now,' he went on. 'Apart

from anything else, it may recently have got more serious, too serious for the ordinary rules of loyalty to apply – even if he hadn't already forfeited any right to your support.' She didn't agree or deny. He'd got to help her begin. 'Does it in some way involve Marcus?'

She took a deep breath, and then let it out slowly in a sigh. 'Yes, I think so. At least, I think that's what's at the bottom of it. Ever since he dropped out of college – oh!' She clenched her fist and thumped it softly on the tabletop. 'Selfish, ungrateful, self-centred little swine! He doesn't care who he hurts. Everything's me, me, me – and Alec gives in, every time, the idiot. He's just besotted with that boy. We argued about it sometimes. "I know you're right," he'd say, "but I can't help it. I love him." Only child, you see – I think Fay couldn't have any more – and he's such a good-looking boy, too, and charming when he wants to be. Have you met him?' Slider shook his head. 'Spoiled, I suppose. Unless it's something inherent. Alec's selfish, and Fay likes to have her own way. Maybe having it on both sides, it got concentrated. His grandfather, from what I heard, was an Olympic-class me-ist.'

'How did Marcus get on with his grandfather?'

'Oh, all right, I think. He liked anyone who flattered and spoiled him. And I think he found it useful to take sides and play one member of the family off against another. Sir Stefan wanted him to be a musician. Fay didn't mind what he was as long as it wasn't anything to do with music. Alec wanted him to go into the law. But Marcus couldn't see why he should have to work for a living at all, when everybody around him had loads of cash.'

'And had they?'

She frowned. 'I would have said so, yes. Sir Stefan wouldn't part with a penny of his, of course, but I thought Fay and Alec between them had plenty. But just lately I've begun to wonder. You were right about that.' She met Slider's eyes. She was plainly very worried.

'What does Marcus live on, now he's not at college?'

'That's it exactly, the same as he's always lived on: Alec. I don't know the details, but I gather a few years ago, when Marcus was still at school, there was a big scandal that it cost a lot of money to hush up. I don't know if he's been in trouble since then, but he's a constant drain, and he doesn't live cheaply. I don't know how he gets through it all, but I do know –' She hesitated. 'I overheard a bit of their conversation on Wednesday. I didn't mean to – I thought they'd finished and picked up the phone to make a call. But I'm afraid when I heard them I carried on listening. Marcus needed money for something – a lot of money – and he was threatening Alec, saying if he didn't give it to him, he'd just have to turn to theft. Breaking and entering, he said. Alec was horrified. The scandal would finish him, of course. He'd lose all his clients. Marcus knows that, the little swine. That's how he puts the bite on Alec every time.'

'So what did Alec say to the threat?'

'He said no, no, don't even think about it. He said to give him time and he'd come up with something.' She shook her head. 'I was so angry with Marcus I didn't listen after that. I put the phone down. Alec sounded so upset I couldn't bear it, even though – well, I suppose I still love him. I haven't quite had time to get over it.'

'And then half an hour later he came out and said he was ill and was going home.'

'Yes. He looked it too.'

'Did he go to meet Marcus before he went home?'

'No, not as far as I know. Why do you ask?' She seemed genuinely surprised.

'I just wondered. So tell me, how do you think he was going to get hold of money for Marcus?'

'Are you asking me in an official capacity, or is this still a friendly chat?' she asked, suddenly curious.

'I hope it's still friendly. But you know that Wednesday is a day I have to be particularly interested in.'

She stared, and he saw her scalp shift back as her eyes widened and her nostrils flared. 'Oh my God,' she whispered. 'Oh my God, you think Alec killed Sir Stefan!'

He looked at her with interest. 'Has it truly never occurred to you before that he might have?'

'No! No, I swear to you! But you're wrong, you must be wrong! He wouldn't do a thing like that, not Alec. He may be a swine in some ways, but he would never harm a soul. He's

134

too soft if anything – that's why he spoils Marcus –'

'But if Marcus had got into some bad trouble and Alec was desperate for the cash –'

'No! Oh no, I promise you, he just wouldn't.' Her voice was stronger, more confident. 'He just isn't that kind of man.'

Slider well knew there was no kind of man, but that was not the discussion he wanted to have with Helena Goodwin. 'All right, then if you really hadn't considered that possibility, what was it about him that's been worrying you so much, that you wanted to tell me about?'

This was plainly difficult. She chewed her lip, staring at him rather blankly as she tried to make up her mind. 'If I tell you,' she said at last, 'it's going to make it look worse for him. And I'm positive he hasn't done – what you think.'

'Then what has he done? Really,' he added when she still hesitated, 'you'd much better tell me. We always find out in the end, and the sooner we can check it all out, the sooner we can eliminate him from suspicion, if he really is innocent. Keeping it from me isn't going to get anyone anywhere.'

'I just don't want it to be me who betrays him.'

'That suggests there's something to betray.'

She was silent a moment longer, and then seemed to decide to take the plunge. 'All right, look, I don't know if this is anything to do with it – it may be nothing at all, but it's been bothering me. Did you know that Alec is trustee for the estate of his godson Henry?'

'Henry Russell?'

'That's right. It's a family thing – Henry's also a sort of second cousin, I think. You know about it, then?'

'Not much more than the name. Is it a large estate?'

'Very. In the millions, I believe. Henry's father was Russell's Pies and Sausages.'

'Ah yes.' Russell's had always been a rather dignified, old-fashioned firm, whose products sported old-fashioned paper wrappers decorated with dull drawings of the various gold medals won in the days of Empire. They made steak and kidney pies and pork pies of the sort Celia Johnson might have bought at the station buffet while waiting for Trevor Howard (though never, of course, actually eaten). But just lately Russell's had suffered a belated panic and gone all trendy, with transparent cellophane packaging and a new range of synthetic fillings which McLaren adored: cheese 'n' potato, chick 'n' curry and crispy bacon bits. Whatever had happened, Slider wondered in parenthesis, to the word crisp? They were all ruled by nursery language these days. 'Yes, I know Russell's Pies,' he said. 'How old is Henry?'

'Twenty-three. And a half.'

'How come the money is still in trust, then?'

'Oh, the trust goes on until he's twenty-five. Apparently Henry's father was a bit of a wild thing in his youth, and expected Henry to be the same, so he wanted the money tied up until Henry had had a chance to sow his wild oats and grow sensible. But in fact he needn't have worried: Henry's never caused a moment's anxiety to anyone in his life. He's so sensible he doesn't even fret about not getting his money for another eighteen months. The only impulsive thing he's ever done is to get engaged rather suddenly, but the girl's perfectly unexceptionable. She's pretty and good, her parents have got a place in Berkshire, and she's called Camilla. Every mother's dream, in fact.'

Slider returned the smile. 'So what's bothering you about this trust?'

'It was something that happened a couple of months ago,' she said slowly. 'Quite a bit of the trust money is in shares in the family firm, as you'd expect, and about two months ago I happened to see a share transfer document, selling a block of them, on Alec's desk. I was surprised, because I hadn't seen it before, and usually I deal with all the routine paperwork. Alec was out of the room at the time, so I had a closer look at it. As trustee, he's quite entitled to buy or sell shares, of course, but share transfers have to have the signatures of both trustees.'

'Who is the other trustee?'

'David Fowles. He's another cousin of Henry's on his mother's side. The thing is, he's one of these lone yachtsmen and he's been sailing round the world for almost the last year. He keeps in touch, of course, but at that time, at that time I saw the transfer document, he was somewhere out in the middle of the Pacific, and had been for weeks. He could be

136

contacted by radio, of course, but there was no way of getting a document to him for signature. But the share transfer had his signature on it all the same.'

'You think it was a forgery?'

'I think Alec forged it,' she said bravely. 'I've handled lots of documents for the trust, and I know David's signature. It didn't look quite right to me. Besides how could it be? And why hadn't Alec passed it through me in the usual way?'

'Because there was something wrong about it?'

'I think,' she said slowly, 'that he was so desperate for money he sold the shares and took the cash.'

Slider nodded gravely. Interesting that she didn't find this hard to suppose, though murder was unimaginable. 'How much cash?'

'I don't know exactly, because I don't know what he sold at, of course, but it wouldn't have been much under a hundred thousand pounds.' She looked at Slider like a puppy hoping not to be kicked. 'And it wasn't long before that that Marcus smashed Alec's car. A sixty-thousand-pound Mercedes. Marcus was drunk – or something worse – and climbed out without a scratch on him, but the car was a write-off. He lost his licence, of course, but there was a hefty fine as well, which Alec had to pay for him.'

'Have you said anything about this to anyone? To Alec?'

'No,' she said, almost in alarm. 'I couldn't be sure – I may have been quite mistaken. Maybe it was a perfectly normal transaction.'

'You didn't want to suspect him.'

'Of course not. I loved him. But I've never been able to put it quite out of my head. I keep – wondering.'

'Where would the money go, if he sold those shares?'

'There'd be a cheque to the trust's bank account. After that –' she shrugged uncomfortably – 'Alec could write a cheque to anyone he wanted. Even himself.'

'And who holds the cheque-book?'

'He does. He keeps it locked in his private filing cabinet in his office, with the other trust documents. Only he has the key to that.'

'Of course, sooner or later he'd have to account for the money,' Slider said thoughtfully.

'He had another eighteen months before Henry came of age. I'm sure he meant to replace it – only where would he get the money from? He'd have to sell something of his own, I suppose; or play the market. I suppose a hundred thousand isn't much to recoup in that time, if you play high enough. The big dealers make millions on a single transaction, don't they?'

Dream on, thought Slider, but he gave her a comforting nod, and she fell silent. Slider pursued his own thoughts. How did the paintings fit in with this? Had he bought them to make good losses to the trust? Christie's had said they would realise a good profit in a year; but he had bought them before the car-crash incident, so they couldn't have been intended to recoup that money. Maybe selling those shares had not been the first time he'd raided the piggy-bank. And if he had borrowed the trust's money to buy the paintings in the first place, he might well have fought shy of reporting their theft to the police. Rifling the fund, abuse of his powers as a trustee: he wouldn't want all that coming out. If that were the case, he had a bit more than a hundred thousand to find before Henry Russell came of age. But there was plenty of time – no need to be panicked into killing Radek for his fortune.

'Do you know what I think we ought to do?' he said at last. She looked up with faint, very faint, hope. 'I think we should go back to the office and see what we can find out.' The hope died. 'You'll feel better for knowing the truth, one way or the other.' And so will I, he added silently.

'I suppose so,' she said. 'But I've told you, all the trust documents are in his private filing cabinet, and I don't have the key.'

'With all that's been going on lately, he might possibly have left it unlocked,' Slider said. 'It's worth a look, anyway.'

Darkness had fallen while they were in the pub, lamplight had come, and the streets had filled with the evening crowds: theatre-goers, diners-out, and throngs of young people looking for the High Life without any clear idea of what it was going to look like when they bumped into it, except that it would probably be making a lot of noise and have an imported lager in its hand.

It was a pleasantly mild evening, so everyone was good-tempered, and already there were groups of sitters-out outside restaurants and bars. The biggest difference the last ten years had made to London, Slider thought as he and Mrs Goodwin picked their way through the backstreets, was in how much more people liked to stay out of doors, given half a chance. Being both naturally fond of company and a Libra, Slider liked the whole idea of sitting at a pavement café watching the world go by; and he enjoyed the lighted windows of the shops that stayed open late, and the smells of coffee and garlic and delicatessen produce that wafted out of the various open doors they passed. In his early childhood everything had stopped at night, there being in the fifties little to sell and no-one with money to buy it. He still remembered when the ban on illuminating shops at night had been lifted, and his parents had taken him up to London for a special treat, for the pleasure of walking along Oxford Street and looking in the brightly lit windows. Ah, simple pleasures! And they'd had fish and chips when they got home, bought at the chip shop opposite the station and hotted up when they got back to the cottage. Mum would never countenance eating in the street. Common, she called it.

Mrs Goodwin was plainly nervous when they reached the door of the office. 'I'm not sure this is right,' she said, turning to him appealingly.

'You're helping the police with their enquiries,' he said. He followed her upstairs, and she let him into the outer office, switched on the lights, and then unlocked the door to the inner office. The filing cabinets were ranged along one wall, rather prissily sheathed in veneered wood so that the sight of raw metal wouldn't offend the cultured client.

'This is his private one,' she said indicating the end cabinet, and reaching out a hand to test the drawer. Slider caught it gently.

'I think it might be an idea if you locked the outer doors, just to be on the safe side,' he said.

'Yes, of course, I should have thought of that,' she said, and hastened away. Slider examined the filing cabinet and smiled to himself. Piece of pie. By the time she returned, the top drawer was open.

'Look at this,' he said cheerfully. 'We're in luck – he did forget to lock it!'

She looked at it, and him, opened her mouth, and closed it again.

'Let's get busy,' he said.

Slider had meant to go straight to Joanna's, but at the last minute he had an attack of nerves, and decided to call in at the station first for a wash and brush-up and a clean pair of socks. He was sorry to see Barrington's car in the yard, and sorrier still to find a message on his desk summoning him to the presence as soon as he came in.

It struck him as he went in that Barrington was definitely showing signs of strain. There was something almost ragged about his movements, and though his face was still as inexpressive as tufa, his eyes were no longer steady, but moved and shifted all the time he spoke.

'You wanted to see me, sir? I was just going off.'

He expected to be asked about the progress of the case, but Barrington had other things of greater import on his mind.

'You've just driven into the car park, I assume?'

'Yes, sir.' This was an odd tack. Slider began to fear the worst.

'And did you notice anything?' Slider was silent. A man does not lime his own twig. 'Did you see my car there?'

'Yes, I did notice it,' Slider said cautiously. Should he add a word of praise? Jolly clean it looked too? I always wanted one of those myself?

'And what did you notice about it?'

Slider lost patience. 'Would you tell me what all this is about, sir?'

Barrington turned like a man goaded beyond endurance. 'What it's about, Slider, is parking! The cars in the yard are so badly parked that I was unable to get into my own space! I had to park half across the space next to it!'

Slider was still groping in the dark. The space next to Barrington's was his. 'That's all right, sir. I just put mine on the end. It doesn't matter.'

'It most emphatically does matter, Inspector,' Barrington said in cold rage. 'What do you think the lines are there for?

140

Do you think they were put there for people to ignore? It only takes one person to park carelessly, and everyone in the yard is affected. Suppose your car had already been there? What would I have done then?'

Slider declined to answer, looking at Barrington with a stark disbelief he was afraid he was not managing to mask.

'Car parking space in the yard is at a premium. To be allotted a space is a privilege, and I won't have the men under my command abusing privilege through sheer carelessness, indiscipline and sloppy behaviour!' He began to walk up and down again. 'I've told you before that carelessness in small things leads to carelessness in larger things. That's where it all starts! Ignore the little faults, and where do you draw the line? The next thing you know, you have widespread corruption. I've seen it happen before. It only takes one rotten apple to contaminate the whole barrel.'

'Yes, sir,' Slider said. 'I understand.' Barrington stopped pacing and glared at him, as if waiting for further answer. 'I'll have the cars reparked,' he said soothingly.

The red seemed to dissipate slowly from Barrington's stare. He straightened slightly. 'Nonsense. There's no need for that,' he said, quite mildly for him. 'Just make sure that the men are told to park straight in future. It's pure inconsiderateness, and there's no excuse for it.'

Slider agreed, and escaped. What the hell was going on with the Demon King these days? These furious attacks on trivia were like little bursts of steam escaping from the safety valve of a pressure-cooker; Slider wondered at how many pounds per square foot he would finally blow, and how much of a mess there would be to clear up. He didn't fancy having Barrington all over the ceiling and down the walls. Maybe he ought to have taken the move to Pinner after all. And he hadn't even told him about the new developments in the case – though that may have been all to the good. Tomorrow was Sunday; perhaps Barrington would have a nice day out on the golf course and come back refreshed on Monday and ready to cope with the petty annoyances of a murder case.

Then Slider remembered that he was on his way to see Joanna, and already late, and it concentrated his mind wonderfully.

141

CHAPTER TEN

If you can't live without me,
how come you aren't dead yet?

Joanna opened the door to him, and she looked so dear and familiar and had been so long longed-for that all he could say was, 'Aunty Em.'

'This ain't Kansas,' she said forbiddingly.

'Oh, don't say that. I've had such a strange dream, and unfortunately you weren't in it.' She stepped back to allow him in, and he walked as so often before into her living-room, where the fire had been kindled long enough to have reached a cheerful red glow. The curtains were drawn and there was one lamp on in the corner, so that the shabby furniture gleamed and winked like conspirators out of the friendly gloom. It was all so different from the neat brightness of the Ruislip house. Here there might be dust in the corners, but the baggy chesterfield opened its arms to you like a dear old mum, and the house rule was that it was pleasure that came next to godliness.

She followed him in and he turned to her. 'I'm sorry I'm so late. I didn't mean to get off to such a bad start.'

She raised an eyebrow at the word 'start', but said, 'It's all right. You don't need to explain – I'm an old hand at this game, remember.'

'Which game?' he asked nervously, thinking of Mrs Goodwin.

But she said, 'Waiting for policemen.'

'I'm not sure I like the use of the plural there, but still. I am sorry to have kept you waiting.'

'It's all right,' she said again, patiently. She reminded him of Irene.

'I wish you'd get angry with me. There's a thin line between tolerance and indifference.'

Her eyes widened. 'You want me to be waiting behind the door with a rolling pin? I think you've strayed into the wrong decade. And the wrong house.'

'And the wrong play. Oh dear. I'm sorry. Let's start again. Have you eaten already?' he asked in a brightly social voice. 'Do you want go to out somewhere?'

Wrong again. 'What d'you think, this is a date? You came to talk, that's all.' She cocked an eye at him. 'I suppose you're starving.'

'I seem not to have got round to lunch.'

'Just as I thought. Sit down, then, take your coat off, and I'll get you something.'

He watched her walk away from him. She was wearing her comfortable velvet Turkish trousers, which were so old the pile was all rubbed off the seams, and a loose, Indian-style crimped-cotton shirt of similar vintage. She was neither tall nor elegant; her feet were bare and her hair was untidy; and she seemed to him to contain every desirable quality. She was home, rest, sanctuary: the place where you were understood and welcomed, the place where you gave and received pleasure. He wanted to talk with her and eat with her and sleep with her and walk along all the sunset beaches in Hollywood with her – things he had never even considered wanting to do with any other woman. By their houses shall ye know them, he thought inconsequentially: designed for living in, his desired person, rather than for display. And desired, by golly – he was anxious to obey her hospitable parting instructions but wasn't sure that he ought to remove his coat yet. He had a promising young erection under there. Don't want to frighten the horses.

She was back very soon with a tray. 'This will keep you going.' She handed him a large malt whisky, and a plate on which reposed a pork pie cut into quarters. He had – as she knew of course – a passion for pork pies, especially proper ones like this with the dark, lean meat and the very crisp

143

raised crust. And she then placed before him a jar of Taylor's English mustard and a knife, and everything was perfect.

'What a woman!' he said. 'How did you just happen to have a pork pie about your person?'

She sat down beside him. 'I'm a very wonderful person. Cut me a tiny piece just to taste.' He cut a piece, dabbed it in mustard, and held it out to her, suddenly doubtful. In the old days he'd have put it in her mouth, but it seemed too intimate a gesture to be attempted without permission. It was unnerving for his brain to be getting all these conflicting signals. That's how they gave laboratory monkeys ulcers.

She saw his difficulty. 'For goodness' sake,' she said, then ducked her head and took the morsel from his fingers. It was a strangely diffuse exclamation and he wasn't sure what she meant by it, but she seemed to know that too, because she said, 'Old dogs and new tricks. With anyone else it would be a deliberate ploy to disarm me by pretending nothing had happened, but with you it's just that you have no idea how to dissemble. Which is what makes you so dangerous.' She was looking at him as she spoke, actually meeting his eyes for the first time, which did nothing to divert the flow of blood back to his head from the eager part of him that was desperately trying to point at her like a game dog; and in fact an unexpectedly game dog he was turning out to be for a man who had been contemplating solitary old age only yesterday. It was on the tip of his tongue to ask her if they couldn't just go straight to bed and sort things out that way, but she caught that thought on its way up too. 'And this still ain't Kansas,' she added sternly, but she was trying to hold down a smile as she said it. She had never been very good at being angry, and positively pathetic at holding grudges.

'So what made you late?' she went on, turning sideways on and tucking her legs under her so as to face him. 'I bet you've been with a woman. I can smell scent on the air.'

'I've been comforting a very attractive divorcée who says she finds me very sympathetic. She's younger than you are, too.'

Joanna grinned. 'I'm younger than I am. This is something to do with the case, I assume?'

'It would be more flattering to me if you didn't immediately jump to that conclusion.'

144

'I wouldn't be interested in a man I thought even capable of entertaining the notion of a thought for another woman. Go on, tell me about the case.'

He would sooner have pursued the intriguing hint that she was interested in him, but he knew there was no help for it. He was not on safe ground yet.

'She's the secretary of Radek's son-in-law, Alec Coleraine. She'd been having an affair with him and now discovers he's been two-timing her –'

'Three-timing her, presumably, counting his wife,' she said with horrible neutrality.

'As you say. Anyway, contemplation of her wrongs was enough to tip her into telling me about something that's been worrying her for some time. She suspected him of being less than a hundred per cent honest in his financial dealings, so I persuaded her to go back to the office and raid the filing cabinets.'

'You dog,' she said. 'And what did you find?'

He told her about the Henry Russell trust. 'All the papers were locked in Coleraine's private cabinet, to which he alone holds the key – and no wonder. There's been a steady sale of trust assets – shares, gilts, real estate – over the last two years, and no purchases, other than the three oil-paintings we know about, which he was careless enough to lose. I've taken down the share names and dates, and with a bit of research we'll be able to find out how much money has gone, but even at a conservative estimate it's got to be two million, given the paintings cost a million and a quarter.'

'And where's it all gone?'

'Where indeed. Unfortunately the cheque-stubs and bank statements weren't there, though Helena –'

'Helena?'

'You get friendly going through someone's drawers together. Helena assures me the bank statements at least ought to have been there, because she's seen him take them out on previous occasions. But we did find one dead cheque-book stuck in the crack at the back of the drawer, and it made interesting reading.'

'Hang on a minute. If he kept all this incriminating evidence firmly locked away, how did you manage to get at it?'

He met her eyes limpidly. 'I think in all his recent anxiety he must have left the filing cabinet unlocked. It's easily done.'

'Like fun he did. I suppose there was a coathanger lying about the office somewhere? Or had you brought your own?'

'I can't imagine what you're suggesting,' he said, shaking his head sadly.

'It's a good job I'm not wearing a wire. Anyway, tell me about this interesting cheque-book.'

'Most of the stubs were uncontroversial. But quite a few had the amount filled in – and large amounts they were – but no payee.'

'Sounds like belated caution. You think Coleraine paid the money to himself, then?'

'Don't you?'

'I'm not in the business of thinking,' she quoted him, and then slipped into Stan Freeberg. 'I just wanna get the facts, man.'

'The fact is that Coleraine's been under severe financial pressure because of his no-good son, who sucks at the parental wallet like a newborn calf –'

'I love your agricultural metaphors,' she marvelled.

'I'm a farm boy, remember. Also Helena told me that business has not been quite what it was because the old partner, Antrobus, had a lot of rich elderly clients who have now died, without being replaced by new ones. So his income was going down while his outgoings were going up.'

She had been thinking. 'But wait a minute, if Coleraine had been defrauding the trust, wouldn't it have been discovered? I mean, what about audits? Don't they have to have them done, by law?'

He shook his head. 'With family trusts, audits are carried out at the request of the trustee, whenever he thinks it's necessary. The last one was done three years ago, according to Mrs Goodwin, and presumably showed up nothing unusual. The other trustee is a sort of sleeping partner who leaves everything to Coleraine because he, the other trustee I mean, is a layman and only knows about boats. So he's not likely to ask for an audit, or want to look at the books.'

'But sooner or later Coleraine would have to come up with the money, wouldn't he? I mean, when the boy comes of age, he's going to ask where it is.'

146

'Ah yes, now that's the really interesting thing. Helena told me the trust went on until the boy was twenty-five, and Henry Russell is only twenty-three. Coleraine still had eighteen months to replace the cash – assuming for the moment he had taken it – and I think that's what the oil paintings were supposed to do, to turn enough profit to fill the piggy-bank again. When he lost them he must have been very, very worried; but he still had time, if he was clever. But then about six weeks ago, disaster struck. Henry Russell suddenly announced he was getting married.'

She grinned at him. 'Oh, you have a lovely way of telling a tale. I liked the artistic pause there. What's Our 'Enery's nuptials got to do with it?'

'While we were going through the filing cabinet, we found a photocopy of the actual trust deed. The trust ends when Henry is twenty-five, or on his marriage over the age of twenty-one, whichever is the sooner.'

'Ah, I see! Nice one. Suddenly he's got weeks instead of months.'

'If it's discovered he's misappropriated the trust funds, he'll be ruined. He'll never practise again. And it'll mean a gaol sentence, and gaol is not something people of his class can easily contemplate. He'd probably think his own death was preferable.'

'Or better still, someone else's death? You're thinking he murdered Radek?'

'Radek had millions, and it was all going to go to Fay anyway. He was an old man, it was only a matter of hastening him on his way. And it was generally believed Radek had a heart condition, and might pop off any time. I don't know whether Radek himself put the story about, but Buster certainly believed it, and would have been sure to tell Coleraine – though the post mortem showed up no evidence of heart disease.'

'What about the gun? Where would Coleraine get hold of a gun?'

'Haven't you heard that bit? I thought Atherton was keeping you up to date on all this.'

'I don't live in Jim's pocket,' she said with a sidelong look at him. 'Besides, he's got other fish to fry at the moment.

147

Didn't you know about him and Sue Caversham – principal second violin in my orchestra? They've been at it like crazed ferrets ever since they met.'

He tried not to feel relieved. He never really thought Atherton and Joanna were – but with Atherton one never knew. He was said to have the social conscience of a dog in a room full of hot bitches, and he and Joanna liked each other very much and had so much in common and – well, Sue Caversham was a very nice person. 'Yes, I remember her. She's very nice.'

'Almost nice enough for Jim,' Joanna said disconcertingly. 'So what about the gun, anyway?'

'Radek's own gun is missing. A Second World War trophy, and the bullet that killed him was the same sort as the ammo we found in his house.'

'Poor old bugger. That's a nasty twist, shot with your own gun.'

'We haven't found it yet, but we know Coleraine had the opportunity to take it. And he has no proper alibi for the time of the murder; and he sure as hell had a motive.'

Joanna nodded. 'It looks pretty black. But what a silly way to murder anyone – in broad daylight in front of a hundred witnesses.'

'Yes,' he frowned. 'But then, Coleraine was an amateur in the business, and he was in a state of mental and emotional turmoil. There's a kind of loony theatricality to it that I can see might fit him. And it probably wasn't planned, you know. He probably thought about it as a tempting way out without really meaning anything serious by it. Then he found himself in the situation and just did it on the spur of the moment. And probably immediately regretted it.' He thought back over past cases. 'People who murder their nearest and dearest generally do it in a very silly and amateur way. The cunning criminal covering his steps, your domestic murderer is not.'

'So what's the next step?'

He shrugged. 'None of this is proof, of course. We have to grind on, verifying everything, and most of all looking for witnesses. That's the footslog of the job. And we have to find the gun, of course. No gun, no proof.'

'But you said the ammunition matched.'

'Yes, but it could have been fired from any compatible gun.

The proof comes from the marks the gun leaves on the bullet and cartridge case when it's fired. Those are unique, like a fingerprint.'

'How so? I don't understand.'

He smiled. 'You should ask Norma about guns. Atherton thinks she's got a fetish. Penis envy, he calls it.'

'I'd sooner ask you. Norma hasn't got your looks.'

'It's jolly kind of you to say so. Well, you know what rifling means, don't you?'

'Going through someone's drawers?' He stirred in his seat. Had she spotted the dog trying to see the rabbit, then?

'Pay attention! A rifled gun barrel has spiral ridges all the way down the inside to guide the bullet. If you like, it's like a screwdriver turned inside out.'

'How graphic! Yes, I did understand that part.'

'All right. Now a bullet is slightly larger than the minimum width of the barrel, and the metal it's made of is slightly softer. So as it's forced down the barrel by the charge, the ridges make marks on the bullet – striations, they're called.'

'Gotcher.'

'And different makes of gun have different arrangements of ridges – the Webley automatic, for instance, has six right-hand thread grooves, while the Colt .45 has six left-hand grooves, and so on. So you can narrow down the type of gun a bullet was fired from. But in addition each individual gun has tiny variations in the rifling which are unique to that actual weapon. The same with the cartridge case – that will bear the marks of the breech-block and firing pin, which are never identical in two separate guns. So if we can find the gun, fire another bullet from it, then compare the marks on that bullet and on the one that killed Radek, we can prove that was the gun that was used.' He smiled ruefully. 'Then we only have to prove it was Coleraine who pulled the trigger.' He was silent a moment in thought. 'One thing, though: it does look as if you were right, that it wasn't a musician who murdered Radek.'

'Of course not. We couldn't do it. We're fools to ourselves, though. If anyone needed removing it was him.'

'Don't say that,' he said. 'I know it's only a joke, but don't say it.'

She looked at him quizzically. 'You really mind, don't you?'

149

'Someone has to care.'

'But nobody even liked him.'

'Buster did. Somebody has to avenge him.'

She shook her head. 'It isn't that, though, is it?' She studied his face for a moment. 'It's holding back the chaos, isn't it?'

He looked at her warily, like a cat eyeing a thermometer. He was about to have his soul probed, and after the events of the last four months it was already feeling delicate. Though she was right, of course. 'I suppose it is.'

'We all have our own ways of doing it. My mother bakes.' It was the first time she'd ever mentioned her mother to him. 'When I left home, for instance, she made a huge batch of shortbread and packed it in a tin in my suitcase, and it wasn't because she thought I might be hungry. Whenever she feels threatened she makes cakes and biscuits and buns – and she's terrific at it, they're always beautiful, symmetrical, really professional-looking. Of course there's only my father at home now to eat them, so mostly they end up feeding the birds, but still she bakes. When she lifts a steaming tray of perfect, golden fairy cakes out of the oven, she knows that she's in control and the Devil is still on the other side of the door with the bolt shot home.'

He thought of Irene, cleaning things that weren't dirty, plumping cushions no-one had leaned against. Why had he never thought of that before? Oh Irene! He felt a surge of sad, guilty compassion, fierce as canteen heartburn. But what could he ever have done, except what he did do?

'Yes,' he said comprehensively.

She went on, 'Do you know that poem by Auden? "The glacier knocks in the cupboard, the desert sighs in the bed, the crack in the teacup opens a lane to the land of the dead."'

'Nasty. There was a wardrobe in my bedroom when I was a kid –' He shuddered.

'For me it's always been music, of course. When I play, I know there's order, symmetry, the things of the light. I can believe the guys in the white hats are going to win and the floor under my feet isn't going to suddenly yawn and tip me into the pit – all common experience to the contrary.'

He smiled at her. 'My father always liked you, you know.'

'You are a master of the non sequitur,' she said. 'What's that supposed to mean?'

'You know what it means.' The moment seemed to have arrived unannounced. 'I love you. That's such an inadequate sentence, but there doesn't seem to be a word for the way I feel about you, which I think you know anyway.' He quickly forestalled whatever she might have said then. 'I know that I put you through two years of hell, though I never meant to hurt you, but please, now that we can be together properly and openly, without hurting anyone at all, won't you take me back?'

'You think it's as easy as that?'

'That wasn't easy,' he said, a little hurt.

She grew impatient. 'Oh don't pout at me! Tell me, do you really, *really* not understand why it's impossible?'

'No. It doesn't seem impossible to me. All the obstacles have been swept away. Now there's only us to please. Why shouldn't we?'

She looked at him broodingly for a while. But when she spoke it was quite gently, as though there was no point in being angry, which on the whole he thought rather a bad sign. 'In the beginning you fell in love with me – so you said. You said you couldn't live without me, but you kept on managing it. You had a wife and children and responsibilities, and I understood that, I honoured you for taking them seriously. But still in the end you didn't choose me. You chose to stay with them. And the fact that you're free now is still not because you chose me, but because you got thrown out. I'm not going to come second with you, because it's too important for that. You should have marched out for me with banners and trumpets and elephants. I'm not going to be your consolation prize.'

'It wasn't like that.' He looked at her despairingly with the recognition of an absolute gulf. Was this a man–woman thing? Or was it just him and her? It was like one of those stories in which someone goes and dies for a completely pointless principle, and you admire their courage and integrity, but you still think they're barmy. How could she want to throw away being together for the rest of their lives for the sake of hurt pride? 'It isn't like that,' he said. 'I don't want you *because* Irene's left me. And actually I did choose you –'

'You could have fooled me.'

'It was just a matter of timing. I mean,' as she looked about to interrupt, 'the way the end bit happened was an accident of timing. Please, listen to me. That last time we met, up in the city, when I was at the Old Bailey and you were at St Paul's –'

'Yes, I remember,' she said tonelessly.

'You said then that I must choose, and on the way home in the car I thought it all through and came to my decision. I realised I'd been procrastinating, and I decided I was going to speak to Irene as soon as I got home, and sort it all out. I was going to tell her I was leaving. But when I got there *he* was there, Ernie, and she got her news in first.' He studied her face. 'You don't believe me?'

'Would you? It's a bit of a coincidence, isn't it?'

'But I was going to leave. I was going to tell her that very evening.'

'You said that to me before, on many occasions, and nothing came of it.'

'But I really *was* going to that time,' he said, his fists clenching with frustration.

She looked away. 'Well, we shall never know, shall we?'

'No,' he said. 'At least, you won't.' She looked at him again. 'Do you think that I don't remember how I felt that day? Or that I'm deliberately lying to you now? A cynical manipulation to get my own way? If you think that, then you don't really believe I love you, because you know I could never do that to you.'

She said awkwardly. 'No, I don't think that. But still, you didn't tell her.'

'Only because I was forestalled. History prevented me, that's all. I would have done it. And now that it can't be proved one way or the other, you have to give me the benefit of the doubt, because it would be unfair not to.'

She went on staring at him, completely at a loss.

'Jo, you must still want to be with me, or we wouldn't even be having this conversation.' He paused to let her deny it, but she didn't. 'And if it's the only thing that's holding you back, I swear to you, I swear that I did choose you, and that I was going to tell her that night.' Pause. Nothing. 'You either have to believe me, or tell me I'm lying.' He held her eyes. 'Am I lying?'

'I don't want to be unhappy any more,' she said in a low voice, and while he was still trying to work out what that meant, they were interrupted by the oven timer going off in the kitchen. 'Saved by the bell,' she said, jumping up.

He couldn't believe it. 'Leave it,' he said, annoyed.

'Leave it? Don't you know what that was?'

He stood up too. 'This is important, for God's sake!'

'So's that. That was our dinner in the oven, and it might burn. Don't you want to eat?'

'What the hell's the matter with you?' he scowled.

'I don't know. I think I may be hungry,' she said flippantly. Then she stepped up close to him and looked up into his face in a way that made the back of his knees ache, because she looked tired and beaten and he wanted to gather her up and make everything all right for her. 'Please, Bill, this is so hard for me. I've been living on my pride for a very long time and it's hard to give it up just like that.' She put her hands up round his neck in what seemed an automatic gesture, and that alone was like an electric shock to the gonads. 'Do one more thing for me, you good man. Have dinner with me before you ask me any more difficult questions.'

'You,' he said unsteadily, 'don't have to ask me for anything. I'm the one who's begging.' He wanted to put his arms round her but he didn't dare touch her at this point. Instead he managed to say, 'What's in the oven?'

'Cassoulet. It's Jim's recipe,' she added temptingly.

His saliva glands started up at the mere thought. Funny how the animal was always hanging around to debunk the spiritual man. 'With those spicy Portuguese sausages?' he asked. 'What are they called?'

'Chorus girls. Something like that. And bits of chicken. I've got a nice bottle of St Josèph too.'

'You must have been expecting company.'

'Nah, I eat like this all the time. Hungry, Inspector?'

'My stomach thinks my throat's been cut.'

'Come, then,' she said, backing off and holding out a hand to him. 'You can open the wine, and we'll eat in here by the fire.'

He took the hand, her fingers curled round his, and the juice of life started to flow again, strong as a river, strong enough to roll rocks away. He followed her towards the kitchen. 'What do you mean, elephants?' he said. 'What elephants?'

CHAPTER ELEVEN

A Stroll down Felony Lane

Secrets can make prickly bedfellows, and Slider had encountered more than once the villain who got to the point where he would sooner face the consequences than go on concealing the deed. So he was not entirely surprised to get a telephone call from Alec Coleraine, before he'd had a chance to call him. Coleraine sounded nervous and depressed.

'I'd like to talk to you, if that's possible.'

'Yes, by all means,' Slider said. 'Go ahead.'

'Not on the telephone. I mean, I want to talk to you privately. In confidence. Is that possible?'

'Do you want me to come to your house?'

'No, no, not here.' He lowered his already lowered voice. 'I don't want Fay to hear. I – it's rather delicate. Look, could you meet me somewhere? At a pub or something?'

'If you like. What about The Mitre?'

'No, they know me there.'

'All right, what about The Kensington? Do you know it, on the corner of Elsham Road? They have live jazz there on a Sunday morning, so it'll be good and crowded.'

'You think – oh, I suppose you're right. But you'll come on your own?'

When he had put down the phone Slider walked along to the CID room, where Atherton and Norma were poring over the lists of shares sold and the stock market prices, working out how much the Russell trust was down. Anderson and

Jablowski were out trawling Covent Garden again, and the rest were going over statements and following up phone calls.

'I may be about to make you redundant,' Slider said. 'I've just had the prime suspect on the dog, wanting to arrange a meeting. He does not sound a happy man.'

'The hounds of hell are on his traces,' Atherton said.

'I think he wants to tell me All,' said Slider.

'Where? When?' Atherton asked. 'Do you want me to come with you?'

'Now. The Kensington. And no. He wants a private chat.'

'Be careful, sir,' Norma said. 'He might be desperate. If he knows you suspect him he might want to eliminate you as well.'

'In a crowded jazz pub? I don't think he's that irrational. But it's nice of you to care,' Slider said.

Atherton looked him over carefully. 'You're very jaunty this morning, guv. Have you won the pools?'

'Oh, better than that,' Slider said with a grin. 'Well, I must be off to the woods. I'll be back soon with fresh supplies. Be good, children, and don't tease the bears.'

Atherton remained staring at the closed door for some minutes, feeling hollow. Norma watched him sympathetically, and at last laid her hand on his arm. 'It's good for him. Be glad for him, at least.'

He looked at her. 'I am.'

'It would never really have worked out with you two, anyway,' Norma said sensibly. 'You're too alike.'

He pulled himself together. 'I'm sorry, who are we talking about?'

'That's right,' Norma smiled and patted him. 'You're a nice bloke. Fancy a cup of coffee? I'll get them.'

There are those whose sartorial standards never slip whatever the vicissitudes of life: they would not willingly meet the Grim Reaper himself without a tie on. Alec Coleraine was standing at the bar in The Kensington trying to get served – the social equivalent of trying to get a Council Tax office to acknowledge a change of address card – and looking as though the hounds of hell had actually got him by the shoelaces; but nothing could be more immaculate and correct for Sunday lunchtime drinkies than the cream turtle-neck sweater, the tweed jacket with the leather elbows, the fawn cavalry twills, and the brown brogues polished so that the toecaps glowed like a bay horse's bum.

His flinching eyes sought Slider's and slid away again, and he had to cough before he could ask, 'What would you like to drink?'

'I'll have a bottle of Bass, please.'

'Oh yes, jolly good. Good idea. I'll have the same. Make that two, will you?'

The band was on the small platform warming up, and Slider looked towards them, as he looked at all musicians now, with a sense of interested kinship, and thought briefly and gloriously of Joanna. They hadn't really talked, not to make plans or agree anything about the future. There hadn't really been time for that yet; they had been too busy catching up on lost opportunities. But there could be no doubt, not after last night, he thought – and short-circuited himself. Last night! Billowy, sensuous memories beckoned, and he caught his mind back hastily like a Labrador from the master bed, gave it a stern shake and sent it downstairs. Not now! He had a case to think about now.

And this poor devil, whatever he had done, was plainly suffering for it as he ought. He must help him get it off his chest. Nasty expression that, whichever way you took it.

'Shall we sit over there? It looks like about the quietest spot.'

'I didn't understand immediately why you suggested this place,' Coleraine said, following him, 'but I see now. If there's a lot of noise, we're not so likely to be overheard.'

'That's right.' Slider sat, wriggling round behind a table, and Coleraine hesitated and then came in beside him, so that they both had their backs to the wall, facing outwards. Slider turned a little sideways so that he was almost facing him. 'There is one thing I must get straight with you, however. You spoke on the phone about confidentiality. Anything I can keep secret I will, but you must understand that if what you tell me is material to any criminal case it will be my duty to report it.'

Coleraine put down his glass and looked at Slider, and

drew a sort of shuddering breath. 'Oh God, what have I done? Why did I ever start on this – this – they call it a slippery slope, don't they?' He gave an unconvincing laugh. 'You go so far and you find you can't stop. But it wasn't for myself, I want you to understand that. I'm not as bad as you think. I didn't do it for myself.'

'It will be much better for you if you tell me everything,' Slider said comfortingly. 'And if it helps you, you can assure yourself that I know most of it already. You won't really be giving yourself away.'

'I – I thought perhaps you did. That's why I – it's keeping the secret, you see. And wondering all the time what's going to happen next. It's got so I'd sooner know the worst than have to go on wondering from day to day when the blow's going to fall.'

'I'm sure I'd feel the same way.' There was a silence while Coleraine stared at nothing, absorbed in his own misery. Slider prompted him, 'So tell me about it, then. Where's the best place to start? With the Russell trust?'

Coleraine came back from his thoughts. 'Ah, you do know about that, then?'

'That you've been taking money from it over a period of years? Yes.'

He took the plunge. 'I didn't mean to defraud Henry, you know. In fact I meant to help him at first. It all started quite innocently with the Miniver fiasco – do you know about that?' Slider shook his head. 'Miniver was a mining company in South America – bauxite, cobalt, things like that. It was more or less exhausted and the shares had done nothing for years, but about three years ago I had a tip that they were going to rocket. Something to do with huge new deposits being found. Well, I like to do a bit on the market now and then, so I decided to have a flutter, but this friend of mine, the chap who gave me the tip, he persuaded me it was no use just dipping a toe in. With big profits to be made he said I ought to go the whole hog and, well, I was persuaded. I put all my spare cash into it; and then I thought of the trust. Why not do Henry a favour too? So I sold a large slice of his shares, and put that into Miniver too.' He took a mouthful of his drink, and stared at the glass as if he hadn't known what it was going to be. 'I suppose I don't have to tell you what happened next.'

'The shares didn't go up.'

'Oh, they went up all right,' he said bitterly. 'They shot up. It was very exciting. And then just as I was thinking I'd made a nice profit and perhaps I ought to get out with it, the whole thing collapsed like a pricked balloon. Up like the rocket, down like the stick. Overnight the shares were worthless. Firelighters. Of course the whole thing had been contrived somewhere along the line to make somebody very rich, and a whole lot of us got our fingers badly burned – including my friend who gave me the tip, so I can't blame him. But it left me feeling –' He paused. 'It wasn't just the money, you see.'

'Wasn't it?'

Coleraine looked at him with a little flash of spirit. 'I know you think that's all I care about, but I wasn't born with a silver spoon in my mouth, you know.'

'I didn't think you were,' Slider said.

'I've had to struggle,' he said defiantly. 'I had nothing to begin with. In fact, I may as well tell you, since I'm telling you everything, that I was a Barnardo's boy. So you see, when I say I had nothing, I mean really nothing – not even parents who would own me. You can't imagine what that's like, can you, to know that right from the beginning no-one wanted you, not even your own mother?'

He seemed actually to want an answer to that, so Slider said 'No. It must be very hard.'

'And I was a shrimp of a kid, too, pale and puny, and you know what kids are like. I was bullied by almost everyone. It's no fun being the smallest. But it made me tough, and it made me determined. I had to think about what areas I could win in. I was never going to beat them on brawn, but I had good brains and I saw how if you had money in this world people had to give you respect. So I worked like a black at school to get on. I swore to myself I was going to be rich enough one day to cock a snook at everyone.'

Probably the other thing he learned, Slider thought, was that while he was never going to be able to beat the boys, he could win with the girls by playing on their sympathy and their motherly instincts. His defects would become virtues.

158

Girls would be comfort and balm to him – and success with them would also be a means of getting one up on the members of his own sex he so hated. It was a syndrome he'd encountered before, the bullied boy becoming a successful ladies' man. Sadly, it was hardly ever because they actually like women. Manipulation is no basis for friendship.

'So you see,' Coleraine went in, 'everything I have, I got for myself with my own efforts. And losing like that in the Miniver crash – being taken for a ride – well, it hurt my pride. It was hard to bear.'

'You also had the loss to Henry Russell to make good.'

'Yes. Of course. Well, anyway, I started speculating. I took trust funds out of the safe stocks and started to make them really work, going into much more volatile areas where the big profits are to be made.'

'And the big losses,' Slider said.

'Yes.' He looked glum. 'It worked sometimes. I did make profits. But I reinvested them – and – well – bit by bit the fund was trickling away.'

'The fruit machine syndrome,' Slider said. 'Everyone always puts their winnings back in and goes on playing until it's all gone.'

'Yes. Yes, I suppose so,' he said rather blankly. 'The trouble was – I don't know how to say it. I don't quite know how it happened. But it seemed as if it wasn't just the money trickling away, it was my scruples. From taking the trust money to invest, and putting it on longer and longer shots, which was unethical if not illegal, it didn't seem such a very long step to taking it for myself. I don't mean stealing it,' he added quickly, looking at Slider. 'I only ever meant to borrow it, I swear to you. And it wasn't really for me, either. You see my son – my son –'

'Got into trouble,' Slider suggested helpfully.

'He isn't really a bad boy at heart. Just high-spirited. And he's been spoiled. His mother and his grandfather between them have spoiled him. I wanted him to go into the law, you know, and he would have followed me into my business and been a terrific success. He's got brains, you know. But they squabbled over him like two dogs over a bone, and the result is he hasn't done anything. I tried to push him, but it just made him defy me. He always knew he could appeal to them, you see,' he added bitterly, 'and they'd always side with him. Talk about spare the rod.' He seemed to feel he had painted the picture blacker than he meant. He looked at Slider quickly. 'But he's a good boy at heart. And when your boy gets into trouble and comes to you, you don't stop to read a lecture, you help him out, don't you? Have you got children?'

'Two. One of each.'

'Yes, well, you understand then. Marcus – he – I couldn't refuse him, could I? I couldn't let them take him to court, maybe lock him up. It would have killed him. He's a free spirit. You can't put sensitive people like him behind bars.'

'So you borrowed from the trust, to pay for his – needs,' Slider said carefully. 'What about the oil paintings. Where did they fit in?'

Coleraine had the grace to blush a little. 'That was – oh, God, I mishandled everything so badly! I suppose you know all there is to know about the paintings. I met a chap, an art dealer, who told me the market was just right for investing in minor masters. The recession had brought prices down, but as interest rates fell everyone was going to look for a better home for their cash, and prices were all set to rocket. As long as you bought soundly, you couldn't fail. I was getting worried about the trust, and it seemed a way to get back on an even keel in one go. I went into it very carefully, you know. I didn't just take this bloke's word for it. But Christie's agreed with everything he'd said, and buying the paintings from them I knew they had to be good.'

Slider nodded sympathetically. 'But why didn't you insure them?'

'I know, I know. It sounds like madness. But at the time – you see, the premiums would have been astronomical, they would have cut into the profits; and besides that, the insurance company would have insisted on all sorts of modifications to the flat, which I could hardly have kept secret from Fay.'

'She didn't know about the paintings, then?'

'Of course not.' He looked aghast. 'How could I tell her where I'd got the money from, and why? Anyway, I thought it would be safe enough for a year or so. We'd never been burgled before. And the pictures were in the back of my wardrobe, all wrapped up. It wasn't as if they were hanging on the wall for all to see. It was just the most wretched bloody luck that we got turned over like that.'

An idea had been forming in Slider's mind, based on a general knowledge of Larry Picket's acquaintances. 'The art dealer who gave you the advice – was he a tall, thin, military-looking man with a sandy moustache? Well spoken – Guards' tie?'

Coleraine looked at him with awful reluctance. 'Bill Hanratty,' he said almost in a whisper. 'Do you know him?'

'I think so,' said Slider. 'I told you we'd got your paintings back, didn't I?'

'From him? He stole them?'

'We picked them up from a fence, but Ginger Bill's one of his known associates. Hanratty isn't his name, but it sounds like him. And the break-in at your place was a professional job.'

'He was so interested in what I'd bought, said I'd been very shrewd. I thought he was a nice guy.' Coleraine put his head in his hands. 'I've been such a fool. God, why was I born? I should have realised it was a bit of a coincidence, a bit odd that the burglars found the paintings. Oh, what have I done? What have I done?'

Slider let him alone for a moment or two, and then prompted him gently. 'All right, so the paintings were gone, and you were in a worse state than ever. So what happened next?'

'Next? I carried on. What else could I do? I thought at least I had a couple more years, I hoped something would turn up, I'd find some way to put the money back. I knew Stefan was filthy rich, and when he went all his money would go to Fay – that was understood. She'd give it to me, of course, to look after and invest for her, so that was no problem, as long as he died before Henry came of age, and there was a good chance of that because he had a heart problem –'

'He didn't, actually.'

'What? What are you talking about? Of course he did.'

Slider shook his head. 'The post mortem showed a perfectly normal heart for his age – no disease.'

'But – but Buster told me –'

'Possibly Sir Stefan made it up as a means to keep Buster in line. "Don't cross me or it might bring on an attack", that sort of thing.'

'Good God,' Coleraine said slowly. 'Yes, it's just the sort of thing he'd do. Poor old Buster. It was a good thing, then –'

'Yes?' A good thing I didn't wait for him to die naturally?

'Oh, nothing. I've forgotten where I was.'

'I think you'd just about reached Henry Russell announcing he was getting married.'

'Ah. Yes.' Coleraine looked suddenly very old and very weary. 'Well, you know, of course, that the trust winds up when Henry marries. Suddenly I was going to have to face the music. I can tell you I was worried sick. I didn't know which way to turn. And in the middle of it all, Marcus came to me again with more trouble, some –' He stopped, looking at Slider warily.

Slider shrugged. 'You may as well tell me everything. How much worse can it be?'

Coleraine sighed. 'I suppose you're right. It was some cocaine dealer who was into Marcus for big money. Threatening him if he didn't pay up. Marcus came to me – I gave him what I had – he said it wasn't enough. We had a bit of a row.' He stared sadly at the table. 'I was so worried already, I said some pretty harsh things to him, about how he'd bled me dry. He said his grandfather had plenty and why didn't I go and ask him. I couldn't bear the idea of that. I hated Stefan, you know, and his attitude towards us. I said I'd sooner die than ask him for money. So Marcus said that if I didn't, he was sure his mother would, especially if she knew what he needed the money for.' He looked at Slider appealingly. 'Fay – she doesn't know everything about Marcus. I mean, she knows about some of his – pranks, but – not the serious stuff. I try to keep it from her. He knows that, Marcus knows that. It would break her heart if she knew he takes drugs. So I said I'd go and see Stefan.'

'And that was the visit you paid him on Tuesday?'

He was very white now. 'Yes. It was useless. I knew it would be. He told me he wouldn't give me a penny, whatever I wanted it for. I went to work. I sat there all day going round

162

and round like a rat in a cage, desperately trying to think of a way to raise the cash. I couldn't think of anything. Then on Wednesday morning Marcus phoned me to ask how I'd got on. I told him Stefan had refused. He said –' Coleraine swallowed. 'He said why didn't I kill the old boy then. Shoot him. Marcus knew he kept a loaded pistol in the house in case of burglars. "Go and get Grandpa's gun and shoot him, then you'll have all the money you want," he said. I thought he was joking, of course.' He stopped. 'Then he said if I didn't do something and get him the money, he'd take to crime. Breaking and entering was easy, he said, and no-one ever got caught. I lost my temper with him, told him to stop being stupid. I told him to come and meet me and we'd talk it out. He'd said he didn't mind taking a free lunch off me, and rang off.'

'You met him where?'

'Tottenham Court Road. There's a café in Hanway Place, somebody's Pantry. Kate's Pantry, I think. I'd have taken him somewhere better but I was afraid he was going to talk wild again and I didn't want to be overheard.'

'And did he?'

Coleraine nodded miserably. 'We had a row. He called me tight-fisted. He said he had to have the money and that didn't I care about him. He said he'd be maimed or killed by the dealer's gang if he didn't get the money.' He shook his head hopelessly. 'Terrible words. Words can hurt, you know, like a real, physical pain. Then he said if I was too much of a coward to kill Stefan, he'd do it, and once the old man was dead, perhaps I'd loosen up and give him what he wanted. And then he stormed out.'

'You really believed he was going to do it?'

'No! No, of course not! It was just talk. He was young and wild and he'd say anything when he was in a temper. But I felt terrible. My head was pounding, I felt sick, I couldn't think. I went straight home. Fay was out, thank God. I walked about the house, up and down, going over it in my mind. I even thought about what he'd said, about killing Stefan. It would be so easy, I thought, and then all my troubles would be over. I could put the money back into the trust, get Marcus out of trouble, maybe even set him up in some career that would keep him out of trouble in future. And Stefan was dying anyway – so I thought. It wasn't so much of a crime, was it?'

'Don't fool yourself. It was very much of a crime, and you know it. It's the worst crime there is. And the worst motive.'

Coleraine looked at him with a sick and beaten look. 'I know. Yes, I do know. I don't think I would really have done it. I mean, you don't know until you're face to face with it, do you? But I don't think I could have pulled the trigger. I've never handled a gun. It's different for Marcus – he's been out shooting, and though birds are different, of course, still it's shooting to kill, isn't it? But with me, even if I could have got hold of the revolver, I don't think when it came to it I could have shot him.'

Slider said, 'But you did, didn't you? You took the revolver out of his desk when you were left alone in his study on Tuesday. And you shot him in the church on Wednesday afternoon.'

Coleraine stared back with blank incomprehension. 'No,' he said. 'No, of course I didn't. That's what I've just been telling you. Good God, did you really think –? But I've just been telling you I went home, and I didn't leave the house again that day. I felt so ill I went to lie on the bed, and I was so tired I fell asleep.'

'If you were at home, why didn't you answer the telephone? We tried to ring your wife there on Wednesday afternoon to tell her about the shooting, and there was no answer.'

'I didn't hear it ring. I turned off the phone in the bedroom, and I was so heavily asleep I didn't hear it ring downstairs. I slept until just before Fay came home at seven o'clock, and that's the first I heard about Stefan being shot.'

Slider studied his face, but it sounded true; he had sounded all along as if he was telling the truth. All around them the wall of noise had built up unnoticed; the band was playing, and people were listening, drinking, smoking, talking, tapping their feet, enjoying their Sunday morning socialisation, with no idea of the drama being run through in this unremarkable corner.

'You suspected me?' Coleraine said now in a dazed sort of way, as if it was beyond belief.

'I was just going to invite you to come back to the station

164

and make a statement,' Slider said grimly. 'I shall still have to, of course, but a different sort of statement now. And the sixty-four-thousand-dollar question is, if you didn't kill Sir Stefan Radek, who did?'

But the answer was written large in Coleraine's sick and suffering face. 'I'm so afraid Marcus must have done it. It's a terrible thing to say, but – but –'

'It's a terrible thing to do,' Slider said.

'If he did it. I can't believe – but if he did, I can't shield him any more.' He looked a desperate appeal at Slider. 'I've got to know. I can't stand it any longer, suspecting him. Please –'

'We'll find out,' Slider said comfortingly. 'You come along with me now, and we'll get to the bottom of it.'

CHAPTER TWELVE

The Domino Effect

'So he came to you to grass up his own son, did he?' Norma asked with somewhat irrational indignation, considering their jobs depended on people giving information about each other. Coleraine was downstairs at this very moment, making a statement to Beevers and Mackay, and considering he was busy unpicking the best case they'd had so far, Slider was taking it very well.

'It all got too much for him. He hates himself even for suspecting Marcus, but he's got to the point where he can't bear the uncertainty any longer of not knowing,' Slider said. 'Of course, he says he's sure Marcus didn't do it –'

'Which is shorthand for he bets he did,' Norma said.

Atherton was jubilant. 'I said it was him, didn't I? Nasty little slime-bucket. Now we've only got to prove it.'

'You take a large size in onlies, my lad,' Slider said.

'Hang on, guv,' McLaren said untidily through a jumbo sausage roll he was eating out of a paper bag. 'Didn't I hear someone say Marcus Coleraine had a flat in Bayswater? We've got a possible sighting of chummy coming out of Queensway station, haven't we.' Flakes of greasy pastry fluttered down from his moving lips and stuck to his powder-blue and magenta striped jersey like terminal dandruff, but he had everyone's attention. 'Well, Queensway station serves Bayswater, dunnit? I mean, Bayswater tube station is in the same road. They're only about a hundred yards apart.'

166

Atherton looked at him almost with affection. 'I knew God must have had some purpose in creating you, Maurice. Of course, that's it! Marcus's flat's in Caroline Place, which is half way between Bayswater and Queensway stations. This is getting interesting.'

'And we know he had the opportunity to take the gun, because Buster said he'd called on Radek on Tuesday afternoon,' McLaren said.

'Opportunity is not proof. And what about his Murray alibi?' Norma said.

'I wouldn't value that above the paper it's written on,' Atherton said happily. 'If Marcus left his father in the café at a quarter past one, he had plenty of time to get back to Shepherd's Bush by half past two to be murdering his grandpa. He even had time to go home first and collect the gun, supposing he hadn't taken it with him for the meet with his dad. And he could have arranged the alibi with Murray either before or afterwards. My personal bet would be afterwards.'

'Tell us why, oh mighty one,' Norma said sourly.

'Well, I don't see him as the sort to plan anything in any detail. I imagine he went storming off in a frenzy of self-pity, shot his grandad, then ran home in a panic. He realised he had to fix himself an alibi, so he rushed off to land his old pal Murray in it; and incidentally indulge in a spot of the doings by way of calming his nerves after the horrid ordeal. That way he really would be at Murray's flat on the afternoon in question, and it would only be a matter of fudging the time he arrived.'

'And what did he do with the gun?' Norma asked.

'God knows. Maybe he stashed it at his flat, maybe he took it to Murray and asked him to get rid of it. But there's all of London on the way, or afterwards. It could be anywhere. It could be at the bottom of the Thames.'

'Not if he meant to put it back,' Slider said. 'Putting it back would still be the safest option, as long as no-one ever discovered it had been missing.'

'Does he know we know?' McLaren wondered.

'If he's been in touch with Buster he probably knows, but there's no reason he should have been. It's a good chance

167

anyway that he doesn't. I think we ought to pay his flat a visit before he does find out. Even if we don't find the gun, we might find a duffel coat and a wide-brimmed hat.'

'I must say it's nice investigating a crime amongst the upper echelons for a change,' Atherton said. 'At least their houses and flats don't smell of urine and their cupboards aren't full of filthy rags.'

Slider was about to answer when Anderson and Jablowski came in. He looked at his watch. Three o'clock. 'You two are back early,' he said.

'We thought we'd get written up before end of shift,' Jablowski said.

'You've got something?'

'Nothing terribly exciting. Just a confirmation of the Marcus–Murray alibi.'

'What?'

'Another good theory destroyed by unnecessary facts,' Atherton said gloomily.

'What theory?' Anderson asked.

'We'd just got Marcus down for chummy,' McLaren said, and explained.

'Oh, bad luck,' Anderson said. 'But we've got a witness sighting of him going into Murray's flat at about half past one. There's a fruit and veg stall on the corner of Russell Street, just opposite the door to Murray's flat. The trader – Ray Tate's his name – knows Murray well. Reading between the lines, I think he gets certain illegal substances from him from time to time. Anyway, Tate says on Wednesday he'd been watching for Murray to come out because he wanted to "talk to him", inverted commas, and he saw a fair young man ring the doorbell at about half past one. He didn't know him, but he thinks he's seen him there before. Murray let the fair man in and shut the door. About half past three Tate takes a break and a cuppa tea, decides to ring Murray's door while he's got five minutes. No answer, which Tate thinks is odd because he's sure no-one's gone out in the last two hours. He rings again, and looks through the letter-box, sees Murray's feet half way down the stairs, just standing there. He shouts out "Steve, it's me, Ray," but the feet turn round and disappear, so he reckons Murray's got his reasons for not wanting

168

company and gives it up. But he keeps an eye on the door all the same, hoping to catch Murray as he comes out. Only Murray never appears, not before Tate closes up at half-five.'

They digested this. 'Well, it's not conclusive,' Slider said. 'Someone could have slipped out while Tate was serving a customer or bending down picking up a box of apples. He can't have been watching every minute of the afternoon. But it's an indication.'

'Anyone slipping out wouldn't be able to tell before he opened the door that Tate wasn't watching,' Anderson said. 'The door panel's hammered glass, you can't see through it. So it would be quite a chance if someone managed to get out unseen.'

'In any case,' Atherton said, 'we're only interested in the time between half past one and, say, two o'clock. If Marcus didn't leave by about two, he couldn't have got back to Shepherd's Bush in time to do the murder.'

'Maybe it wasn't Marcus that Tate saw go in,' McLaren said hopefully.

'We showed Tate the mugshot, and he said he thought that was him,' Anderson said. 'It's as close as you'll get.'

'Never mind, I still think it's worth taking a look at Marcus's flat,' Slider said. 'It isn't what you'd call a water-tight alibi, and there's definitely a connection there somewhere. At the very least, instinct tells me that Marcus knows more about it than he's said.'

The house in Caroline Place had once been a handsome thing, but was showing the symptoms of being divided up into too many flats. The steps and rendering were cracked, the door and windows needed painting, and the heterogeny of curtains at the different windows gave it a shabby air. Still, it was central, close to a tube, and would probably be bringing in about a hundred pounds a body per week to the landlord.

The landlord came scuttling out from the basement like a crab out of its rock crevice as Slider and Atherton reached the foot of the steps up to the front door. He was stout and short, so that he looked almost spherical, a round head stuck onto a round body without benefit of a neck in between, like something a child had made out of Plasticine. He was dressed in a white shirt open at the throat and with the sleeves rolled up, black trousers and a black waistcoat with a gold chain across the extreme point of his circumference, which for some reason made Slider think of undertakers. His face was pudgily white, his head almost hairless, and yet he managed to give the impression of being exotically swarthy, perhaps because his eyes had the dark melancholy of an ancient race. He stuck his arms out, pumping his elbows and waving his thick fingers to help him up the steps out of his hole, puffing and calling, 'Yes, yes, I'm coming, vait, don't be so impatient!'

Slider stopped and looked at him with mild enquiry. He stood before them, looking them over with quick, suspicious eyes. 'Yes, yes, vot do you vont? I am Mr Rose, this is my house. Vot are you, police? Not customs, no, policemen, I think. Plain clothes. Vy you calling at my house?'

'We came to see one of your tenants, Mr Rose,' Slider said, somewhat amused at the quick identification. It spoke long experience.

'On a Sunday?' he protested, spreading his hands. 'It must be serious. Vich one you vont? I don't vont no trouble here. I keep a quiet house, I am honest landlord, trying to make honest living. Don't come here making trouble at my house.'

'No trouble, Mr Rose,' Slider said soothingly. 'We just want a little chat with Mr Coleraine. What number flat is he?'

The thick face sharpened, a quick intake of breath hissed between the teeth. 'Ah, so, number four. I knew it! Ven I see policemen coming, I knew it must be number four.' He gave the impression of leaning closer, though he could hardly have got closer than he already was. 'A bad boy that! I vood have got rid of him, but he pays, he pays, always on time, no trouble, and I am a businessman.' A shrug. 'I cannot turn away good money. But now he has someone sharing vid him, and this is forbidden. I say to him, Mr Coleraine, you know I let this rooms to you and you only, no others, no lodgers, and he denies. I cannot catch him, but I know there is another up there. If I can catch him, I get rid of him, I promise you. He's a bad boy. In a minute, he goes. Like this.' He made the gesture of snapping his fingers, but it was like trying to snap two grilled pork sausages.

170

'How do you know there's someone sharing with him?' Slider asked with interest.

Mr Rose shrugged again, and tapped his nose. 'This tells me. I let rooms all my life, and my mother before me. I know. I cannot catch him, but I know.' He slid his eyes sideways and up, glancing significantly at Slider's face and away again. 'I think he gives him key. This is forbidden, *absolutely* forbidden. I vont him out of my house.'

He folded his arms round his chest, a smouldering bonfire of ancient grudges, and watched broodingly as Slider and Atherton mounted the steps. The front door was on the latch, and Slider pushed it open. A communal hall, smelling of floor polish; institutional green lino, a large speckled mirror on the wall beside the door, a battered side table below it on which reposed a collection of leaflets which presumably had been pushed through the letter-box and picked up by some resident public spirited enough not to walk over them but too indifferent to dispose of them. Beyond the mirror was the door to the ground-floor flat with a plastic number 1 screwed to it; stairs leading up straight ahead; on the first floor doors numbered 2 and 3. Narrower stairs, and on the second floor a door numbered 4 and a very narrow, precipitous flight going on up to the attic.

Atherton laid his ear to the door and after a moment nodded to Slider. 'Music,' he murmured. 'Shall I knock?'

The door was opened after a few moments, just enough to reveal Marcus Coleraine in jeans, a purple singlet, bare feet and hayrick hair, blocking the view into the flat. At the sight of Atherton his face shut down. 'What do you want?'

'First of all, Mr Coleraine, we'd like to come in,' Atherton answered.

'What for?'

'We'd like to talk to you, son,' Slider said gently. 'I'm Detective Inspector Slider of Shepherd's Bush Police Station. Sergeant Atherton you know, of course. Your father's at the station at this very moment making a statement, and from what he's told us, we think there are some things you might be able to clear up for us.'

Marcus still didn't move, looking from face to face with an air of trying to calculate the incalculable. Finally Slider said,

'Can we come in? Or is there some reason you don't want us to see behind you?'

A moment's more resistance, and Marcus stepped back and opened the door. 'Come in if you must,' he said. Inside there was a sound of music playing very quietly – Dvořák, the New World Symphony – and an agreeable smell of bath soap. The short passage had two doors opposite each other, both open – one on the kitchen and the other on the sitting-room – and then bent round a right-angle up ahead, presumably to the bedroom and bathroom. All the walls were painted cream, the woodwork white, there was oatmeal Berber underfoot, and everything seemed clean and fairly new.

Marcus had backed up as far as the sitting-room door, but was not inviting them any further in. The assumption that they might be prepared to stand in the hall and talk annoyed Slider. What was the point in this time-wasting, unless it was simply meant to annoy for annoyance's sake?

'We'd like to look around, if you don't mind,' he said evenly.

'Have you got a warrant?' Marcus asked. Atherton gave Slider a look. Would they never learn?

'No,' said Slider patiently. 'I can get one if I have to. Is there some reason you don't want me to look around? Is there something you have to hide?'

Marcus hesitated. 'What are you looking for?' he asked, trying for a reasonable tone of voice. 'Maybe I can save you trouble.'

Slider held his eyes. 'For one thing, we're looking for your grandfather's revolver.' Marcus's eyes flinched slightly, and Slider felt a surge of triumph. The boy took an instinctive half-step backwards, and Atherton, adjusting his position accordingly, was able for the first time to see into the sitting-room.

'Guv?' he said, touching Slider's arm. Slider followed the direction of Atherton's nod. On a table just inside the sitting-room door was the telephone, and beside it a brown, broad-brimmed trilby-type hat. From where he stood, Marcus could not see what they were looking at, but there was alarm as well as enquiry in his eyes.

'What's the matter?' he asked quietly.

'What's the matter? You're in a world of grief, son, that's what's the matter,' Slider said gently. 'Why don't you tell me all about it, and get it off your chest? You know we'll find out in the end.'

'Yes, I suppose you will,' Marcus said rather blankly, his mind evidently working. And then suddenly, shockingly, he grinned. 'Oh well, it couldn't last for ever. I did my best, that's all.'

'Your best?'

'It wasn't me killed Grandpa,' he said cheerfully. 'You're barking up the wrong tree there. But I'm not going to get into trouble over it. I didn't mind helping as long as it didn't come back on me, but if Dad's fingered me, the simp, I'm getting out from under.' He turned his head and shouted towards the back of the flat. 'Lev? Lev! Come here, will you? It's all right, come on out!' Nothing happened, and Marcus turned back to Atherton and Slider. 'He's hiding in the bedroom, the dumb bastard. Doesn't realise the game's up. Go in and sit down and I'll fetch him.'

But at that moment someone appeared at the turn of the passage, a small, slight young man, smaller than Marcus, with a narrow, pale, thin-skinned face, fine hair the colour of cornsilk, and over-large blue eyes set in delicate orbits of mauve shadow. His mouth was curious, wide and almost without a top lip, except for a small pink mark in the centre where there ought to have been a peak. His lower lip was soft and childlike and drooping, and when he saw the two men it began to tremble. He flung Marcus a look of mingled reproach and fear, to which Marcus merely shrugged with robust indifference.

'It's the police. Sorry, Lev old mate, it can't be helped.' He turned to Slider, completing the introduction in a parody of formality which he was obviously enjoying. 'Gentlemen, may I introduce Lev Polowski, who shot my grandfather?'

Transparent, unsullied tears slipped over Lev's lower eyelashes. 'I didn't mean to. Honest I didn't mean to,' he said in a husky voice.

Marcus grinned the wider, and slipped an arm round his shoulders. 'It's all right, don't worry, they don't hang you any more,' he said, and Lev broke into shuddering sobs.

Slider stepped in. He caught Atherton's eye and jerked his head towards the kitchen. 'Mr Coleraine, I wonder if you'd be so kind as to make some tea?'

He made a moue. 'Oh God, do I have to? I'm not a skivvy, you know.'

'And while you're in the kitchen, I'd like you to tell Sergeant Atherton your side of the story. Meanwhile, Mr Polowski, we'll go in here where it's quiet and you can tell me all about it.'

Lev Polowski sat on the sofa, his hands between his knees, his bony shoulders hunched up around his ears. He looked so fragile and innocent it was hard to think of him as a grown man.

'Stefan did everything for me. I owe him everything,' he said. He had a slight, attractive accent, but his English was excellent. 'I was a student at the Academy in Warsaw. I had a scholarship, which paid my fees, but things were very hard at home with me not earning and my brothers and sisters growing up. My father died, you see, when I was twelve, and Mamma found it harder and harder to make ends meet, and it was getting to look as though I must give up music and try to get a job. My father was a musician, and Mamma wanted me to be one too, but there are so few openings for a trumpet player, so little solo work, and a hundred good players after every orchestral place. And then – Stefan came.'

A rapt look crossed his face, and his hands clasped each other harder. They were large and strong compared with the rest of him, capable-looking, a man's hands grafted on to a boy's narrow wrists.

'You met him in Warsaw?' Slider asked.

He nodded. 'He came to conduct a public concert with the Philharmonic, and the next day to give a master class at the Academy. Everyone was so excited, for he is a great national hero to us – the poor Polish boy who fled into exile and became the greatest musician of our age. And also, we all knew he sponsored talented young musicians. Everyone hoped he had come to talent-spot, but how to catch his eye? He was going to walk about, look into classes, and so, and so; but also we were to give a concert for him in the lunch hour,

174

we the senior orchestra. Everyone was practising as though their lives depended on it, and I –' He shrugged. 'I went over and over my part to make it perfect for him, but I had nothing to hope for. I was not a violinist, not even an oboist or clarinettist to attract his notice, to be taken up and polished as a soloist. We all thought that if it would be anyone, it would be Marta he noticed, our star pianist, who was going to play the Sans-Saens concerto for him, and we were glad, because Marta was so very, very good, and a lovely person too, worthy of being given her chance. No-one would have begrudged the luck to Marta.'

He lifted his head and his eyes were wide and distant. 'I did not dream – no-one dreamed – that he would notice me. It is a nice trumpet part in the Sans-Saens, very prominent, and pretty, echoing the piano and completing the tune. And I was good that day, I knew I was good, and I was glad to have made something fine for the great man. But afterwards, when we were walking from the platform, our Director of Music came to me and said, "Sir Stefan would like to speak to you."' He was reliving now what Slider could see had been the best moment of his life. His husky voice caressed the words like a lover. 'I was taken to the Director's office, and sent in alone. There was Stefan – so tall, so noble, his white hair, his fierce eyes, like a great eagle – and he was looking at me so piercingly, as if he could see into my soul. "You sent for me, maestro," I said. And he held out his hand to me, he took my hand in his –' His hands rehearsed the moment quite unconsciously in front of him. 'And he said, "You played today like an angel. Great trumpet players are very rare. I wish to help you become a soloist. Will you leave Poland and come with me?"'

He stopped. 'And you went with him?' Slider prompted after a while, and Lev sighed and looked at him as though he were waking from a deep sleep.

'Yes, of course,' he said with an effort. 'Since then he has done everything for me. He brought me to England, paid for me to have the best teachers, arranged my solo debut, took me with him on tours to play with him with some of the greatest orchestras in the world. And he gave Mamma money, too. He is a great, great man.'

'You must have been grateful to him.'

'Of course. Of course.'

'You admired him. It would not be too strong a word to say you loved him,' suggested Slider.

The boy's gaze grew troubled. 'Yes,' he said, his voice barely audible. 'I loved him.'

'And he loved you? He wanted you to show your love in a physical way, perhaps?'

Lev nodded, and then his eyes filled with tears again and he dropped his head, hiding them. 'I was –' He began and stopped, drew a shuddering breath, began again. 'I didn't want Mamma to know. She wouldn't understand. But I was not ashamed. I was proud to be his lover. Only –' He stopped again.

'How long did this go on? When did it begin?' Slider asked.

'Two years. It began almost as soon as I came to England. I was happy – I had my music, I had my career, I had Stefan. But then it seemed that I saw less of him. He changed towards me. He was still kind, but distant. He said I could stand on my own feet now, and I could, in a way, but I thought – I was afraid –'

'That he had someone else?' Slider suggested.

He nodded again, chewing his lower lip. After a moment he said, 'I tried to tell myself I could not expect – he was so much greater than me – I was nothing compared to him. I should not judge him. But when I remembered the things he'd said to me about love, I could not bear it. And then Marcus told me – he told me – that Stefan was – that he was having an affair with a woman. I thought he was lying at first, but when I faced Stefan with it, he admitted it. He said – *terrible* things to me.' He shook his head to shake away the memory.

'How did you meet Marcus?' Slider asked.

'At Stefan's house, of course. Stefan wanted us to be friends. I was pleased that he did. I thought he wanted it because I was important to him. But I think he hoped Marcus would distract me, keep me from finding out about the others.' He gave a short, humourless laugh. 'He never guessed Marcus would be the one to tell me.'

'How did he come to tell you?'

'It was on Tuesday – last Tuesday. We'd been out together, Marcus and I, just messing around and he asked me to go with him to visit his mother at her shop. I think he wanted to ask her for some money. I didn't want to go, because I was shy of her. Stefan had said she mustn't know about him and me, because she wouldn't approve, and I was afraid she might guess. But Marcus persuaded me. We went to her shop, and she was very nice, friendly to me, but I felt awkward. She told me about the concert Stefan was giving at the church for the charity she was interested in, and asked me if I would be going to it, and I said maybe. But really it was the first time I'd heard about it, and I wondered why Stefan hadn't said anything to me. And afterwards, when Marcus and I left, I said to him that I thought I would go along to the final rehearsal, because I hadn't seen Stefan for such a long time, he'd been so busy, and it would be a chance to catch up with him. Marcus said it would be a bad idea to go, and I asked him why, and that was when – when – he told me that Stefan was having an affair with a woman, his agent, and that she'd be there.'

'Kate Apwey,' said Slider.

'Yes, that's her.' He lifted his flamey eyes to Slider's face. 'I hate her name! I hate her! She could be with him all the time, any time! But how could he do it?'

'So what did you do when Marcus told you? You said you went to confront him with it?'

'Not straight away. I was too upset. I told Marcus I wanted to be on my own for a bit, and I left him and went for a walk.'

'Where?'

'On Hampstead Heath. That's where we were. His mother's shop is in Hampstead, you see. I walked about, thinking and thinking, and then in the end I decided I had to go and face Stefan, and ask him if it was true. I thought Marcus might be mistaken. Or that he might – be making mischief.' He bit his lip. 'Marcus likes to tease, you see. He likes making trouble. He doesn't mean any harm, really, it's just – it amuses him.'

Slider nodded. He remembered Marcus's glee when he called Lev out from the bedroom. 'What happened next?'

'I took the tube and went to Stefan's house. When I got

there I saw Marcus coming out. I almost turned away, but he saw me and called to me. I went up to him, and he said, "Grandpa's at home. You'd better go in and have it out, hadn't you?" And he laughed. It made me angry. So I went in.'

'Wait a minute, you said this was Tuesday afternoon?'

'Yes.'

'Sir Stefan was alone?'

'Yes. Except for Buster, of course.'

'Did Buster see you?'

Lev looked puzzled. 'He let me in. Why?'

'No, nothing, it doesn't matter. Go on please.'

He resumed slowly. 'Buster showed me to Stefan's study, and in a minute Stefan came down. He was in a bad temper, I could see straight away. He said he was just going out to rehearsal, that he was in a hurry, and asked me what I wanted. I said that I would come with him, that I would like to watch the rehearsal, and we could talk afterwards, but he said he would be busy and that it wasn't convenient. He was so cold, I couldn't bear it. I said he was always too busy to see me these days, and so it began. We quarrelled. I accused him. He admitted it, and said it was none of my business, that I should be grateful to have been noticed by him. I asked how he could bear to touch a woman in that way, and we – he –'

'Yes, I understand. Things grew heated. You both said things you didn't mean.'

Lev shook his head. 'He meant them. That was the worst thing. He meant them. And then he told me to leave, and said he never wanted to see me again. I said he'd be sorry, and I ran out. I was crying, but I was angry too. I wanted to kill him, Just then, I wanted him dead.'

Slider nodded. 'You knew about the revolver?'

'I knew about it, but I didn't think of it then. He'd showed it to me once. He was very proud of it, and he liked to get it out and touch it. He made me hold it once and it – it – excited him.' The transparent cheeks showed a rush of blood. 'But I didn't think of it then. It was afterwards, when I went out into the street, Marcus was waiting for me. He asked how I got on. I told him everything. I was so hurt and angry, you see, and I said to Marcus I wanted to kill Stefan, forgetting it was his

178

grandfather. But Marcus didn't care about that. When I said I wanted to kill him, Marcus took the gun out of his pocket and said, "You'll need this, then."'

'He had Sir Stefan's revolver in his pocket?'

Nod. 'I asked him where he'd got it, and he said he'd taken it just now in case I needed it. I didn't want to touch it, but he shoved it into my pocket, and when I tried to stop him he said to be careful, it might go off, and when I tried to take it out again he said not to be a fool because someone might see it. And then he patted me on the shoulder and said good luck and left me.'

'And what did you do?'

'I went home. I got the bus and went home, with the gun in my coat pocket, feeling huge and hot and as if it was burning a hole. I thought everyone looking at me must know. When I got home I took it out and put it on the table and I thought I could never touch it again. But when I remembered what Stefan had said and how he had treated me, I was so angry and miserable I wanted to die. I picked it up again, thinking I might shoot myself. Oh, I don't know what I was thinking! And then I remembered the time Stefan had first shown it to me, and then I really wanted to kill him. I decided I would go to the rehearsal the next day, and I would shoot him in front of everyone, shoot him down in public, and then shoot myself afterwards.' He nodded, his eyes dreamy again. 'It seemed so good, and I was quite calm then. We would be together for ever, and no-one else would be able to have him. I sat up all night, and I smoked – Marcus had given me a bit, along with the gun – and I thought about it, and in the morning it still seemed very good to me. So I had a shower and dressed myself and put the gun in my coat pocket and got the bus back to Shepherd's Bush. It was the forty-nine, the same bus I always took when I went to see him at his home, and that seemed right, too, like a pattern.'

Yes, Slider thought, that was the missing element. The theatricality of the act – shooting Radek down in front of witnesses – had always seemed ludicrous: it did not fit quite comfortably with the notion of Alec Coleraine killing for financial gain. But as the final, suicidal act of a jealous lover, particularly of one so young, ardent, idealistic, and half out

179

of his peanut with illegal substances, it made perfect sense. Like a pattern.

'And so you went to St Augustine's church, and you shot him,' Slider said.

Polowski's eyes widened. 'No! I didn't! At least, I suppose I must have, but I didn't mean to. I swear I didn't mean to kill him.'

'All right, son,' Slider said. 'Just tell me about it.'

CHAPTER THIRTEEN

Some Enchanted Afternoon

In the kitchen Atherton had been hearing the story from the other side. It was an account to amaze but not much to delight.

'How did you know what the relationship was between your grandfather and Lev?' he asked, at the point in the narrative when it was evident Marcus knew.

Marcus, sitting on the kitchen table and swinging his legs with deliberate insouciance, said, 'Grandpa told me himself, of course. I think he saw it as part of my education to corrupt me – not that I saw it as corruption. I mean, who cares these days? I'd have guessed anyway. He didn't keep anything from me. God, if his adoring public only realised what a filthy old goat he was! He'd do anything, with anything, to anything, and he didn't care if we knew it. Well, apart from Mum, of course.' He screwed up his forehead in perplexity. 'For some reason he really minded what Mum thought of him – and she's so strait-laced, she'd have done her pieces if she'd ever discovered he was bi. I think she may have guessed that he had the occasional bonk with a female – I mean she's not totally naïve – but it would never cross her mind that he'd do it with a boy.'

'And you kept the secret from her too?'

He looked indignant. 'What d'you take me for? Do you think I'd deliberately upset her? I love my mother, I'll have you know.'

'I suppose everyone's got one weakness,' Atherton remarked.

'Besides, Grandpa would have killed me if I'd split on him. He had a filthy temper, you know – not something you'd provoke twice.'

'So if you knew about Lev and your grandfather, why did you tell Lev about Kate Apwey?' Atherton asked.

'Oh, just for fun,' Marcus said indifferently.

'Weren't you afraid your grandpa'd find out it was you who spilled the beans?'

'Even if he did he wouldn't have cared. He'd finished with Lev. He'd got bored with him, only Lev didn't realise it, of course. I was doing Grandpa a favour really, getting Lev off his back.'

'And Lev? Weren't you supposed to be his friend?'

'We knocked about together, but he was a bit of a geek really. I thought it'd be fun to stir him up. He had no idea what Grandpa was really like – he thought he was a genuine saint. So I painted him the real picture and watched him go green. Then I went round to Grandpa's and wound him up. It worked a treat – better than I'd expected, actually, because Lev arrived just as I left, so he came in for it all hot and steamy, before the old boy had had a chance to cool off.'

'God, you're a sweetheart, aren't you?' Atherton said, amazed.

'It was fun. You had to be there. I hung around outside and waited for Lev to come out, and when I saw the expression on his face! If looks could kill! So I gave him the gun and said if he –'

'You what?'

'Grandpa's revolver. He always kept it in his desk drawer, loaded. I took it when he wasn't looking and gave it to Lev.'

Atherton controlled himself. 'I suppose you had a reason for doing that?'

'Yeah, I told you, it was all a bit of fun. I thought Lev was so mad he'd go and wave it under Grandpa's nose and give the old boy a fright.' He slid his eyes sidelong at Atherton and, evidently feeling something less warm than total approval emanating from him, attempted justification. 'Well, he deserved it, stingy old bastard: all that money he had, doing nothing, and wouldn't give me a measly penny. Of course, Lev's such a wimp I didn't really think he'd actually shoot him –'

'But if he did it wouldn't matter?'

'Well, we've all got to go some time,' Marcus said virtuously. 'Grandpa's had a good innings anyway. And Dad says he's got – said he had a heart condition,' he corrected himself. 'He could have gone off any minute. It's not like he was young or anything.'

Youth was, of course, the only justification for being allowed to go on existing. Atherton had come across enough villains in his career to know that while they were all utterly self-serving, most were too stupid to be anything else. Marcus was a new phenomenon, and he stared at him with the professional detachment of a naturalist observing something particularly horrific in the insect world.

'I don't think you realise it,' he said gravely, 'but you are into serious naughties. By taking the gun and giving it to Lev you've made yourself an accessory.'

Marcus sniggered. 'You make me sound like a bloody handbag or something. Accessory!'

'It's no laughing matter, I can assure you. You could even be facing a charge of conspiracy to murder. That's twenty years in chokey.'

But it was impossible to frighten this appalling young man. 'Crap,' he said robustly. 'I didn't think for a minute Lev would do it. And in any case, he didn't mean to. It was an accident. He'll tell you.'

'We'll see,' Atherton said. 'In the meantime, you'd better tell me what happened on Wednesday.'

Marcus shrugged indifferently. 'Well, I got up, got dressed, went down to the shop and got some stuff for breakfast, messed around a bit – you don't want to hear all this, do you?'

'Not at this point. You can skip to the interesting bit.'

'All right, at about half-eleven I got a phone call from this bloke who said he had some gear to sell me, really good stuff, but expensive. Only I was brassic, of course, and he said he'd let it go to someone else if I didn't take it quick. So I telephoned my father and told him I owed some bloke and he was after my blood. Well, to tell you the truth, I'd already spun him that one a couple of days ago, to try to get him to cough up, and he hadn't, so I upped the stakes a bit: I said the bloke was threatening to carve me up if I didn't come up with the money. Poor old Dad believes all that stuff, you know. He thinks he's Philip Marlowe, poor old geezer! Anyway, he said come up and see him right away and he'd see what he could do.' Marcus's mouth turned down. 'That was a wasted journey. It turned out he was just playing me along. He dragged me all the way up to Tottenham Court Road and then said he couldn't give me anything. I was furious! We had a row, and I told him what a bastard he was: he didn't even care if I got cut up. He said he just hadn't got it. I said in that case why didn't he kill Grandpa –' He stopped and smiled at Atherton. 'Which was amazing irony when you consider, wasn't it?'

'Amazing,' Atherton said hollowly.

'Well, eventually I saw there was nothing to be got out of Dad, so I left him and went off to see my mate Steve. I'd given my last bit of brown to Lev last night to cheer him up, you see – which I thought was pretty generous of me – so I went to see if Steve had got a bit in the house, which he usually did. I thought a smoke would calm me down. I mean, I don't like rowing with Dad, you know, only he's such a schmuck, I just lose patience with him. Anyway, I was still there, at Steve's, when Lev phoned me from my flat to tell me he'd killed Grandpa.'

'How did he get in to your flat?'

'Oh, I'd given him the key a couple of weeks before. We were mates, I told you.'

'Mates. I see. And how did he know you would be at Steve Murray's?'

'Good guess. I spent a lot of time with Steve. Anyway, Lev said he'd shot Grandpa and he didn't know what to do. So I told him to stay put, do nothing, speak to nobody.'

'In your flat? That was a bit risky, wasn't it?'

'Well, to tell you the truth,' Marcus said with a grin, 'we'd had a bit by then, so I probably wasn't thinking straight. All I know is, when I put the phone down and told Steve about it, we both thought it was terribly funny. We rolled about and laughed ourselves nearly sick. You know how it is when you're high.'

Atherton offered no response, and Marcus shrugged. 'Anyway, as it turned out no-one had seen Lev properly or recognised him, which was amazing when you think he goes about in that geeky duffel coat, which nobody but him would wear. And he'd worn that hat before, too. But no-one came looking for him, so I just let him stay. I thought eventually if he didn't get found out he could go back to Poland. I could probably get Mum to cough up enough for that, once she'd got Grandpa's money, and I thought it would be sort of appropriate really, for his money to pay to get Lev away. It was quite fun when you came round to Steve's and you obviously hadn't a clue what you were looking for. But when you turned up here, I knew the game was up. It's been a laugh, though.'

'You are, without exception, the most appalling animal I've ever met,' Atherton said with a mild, David Attenborough sort of interest.

Marcus looked sulky. 'Save that for Lev. He's the one who killed Grandpa, not me.'

Slider had found a box of tissues under the television, and Lev was now on his fourth. His eyes and nose were pink in his white face, so that he looked like an albino mouse; but he was talking freely, evidently glad of the chance to get it off his chest. Slider remembered Freddie Cameron saying, 'They like to tell the tale, old chum, they like to tell the tale.' Murder bestowed a kind of celebrity on both doer and done to. He had interviewed murderers in his time for whom it had been the one significant event between their birth and their death, and they had recounted it, not exactly with pride, but with a sense of occasion, like the Queen's Jubilee or When Gran Won the Premium Bonds. And when the murder was a *crime passionel*, of course, it was an integral part of the affaire, to be told along with the first sight, the first kiss, the first quarrel. Oh darling, they're playing our tune. 'When you shoot your true love, across a crowded room . . .'

'I don't know if I would have done it if I'd met him face to face when I first got there,' Lev said, hunching miserably over

185

his soggy tissue like a bird in the rain. 'Maybe if it had been an ordinary hall . . . But that church – do you know it?'

'Yes.'

'Oh, of course, you must have been there. I was forgetting. Well, it is not like an English church, is it? It's very Russian in a way. We are Catholics in my family, but there are Orthodox churches in Poland too, and it made me think of home, and Mamma, and my brothers and sisters. When I first went in, the orchestra was there, but there was no sign of Stefan, so I had to stand and wait; and it was dark and smelled of incense, and there were the saints and the icons and the statue of Our Lady. And bit by bit all my anger and hate drained away and I felt very small and frightened, as if I was a little boy and God was watching me. And then Stefan came in. He stood at the side talking to some people, and when I saw him I remembered how much I owed him, how he had given me everything, brought me from Poland, given me the best teachers, arranged concerts for me. And then when I saw him walk across to the podium, as I had watched him so often, I knew I loved him, and I could never hurt him.'

'You were still standing at the back of the church?'

'Yes. I hadn't moved. I had planned to walk down right to the front and call his name, and when he turned round and saw me, then I would shoot him. I don't know if I would have. I don't know if I could ever really have pulled the trigger. It isn't a thing you can know ahead of time, is it?'

Slider shook his head. 'I've never been in that position.'

'No. No, I suppose most people haven't.' He blew his nose and continued, his drowned eyes staring at nothing. 'When he appeared I had taken the gun out of my pocket, but still I didn't move. And when he walked across the platform, all that filled me was love and care for him. He looked ill, and old, and frail, and I was suddenly afraid he might die – isn't that ridiculous? After planning to kill him, now I was afraid he might die.'

He stopped, and Slider had to prompt him. 'So what happened next?'

Lev looked at him with sudden blue. 'I don't know. Truly, truly I don't know. I must have been pointing the gun at him

186

automatically, because I didn't know I was. I was tense and anxious, seeing how ill he looked – worried for him. Maybe I was squeezing the trigger, but I didn't mean to.' His hands were clenched with it now. 'He picked up the baton, and then he stopped. I know all his movements, I have watched him in life and on film a thousand, thousand times, and I knew something was wrong. I started forward, a step, one step only, and he collapsed and – and I heard the explosion.' He put his hands up to his face, flinching at his own touch as if he hadn't known he was going to do it. 'I didn't know what it was at first. I thought it was a bomb or a mortar or something. I thought of the IRA. It was so loud, you see, and close. I thought the roof would fall in on me. And then I smelled the smoke, and I looked down and saw the gun, and I realised I must have pulled the trigger. He was lying there, so still, and I was standing here with a revolver in my hand, and I almost died of horror. I realised I must have shot him, and I couldn't think of anything to do except run away. But truly I didn't mean to. You must believe me.'

The blue was desperate with appeal now. They like to tell the tale – and it matters how it is received.

'Yes, I believe you,' Slider said. 'What did you do next?'

'I ran. Just away, down the street, I wasn't capable of thinking. Then when I found myself at the tube station I thought of Marcus. He's so sophisticated, I thought he would know what to do. So I went to his flat. He wasn't in, but I had the key, so I went in and sat for a bit until I stopped shaking. Then I telephoned Steve Murray, to see if Marcus was there, and he was. He told me to stay put and he'd come to me, but he didn't, not till next day.' His face darkened with the memory. 'It was the worst night of my life. A hundred times I was going to telephone the police and give myself up. I wish I had. I didn't even know whether Stefan was dead or alive.'

'You could have watched the television news, or turned on the radio.'

'I didn't think of it. Not till the next day. I fell asleep eventually, you see – not having slept the night before I must have been tired. And when I woke in the morning I put the radio on and heard – heard he was dead.' Tears welled again in an amazing, easy flood. 'I was going to give myself up then, but Marcus came home and talked me out of it. He said to think of the scandal, and how upset his mother would be if she knew about Stefan and me. And how upset my mother would be to have a son a murderer. And when I thought of Mamma I just wanted to go home. So Marcus said I should lie low for a while, and that after a bit you – the police – would give up on the case, and then he would get me back to Poland somehow.'

Slider shook his head. 'You seem to take that young man's word for most things. But what would have happened when you were missed? You couldn't just disappear without anyone asking questions, and then the connection would have been made.'

'Did you make it? Is that why you're here?'

'We came here to search the flat for the revolver.'

'You suspected Marcus?' Lev seemed horrified. 'But how could you think he would kill his own grandfather?'

Slider passed on that one. 'Where is the gun, by the way? Have you still got it?'

'Yes,' he said, to Slider's deep relief. 'It's in the bedroom. Shall I get it?'

'No, it's all right, we'll get it in a minute.'

Lev looked at him cannily. 'Yes, there are five bullets left. You think I might shoot myself?' Close, son, close, Slider thought. 'No, not now. The moment has passed. Telling you all this has made me feel much better.' He thought a moment. 'What will happen to me now?'

'We'll take you back to the station and you'll make a statement, and then I'm afraid you'll have to be kept in custody until the powers that be decide what to charge you with.'

'Will they send me to prison? Will I be accused of murder?'

'That isn't for me to say, son.' Looking across the hall he could see Atherton just inside the kitchen, and gave him the nod to come in. 'Let's take one step at a time, shall we?'

Polowski nodded meekly. 'It's right that I should be punished. But I didn't mean to kill him, you know. In fact, I could almost swear he fell before I pulled the trigger.'

Barrington listened in silence, his massive face, pitted like lava, as mobile and expressive as a mountain side. Quinbus Flestrin, the Man Mountain, Slider thought suddenly, out of the far past and his education at the conscientious secondary modern in Timberlog Lane. All the things they used to force children to read that you hated at the time and were grateful for later. His mind was like the lumber-room of an old family house: comfortably crammed with odd and interesting stuff, most of which he'd forgotten he'd got, but which might come in useful one day. He thought of his own children and was sorely afraid that such rational, modern, purpose-built creatures would have nothing in their attics but triple-thick insulation: very useful, but not providing much amusement for a rainy Sunday.

'Right,' Barrington said, 'so what have we got besides the confession? The CPS won't go on a confession alone these days, and we don't want any mistakes over this one: Radek was a world celebrity. Let's tabulate.' He lifted his strong hands ready to count off on his fingers. 'You've got the gun?'

'Yes, and the ballistics report confirms the bullet taken from Radek was fired from that revolver. It's the same make as the remaining bullets in the chamber. There's no doubt that was the gun used.'

'Fingerprints?'

'Messy,' Slider confessed. 'It's been well handled. We can identify some individual ones, but there are prints from both Polowski and Marcus Coleraine. The duffel coat and hat definitely belong to Polowski – we've got a witness who lives in the same house in Earl's Court to identify them – but we can't prove it was him wearing them at the time. And the coat originally belonged to Marcus.'

'What about the witnesses who saw him between Shepherd's Bush and Queensway?'

'It's the same as the witnesses at the church: none of them got a really good look at his face. The best is the women who saw him coming out of Queensway station, because he'd taken the hat off by then and had it stuffed inside his coat. Her description tallies, but I don't know whether she'd pick him out of an identity parade if Marcus was in it too. Superficially they are very similar – small, slight and fair. We'll try it, anyway. And there's Marcus's alibi, too. It isn't

189

perfect, but as long as no-one wants to deny it, it'll just about stand up.'

Barrington frowned. 'You think there is some doubt as to which of them did it?'

'No, sir. I'm sure in my own mind it was Polowski at the church. And they're both telling the same story at the moment: as long as they continue to agree I think the external evidence is sufficient. I think the problem could arise when Coleraine realises how much trouble he's in. He may then want to back-pedal and deny any involvement at all, and defence would jump on that, of course.'

'Yes,' Barrington said judiciously. 'There's also the question of whether he can be allowed to incriminate himself. We mustn't forget his father's a solicitor.'

'Even if he is a bent one,' Slider added.

Barrington looked at him suddenly – at him, rather than in his direction. 'Yes,' he said thoughtfully. He drummed his fingers on his desk top, and Slider feared an outburst might be on its way, but in fact what he said was, 'This has been quite an unpleasant case. A lot of people have come out of it very badly.' Slider said nothing. 'Is there something particular about it that's bothering you?'

Slider was startled. Insight, sensitivity, sympathy – from Barrington? That would be an intriguing new sensation, though not necessarily pleasant – like having a hedgehog down your trousers. 'Sir?'

'You don't seem comfortable with the result.'

'Oh, I just don't like how much reliance we're having to place on Marcus Coleraine,' he lied.

'It's a good result, though,' Barrington said. 'And quick, too. It looks good for us. The Commander will want to give it publicity – and I want you to know that I shall make sure the credit goes where it's due.'

Slider was so surprised he only just managed to reply. 'It was a team effort, sir. Everyone's pulled their weight.'

'Good teams only exist because they have good leaders,' Barrington said. 'I've seen how your people work for you. You inspire loyalty, and that's the sign of a good officer.'

Wilder and wilder. Slider felt as though his head was rolling about the room like a bowling ball. He was so accustomed to taking the shinola shower that he never even took off his bath cap any more when entering the sanctum. Something strange seemed to be happening to Barrington, because he seemed to be suffering some mild spasms of the face. He looked at Slider and then down at his blotter and then at the portrait of the Queen on the wall to his right, and then at Slider again. And it was at that point that Slider realised the spasms were Barrington trying to smile. It was a ghastly sight and an even more ghastly notion.

'I think I've sometimes been too rigid in my ideas of what makes a good officer,' Barrington said at last. 'I took certain precepts and had them carved in stone, and when you're dealing with people, that can be a mistake.'

Oh shit, Slider thought, he's going to pour his heart out to me. He didn't think he could cope with that.

'Especially in civilian life. You can't apply battlefield rules to guerrilla fighting. What I'm trying to say is that I may tend at times to hold up an ideal, a template, and measure people against it, rather than valuing what they're good for in their own way.'

Slider could have translated for him: I worshipped my old boss, and anyone who wasn't like him was nothing; now I've found out that my old boss was nothing, I've been left all at sea. And looking more closely at the Man Mountain, Slider could see how far out on a Donald Duck lilo Barrington must have drifted in the past weeks. There was a strained expression in his eyes and his face looked thinner; his clothes seemed a little too big for him – even the ring on his wedding finger seemed loose. He had plainly been suffering, and Slider realised suddenly how little he knew about his chief's private life. Had he had someone at home to comfort him after a hard day making subordinates miserable? Was he married? Had he ever been? It was difficult to imagine him doing anything so normal as putting on striped pyjamas and going to bed with a wife. Slider knew that Norma, to her own annoyance, found him unaccountably sexy, and violent passions did not seem necessarily incompatible with that asteroid façade; but it was impossible to visualise him ever unbending far enough to pop the question to anyone. He'd probably have to send a memo.

191

No, that was unkind. If the poor old bean was trying to break the shell and emerge into humanity at last, it was only right to encourage the transmogrificaton. Thinking back to the last sentence, Slider decided he could hardly say yes sir or no sir, so he said, 'I understand, sir.'

'Do you,' Barrington said. And then as though the first had not been a question, 'Do you?' He paused, stood up, walked up and down the space between his desk and the window, looking as incongruous as a tiger in an estate agent's office. 'What I want,' he said slowly, 'if it's possible, is to start again. Clean slate. Do you think that's possible – Bill? Pretend these unfortunate – er – *tensions* have never existed between us. I want us to work together in future without prejudice. I promise you I'll back you all the way, and you'll find me a good man to have on your side.'

The smile finally broke the surface, and it was not a thing to dwell on. Slider wanted it over with as quickly as possible, before Barrington tried to shake his hand or something. 'Sounds good to me, sir,' he said, hating himself rather. But it was that or throw himself out of the window, and it was nearly teatime and they had Danish pastries in the canteen on Mondays.

'Fine. Good. Well, then – we start again from here, right?' Barrington stopped in the middle of his walk and thrust his hand out across the desk. Whimpering inwardly, Slider grasped it.

'I'd better be getting on with it, then,' he said, backing off. 'Getting this case together.'

He didn't manage to get very far before Barrington, with a great effort, said – or rather blurted out – 'I don't suppose you'd be free this evening, would you? To have dinner? We could talk over any problems you think I ought to know about. I'd like this to be a happy station.'

Come, Slider thought Alice-like, that's going too far. Enough is enough. 'I'm sorry,' he said, 'I've already got plans for this evening.' Which was true, actually and fortunately; and the conviction evidently carried.

Barrington looked for a fraction of an instant disappointed and Slider felt for an equivalent space of time rather mean. But then the fissures in the rock-face closed up, he barked,

192

'Some other time then,' and sat down and pulled some papers towards him; the silent dismissal.

Atherton stuck his head round the door. 'I wondered what you were doing tonight. Only Sue's coming round for dinner, and I thought you might like to join us. Little celebration, perhaps.'

Blimey, what it is to be popular, Slider thought. Suddenly I'm the Prom Queen. 'Thanks,' he said. 'Much as I hate to turn down anything you've cooked, I've already got a date for tonight.'

Atherton realigned his body vertically with his head, and leaned against the door jamb. 'Oh? Is it anyone I know?' he asked with elaborate unconcern.

Slider's grin would not have looked out of place on a Norman Rockwell paper-boy. 'Yup. She's forgiven me, and I think she's going to take me back. We're going to talk about it tonight – if we get round to it.'

Atherton felt as though his intestines had suddenly gone off without him. 'Oh, that's wonderful,' he said. 'That's really wonderful. I'm so glad for you.'

'Don't be too glad too far ahead of the game. You know how strong-minded she is, and how dumb I am. But it's a foot in the door. I'm going to depend on my hunky torso to argue the case for me.'

Atherton managed a smile. 'She's a gone goose, then.'

'What's this with you and Sue?' Slider asked. 'Is that serious?'

'When have you ever known me to be serious?'

'I thought perhaps it was a case of imitation being the sincerest form of flattery.'

'Oh well, you know how I feel about you, guv. Talking of cases, by the way –'

'Don't. It leaves a bad taste in the mouth.'

'I hate to think what a good defence counsel will make of it,' Atherton agreed. 'But I was just going to say that you should remember to tell Joanna she was wrong. You told me she said we'd discover it wasn't a musician who killed Radek.'

'She was wrong, and she was right, because he didn't mean

193

to do it. I'll tell her that.' Slider stared away at nothing. 'I should think they'll let him off lightly, don't you?'

'Whether they do or not, he'll serve life in his own mind. What's done can't be undone.'

'And I still don't really know whether he was a great conductor or just a showman. How much has the world been robbed of?'

'You'd better ask Joanna,' Atherton said shortly.

CHAPTER FOURTEEN

There's no Police like Holmes

'I wonder if anyone has ever written about the rôle of spag bol in the process of seduction,' Slider said, stirring in the tomato paste. 'It does seem to me that once you've cooked and eaten it together, you're bound to each other for life.'

Joanna, wrapping the garlic bread in foil ready for the oven, said innocently, 'You never cooked it with Irene, then?'

'That,' Slider said, 'was well below the belt.'

She grinned quickly at him. 'Sorry. It just slipped out.'

'And actually, the answer is no. I've cooked it *for* her, years ago when we were first married and lived in a bedsitter with a gas ring, but never *with* her. So my case remains sound.'

'You really think,' she said, 'that once we've had dinner I won't be able to resist you? That I'll tumble into your arms like a ripe plum falling off a tree?'

'Counting on it,' he said, adding oregano like a man with palsy.

'Oh Bill, don't rush me.'

'Rush you?' he said indignantly. 'It was me that suggested we ate first.'

'What's this "first" business?' she objected. He put down the spoon, turned and put his arms round her waist, lifting her slightly off her feet and pressing her hard against him.

'Listen to me, woman,' he said. 'I've apologised for being such a complete and utter waste of space these last two years, and I'll apologise again as often as you like, but I'm not going

195

to let you ruin the rest of both of our lives by making us live apart.'

She looked him straight in the eye, which given her position was all she could look him in. 'I suppose you think that being masterful is going to –' There was quite a long silence. 'My, you are strong,' she murmured at the end of it.

'I've always been strong in the arms and shoulders,' he said. 'It comes of shovelling muck all through my formative years.' He lowered her, still held against him, to the ground.

She looked up at him with a faintly troubled expression. 'It still hurts, you know.'

'I know.'

'I didn't want you to think it was just that easy.'

His smile faded. 'I had two children. I was married for fifteen years. No, I didn't think it was just that easy.'

'I'm sorry,' she said in a small voice.

'No,' he said. 'I'm not laying that on you. And I've no regrets. But I don't want to waste any of the time we've got. I –'

'Yes? You what?'

'No, it sounds pretentious.'

'So sound pretentious. You think someone's writing all this down for posterity?'

'I was just going to say, I deal so much with death and sadness in my job, I want everything we do to be a celebration of life.' He made a face. 'Yeuch, I can't believe I just said that.'

She smiled seductively. 'Your sauce is catching. I can smell it.'

He dropped her precipitately and grabbed the spoon. 'Just in time. How long is your bread going to take?'

'Ages. The oven isn't up to heat yet. We've time to sit down and have a glass of wine. And you haven't told me about the case yet. You must be pleased to have got it all sorted out so quickly.'

'The sorting out hasn't begun yet. Now we've got the real plod of putting all the documents together and trying to get it into a form that won't send the CPS into fits. Of course, I know in detective fiction it's all over once Sherlock fingers the villain and swans off for coke with Watson, but it's not like that in real life. In real life working out who dunnit is the least of our troubles – certainly in this case.'

'Well never mind, sit down here, take hold of this, and tell me the latest developments,' she said, handing him a generous glass of Dolcetto d'Alba, glowing liquid ruby in the firelight and smelling of the warm south. Ensconced in the depths of the chesterfield – it wasn't the sort of sofa you could apply a meagre verb like 'sit' to – with Joanna's thigh against his, he sipped and told her the tale.

'Atherton thought it was a nice change to investigate amongst people whose houses didn't smell of urine,' he finished, 'but I've found it depressing to see how badly all these people have behaved, people who ought to know better. Casual sin and casual lawbreaking – drugs, embezzlement, greed, adultery, murder – looting their way through life and dropping the litter behind them like tourists. Not one person's shown any compassion or had one thought to anyone else. It was just me, me, me.'

'All sin is selfishness. And selfishness is the root of all sin,' she said.

He gave her a tired smile. 'Oh, and by the way, Atherton told me to remind you you were wrong – about the murderer not being a musician.'

'He'd better not bank on collecting. Maybe Polowski didn't do it,' she said. 'Maybe it was Marcus all along, and he was only covering for him.'

'No, no, it was Lev Polowski who pulled the trigger all right.'

'But?'

'But what?'

'No, that's my line. You sounded as if you wanted to say "but". Is there something funny about it?'

'How well you know me.' He sighed. 'There's lots that's funny about it. I know we've got the right man and he's confessed of his own free will, but I just don't feel right with this case. There's something unsatisfying about it – like watching a film where the hero and heroine meet in a restaurant, and they keep loading the forks, but you never see the food go down. Nobody's actually chewing and swallowing.'

'All right.' She swivelled round to sit cross-legged facing him. 'Go through it with me, then, item by item. What doesn't feel right?'

'Well, to begin with, there's the question of why Buster didn't recognise Lev.'

'He was a long way away, and it was dark,' Joanna said. 'Remember we were sitting under the lights – you can't see out into darkness. And Buster had no reason even to look that way until after the shot was fired.'

'Oh, I know. I didn't mean that. But the description of the murderer included his small size, the duffel coat and the hat. Now wouldn't you have thought that would ring a bell?'

'Why should he know anything about Polowski's ward-robe?'

'He'd called on him just the day before. And duffel coats aren't that common any more.'

'Maybe he wouldn't know that. But probably he wouldn't even think of it. With the shock of the shooting itself, and then he's been devastated with grief ever since – he's hardly in a state to ponder sartorial niceties.'

'You sounded just like Atherton then. All right, I accept that – but then why didn't he tell me that Lev had called at the house on Tuesday? He mentioned Marcus and Alec Coleraine, and when I said was there anyone else, anyone at all of any description, he said no.'

'Forgot, maybe. People do.'

'Forgot? Marcus had, in his own words, "wound Radek up". They were about to go out and already late, and there's another interruption, and an emotional scene, and Keaton doesn't remember it, even when prompted?'

'Well then, why do you think he didn't mention it?' she asked Socratically.

'I don't know. I wish I did.' He sipped his wine thought-fully, and she took the opportunity to go out to the kitchen and check on the oven. When she came back, he said, 'Polowski says Radek looked ill when he got up on the platform. Did you think so? Did you notice anything in particular?'

She frowned. 'Well, I told you he was sweating a lot, but he always did. Maybe it was more than usual. He wiped his face

198

with his handkerchief before he began. I don't know. It all happened so quickly, and I wasn't really looking at him to notice him. He wasn't a man to gaze at.'

'Lev gazed at him. He said his behaviour was different from usual.'

'So what are you trying to suggest – that he knew he was going to be shot? But that wouldn't alter the fact that he was shot, would it? I mean, that is a fact, isn't it? You took a bullet out of him?'

'Not me personally. Jenkins the pathologist did, though. I wish it had been Freddie.'

'Why, don't you trust this new one?'

'He hasn't got so much experience. Maybe he missed something.'

'But I thought he had more firearms experience. Wasn't that his specialist area?'

'True.'

'Well, then. I don't understand what the problem is.'

'Nor do I really,' he said ruefully. 'Maybe I'm hungry.'

'There's always that,' she agreed. 'Combined with the fact that your life has been turned upside down recently, and you've been working long hours and probably not sleeping much.'

'And I haven't even told the worst yet. Mad Ivan wants to be friends with me.'

'What?'

'He asked me if we could start again with a clean slate, and then he invited me to dinner.'

She smiled slowly 'And you chose me! Well, I need never doubt again.'

He reached out a hand for her. There was some extremely urgent unfinished business rushing about his bloodstream. 'We don't have to eat now, do we?'

'Yes, we definitely do. Try to be a little sophisticated. Anticipation is half the dish – didn't Sophocles say that?'

'I doubt it. He was Greek, wasn't he?'

Atherton lay on his back feeling – feeling – well, feeling like he'd never felt before, actually. 'I'm sorry,' he said.

Sue turned onto her elbow and looked at him over her

plump shoulder like a partridge hiding behind a pink rock. 'Don't worry,' she said. 'There'll be plenty of other times.'

'It's never happened to me before,' he said with a voice driven by humiliation.

'It has to me,' she said. He glanced at her, unwilling to meet her eyes in case it was embarrassing.

'Has it?'

'Yes. But it's not a contest, you know.' She wriggled herself into a more comfortable position. 'The difficulty is knowing what to say. After all, if I say it doesn't matter it sounds as if I'm not disappointed, and if I say I'm disappointed, it sounds as if I'm blaming you. It's a bit like time travel, really. The danger is not that you might come face to face with yourself, but what on earth you'd find to talk about with someone who knows all your best lines.'

He grinned unwillingly. 'You really are a complete nut.'

'I know,' she said complacently. 'Did I dream it, or was there some of that pudding left?'

He sat up doubtfully. 'You want it now?'

She sat up too, the sheet miraculously continuing to cover her breasts just as if she was in a movie. 'Why not? It's the second most indecent thing I can think of to do at the moment. Can I have it in here, out of the serving bowl?'

'Yes, of course,' he said. He felt quite relieved. At least he knew he could cook. It was a mystery really, why he'd failed; and it wasn't because he hadn't really fancied Sue – after all, they'd been bouncing the springs every spare moment since they met.

He opened the bedroom door and Oedipus shot in and jumped up onto the bed, giving him an affronted look over his shoulder. He stalked up to Sue with his tail straight up like a broomstick and began rubbing himself against her, purring like a geiger counter. She laughed and looked up at Atherton. 'That'll learn you!'

'Nothing of the sort,' Atherton said. 'He's just showing his good taste.' Their eyes met and he felt better. He really, really liked her. More than anyone else he'd met in years.

He began to turn away to go to the kitchen and she said casually, as if quite at random, 'Did you ever sleep with Joanna?'

He stopped very still. His back was to her so she couldn't see his face, and the pause seemed to go on for a very long time.

'No,' he said at last.

'Well, that's okay then,' she said lightly. He forced himself to turn and look at her, to find out the worst, but she was smiling an all-embracing smile of perfect understanding. He felt comforted and comfortable, as if he'd been to confession and had all his sins cancelled.

'Bring two spoons,' she said.

Slider woke with a violent jerk. His head had fallen right back onto the arm of the chesterfield, and his neck hurt. He sat up, bewildered, met Joanna's eyes, and found the memory of a recent gigantic snore sculling about his brain. It must have been the noise of it that woke him.

'You fell asleep,' she said kindly.

'I'm sorry,' he said thickly. 'Bad manners.'

'It's all right. You're tired and full of good things, and its warm in here.' She eyed him curiously. 'Were you having a dream? You were twitching and muttering.'

His absent brain cells started to ooze back into their usual crevices. 'Yes,' he said. 'It was – yes, I remember now! I was playing in your orchestra. We were doing a concert.'

'What were you playing?' she asked, amused.

'The trumpet.'

'You can't play the trumpet.'

'I can't play anything, but it was all right in the dream. I knew I could play it all right. That wasn't the problem. There I was sitting at the back with the others and –' He frowned. 'Oh yes, I remember, the problem was that I had the wrong music in front of me. Any minute the conductor was going to start waving his hands and I'd have to play, and I knew my bit wouldn't fit in with everybody else's.'

'That's what you were muttering, I think – "It won't fit, it won't fit."' She looked at him patiently, seeing by his frown that he was far away in thought. His hair was ruffled, his eyes bloodshot, the muscles of his face slack with tiredness. A fine stubble was just beginning to show at this distance from this morning's shave, and she could see that if he grew a beard now quite a bit of it would be grey. She had one of those infrequent moments of seeing him whole and separate, something complete and absolutely outside herself, as if he were rimmed with light; and she loved him so hugely she could only sigh, as one sighs sometimes with pain. That was why he'd gone on pursuing her in spite of her best efforts, she thought: because, being logical and clear-sighted, he saw that being apart wouldn't stop them feeling like that about each other, so there was no point to it. She was going to have to accept love with all its inconveniences, and she had a moment of panic, because she'd got used to living on her own and liked her independence, and the safety that came along with it. But on the other hand, there was a sort of reprehensibly girly excitement about the thought of setting up home together and doing the things ordinary people did, like choosing wallpaper and buying carpets and deciding where to go for their summer holidays. Doing things with Bill. Alice in Magazineland. Suddenly she felt like crying.

He came back from his long journey. 'Jo, I'm sorry, I'm going to have to go,' he said. He looked at her with such tentative apprehension, as though he thought it might be rolling-pin time again, that any indignation she might have felt expired in a puddle of amusement.

'Go where?'

'I've got to go back to the station. I need to have all the papers to hand.'

'It's the case, is it? Is there something wrong?'

'It doesn't fit,' he said. 'There's something that doesn't fit. I've just got to go over it again and –' He was away with his thoughts again. Joanna got up and went silently to fetch his coat. She thrust it into his arms and turned him towards the door.

'Go,' she said. 'And drive carefully.'

'I'm sorry to mess up your evening,' he began, trying to look over his shoulder at her.

'Your evening too. It's all right, I understand.'

'I'll make it up to you.'

'I know you will. Just promise me one thing? Phone me later – when you can, when you've something to tell me.' She reached past him to open the door, and he turned in

202

the confined space and kissed her.

'I love you,' he said. And went.

Seven o'clock in the morning is usually a quiet time in a police station. The CID office is unmanned, night shift ending at six and early shift not coming cn until eight. Slider lifted his head from the sea of papers and looked towards the windows, seeing the early sky pale and sunless, hearing the morning traffic getting into its stride along Uxbridge Road. He picked up the telephone and dialled.

'Freddie! I'm sorry to bother you so early. Oh good. Did you have a nice holiday? Well, it's something that happened while you were away. Oh, you heard about that? No, I don't know that there's anything wrong, exactly, but I wondered if you'd have a look at the PM report for me. I don't want to say until you've looked at it – I want your unbiased opinion. If I fax it to you now, could you look at it right away and ring me back? Yes, I know, but I do think it's important. All right. Thanks a lot. I'll go and do it right now. Thanks, Freddie. Bye.'

It was almost eight o'clock when Cameron called back. 'You were a long time,' Slider said.

'My dear old boy, you didn't expect me to sit and read your blasted report in my skivvies, did you? I had to bath and shave and dress, and then I read it while I had my breakfast.'

'Breakfast,' Slider said in a mixture of exasperation and longing. The spag bol of sacred memory was now a long way in the past.

'Certainly breakfast. Martha promised me kedgeree this morning. Only a certified madman passes up on Martha's kedgeree.' Even his voice was replete, Slider thought bitterly. 'Anyway, I'm here now. What's the problem with this PM?'

'Do you think the conclusion is all right. The cause of death?'

'I didn't examine the body, old chum. But it looks all right to me. Laddo James knows what he's doing. I don't know much about him personally, but his reputation is certainly sound.'

'But the bullet – it was hardly more than a flesh wound. It

203

was at extreme range and it damaged no organs. Could it really have caused his death?'

'Let's be accurate: it was the shock that caused his death, and there's nothing surprising about that. He was an old man. Shock is a very individual thing. You can never be sure how it will affect people.'

'But Radek was very fit, and there was nothing wrong with his heart. Look, Freddie, you're a bit of a music buff. You know how healthy conductors usually are.'

'Yes, I know. They do tend to live for ever. I grant that on the surface it may seem surprising that such an unimportant wound should have led to his death, but as I said, shock acts very idiosyncratically.'

'All right,' Slider said, changing foot, 'but then there's something else. The cadaveric spasm. His left hand was clutching the neck of his jumper, his right hand was clenched on nothing.'

'That's right.'

'Just visualise it, will you, Freddie? He's standing there in front of the orchestra waiting to begin, with his baton in his right hand, his left hand poised in the air. There's a loud bang and he's struck in the lower back by a bullet, and in the emotion of the terrible shock he clutches at his sweater so violently that the spasm remains after death, but he *drops his stick*.'

There was a silence at the other end. 'Yes, I see what you mean. It is odd.'

'He must have dropped the stick before the death spasm. If it was the shot caused the spasm, why did he drop it?'

'I don't know, chum. Is this leading where I think it's leading?'

'Is it possible,' Slider said, 'that it wasn't the bullet that killed him?'

'I keep telling you, what killed him was the syncope.'

'All right, is it possible that something else caused the syncope? Could James have missed something?'

'It's possible, old boy, anything's possible. But are you suggesting the shooting was a belt-and-braces job, or just an accidental concurrence? For someone to have shot him at that precise moment would be a bit of a coincidence, wouldn't it?'

'Coincidences are coincidental. That's the thing about them. Anyway, the man who fired the shot says it was the surprise of seeing Radek fall that made him pull the trigger.'

'Sounds a bit thin to me.'

'But it's medically possible?'

'It's possible. So what are you thinking?'

'I don't know yet, only that I can't make it come out straight as it is. There's the cadaveric spasm. There's the fact that the gunman – and I admit he's not the most reliable witness – says Radek fell before he pulled the trigger. And there's the way he fell, too – he crumpled forward quite gently, didn't even knock over the music stand. If you'd been hit in the back by a bullet, wouldn't you arch backwards? Wouldn't you automatically clutch at it?'

'One would have thought so, yes. But I've never tried it, so I can't swear to it.'

'What else could have caused the syncope, Freddie?'

'Well, some other kind of shock or insult. Something that attacked the central nervous system. A virus or a bacterial invasion could do it. Or some kind of toxin. Did he drug?'

'Apparently, but not to excess. I don't think it's likely he took anything of that sort beforehand, though. It wasn't his way – he took stuff afterwards to wind down. But he might have taken something medicinal. He was a bit of a hypochondriac.'

'Accidental poisoning, then. Were there any symptoms?'

'No,' Slider said uncertainly. 'Not really. We've one witness says he looked unwell, another says he was sweating a lot, but nothing concrete. But even if they were symptoms, he was apparently all right up to about five minutes beforehand.'

'It could be a quick-acting toxin, with or without the added insult of the bullet – given his age, even though he was fit, the combination might bring on a syncope before any strong symptoms developed.'

'But if he was poisoned,' Slider said, 'wouldn't it leave post mortem signs?'

'Not necessarily to the naked eye. But all poisons are detectable in one way or another.'

Slider was silent a moment, thinking of the trouble it would cause, thinking of the resistance from the family, from his

205

seniors, the ruckus in the press. But as it was, it didn't fit, it didn't fit. And Radek was still above ground. Just. It would make it much worse to have to get an exhumation order later. If he was going to go any further, he had to act today.

'Freddie, if I get the paperwork, could you do a re-examination? Could you test for poisoning?'

'Certainly, Bill, certainly. You just tell me which poison.'

Ah, yes, there was the rub. 'I don't know.'

'Can't test for that one, chum.'

'I'll find out,' Slider said, 'I've got to give it some more thought.'

'You certainly have,' said Cameron. Slider could hear in his voice the quizzical edge of a man who thinks his friend's got a chimera by the tail.

'But you'll hold yourself ready?'

'I'll have the bleeper with me, and I'll come running at the sound of your lovely voice,' Freddie promised.

Slider put the phone down dazedly. Which poison? Ah yes, and if there was a poison, who administered it, and how, and when, and why? It occurred to him that if Radek had been killed other than by shooting, it opened up the whole field of suspects again. It could be anyone. It could even be Fay Coleraine, and eliminating her from suspicion had been his only comfort from the beginning of the case.

CHAPTER FIFTEEN

Morning becomes Electric

Norma was the first in. Slider called her into his office and gave her a job to do. She listened gravely, nodded, and went away without comment or protest. Thank God for Norma, he thought, as he had so often thought before. Then he dialled Barrington's number, but there was no answer. Slider contemplated calling his bleep, but then decided he was probably on his way here anyway, so he might as well wait until he arrived before tackling the delicate problem.

As he put the telephone down, it rang again. He thought immediately of Joanna, whom he hadn't called yet; and then felt an absurd flush of guilt as it turned out to be Irene.

'I thought you'd have called me over the weekend.'

'I'm sorry. I didn't have time. The case broke, and I was working twenty-four hours a day.'

'You've got a result?' It was the most interested she'd sounded about his job in years.

'Yes. And a full voluntary confession.' No point in telling her his doubts.

'Oh good. I am pleased for you. And Matthew will be. He keeps badgering me for details.'

Slider thought briefly and painfully about the empty bedroom and the poster. 'How is he? And Kate?'

'They miss you,' Irene said, surprisingly generously. But then, he reminded himself, she thought she was the guilty party.

'They always did,' he said. 'Even when I was there.'

'Bill, don't. I don't want to revive old quarrels. I want us to be friends now. Can't we?'

'Yes,' he said. 'I want that too.' He made an effort. 'We must meet. I've got a lot of things to tell you.'

'We've got to talk about the house. And the divorce. I'm sorry, Bill, but we have to talk about that.'

'Yes, I know.'

'Have you got somewhere to stay yet?'

'Nearly. I'm working on it. I've got a bit of work to do on the case first, but I should be clear by the end of the week.'

'Then come and see us. All of us, I mean. Come on Saturday so you can see the children.'

'I don't – don't want to come to Ernie's house.'

'Oh *Bill* –!'

'I'm sorry. I don't want to hurt your feelings, but I don't want to see my children in his house.'

He surprised himself by the firmness with which he said it, and it seemed to surprise her, too. After a moment she said, almost respectfully, 'Whatever you say, darling. We'll meet you anywhere you like.'

'Thanks,' Slider said, and meant it. 'Look, I must go now. I'll ring you later in the week and arrange something for Saturday. We'll go out somewhere nice. Have a think meanwhile where the children would like to go.'

'I'll ask them.' A slight pause. 'Are you all right? Are you eating properly and everything?'

'I'm fine.'

'Only I know what you're like when you're in the middle of a case. You must take care of yourself.'

It was making him want to cry, all this tender concern. The sooner he confessed his guilt to her the better. 'I'm fine, really. I'll ring you on Friday.'

When she'd rung off, he pressed the rest for a dialling tone and called Joanna. The sound of her voice settled his ruffled feathers. 'Nothing's happened yet. I'm still working on my doubts. I'll let you know as soon as I've got somewhere.'

'All right. Have you had breakfast?'

'Not yet.'

'Have some. You must feed the inner man.'

He smiled. 'Not you as well! All this tender concern.'

'I love you more than Atherton does,' she said sternly.

'He's not in yet. I was talking to Irene.'

'Oh. Now you've made me jealous. You called her before me.'

'No, it's all right, she called me. But I'll have to go and see her next weekend. Her and the children.'

'That's all right. You don't have to ask my permission.'

'I'll have to tell her about us.'

'What about us?' She sounded suspicious.

'Well, everything.'

'Oh no you don't!'

'But I have to. It isn't fair. She thinks she's the guilty party,' Slider protested.

'Don't be such a gimboid! She probably enjoys it – all women like to feel dangerous, and precious little chance she's ever had before. If you tell her all our past history, just to ease your own conscience, you'll make her miserable and probably foul up the divorce into the bargain, and what good will that do? And the children will find out that you were unfaithful to their mother and they'll be miserable too. Then she'll probably try to stop you seeing them – and they'll probably agree with her.'

'You think so?' he said doubtfully.

'I know so. Leave well alone. Tell her nothing. You can pretend to meet me later on, and then she'll be able to feel good about being glad you've found someone.'

'That's so devious.'

'It's common sense.'

'But I'll feel bad about deceiving her.'

'So feel bad. That's the price you pay. But don't make her suffer for your sins.'

'You're a strange person. I should have thought most women would want to gloat.'

'I'm a very remarkable person. And you don't know anything about most women, whoever they are. Go and have some breakfast.'

The canteen was quiet, warm and steamy. Still glowing a little from being blessed by Joanna, Slider found himself with a huge appetite and wolfed down eggs, bacon, sausages, beans, double fried bread and two cups of tea as though everything in the garden was rosy. On the second cup, Atherton found him, looking worried.

'They said you were up here. And they said you'd been in all night. What's up, guv?'

Slider told him, and Atherton's frown deepened.

'There's nothing to go on, guv,' he said at last. 'Nothing at all.'

'It's the cadaveric spasm that bothers me most, I think,' Slider said, almost as if he hadn't heard him. 'And the way he fell. It was as if he didn't even notice he'd been shot. Look at the sequence of events: he drops his stick, clutches at his throat, collapses and dies with both hands clenched. Now what does that look like to you?'

'He was shot in the back. The shock caused a fatal syncope. Why look any further?'

'Why did Buster not mention Polowski's visit?'

'You want to make him the murderer? The only person who's actually mourning Radek?'

Slider shook his head, not in denial but exasperation. 'There's something not right about it.'

Atherton looked doubtfully at the top of Slider's head. 'Guv, you can't go to Mr Barrington with no more than this.'

'Can't go to him with anything. He's not here – still in transit, I suppose. I telephoned his house and there's no answer.'

That was a stopper, Atherton thought. If he'd tried to talk to Barrington, he must be serious about it.

'All right,' he said, sitting down opposite and putting his elbows on the table, 'let's have a look at it. If Radek was poisoned, because of the time factor he must have taken the poison in the dressing-room, otherwise he'd have developed symptoms sooner. So that narrows it down to Buster, who's got to be prime suspect because of his closeness to the victim, or Des Riley, who comes in at number two, or Tony Whittam. No-one else came near him.'

'Not Tony,' Slider said. 'He wasn't alone with Radek at any point.'

'Nor was Des, for that matter. But he might have gone into

210

the dressing-room before Radek arrived and planted – whatever it was.'

'In that case,' Slider said, 'it could have been anyone. Anyone in the orchestra. The verger. Anyone who knew Radek would be there.'

'Ah, but what could they have planted? I went in there and clocked everything. There was nothing to eat or drink, not even a carafe of water. Only the water in the tap.'

'It would be hard to poison that intentionally,' Slider acknowledged. 'I wonder if Marcus could have spiked something the day before, something he knew Radek would take with him?'

'But what? Again, there was nothing in the dressing-room that he would have swallowed.'

'I know. I've been over the list and I can't work it out.'

'Unless Buster took it away with him. We looked in Radek's pockets but we didn't frisk him.'

Slider pondered. 'But look, if Buster – or anyone – deliberately poisoned Radek, they couldn't have known Polowski was going to shoot him and cover the trail. So they'd have had to do it in some way that wouldn't be found out, or at least that wouldn't be traced back to them. If Radek had collapsed with symptoms of poisoning, everything in the dressing-room would have been impounded and analysed, and questions would have been asked as to where it came from. And in that case Buster would certainly have had to empty his pockets –'

'Yes, if the symptoms had looked like poisoning,' Atherton said. 'But suppose it only looked like a heart attack? Everyone knew Radek had a bad heart –'

'Because Buster had told them so,' Slider finished triumphantly.

Atherton spread his hands. 'Brilliant. QED. Except that Buster's the only one without a motive to kill Radek.'

'Forget motive.'

'If you say so. But I repeat, you've still no real reason to think Radek didn't die as a result of the gunshot.'

Slider's face shut down. 'Go along with me on this,' he said tersely. 'Humour me. I've just got a feeling about it.' He got up, and walked towards the door.

Atherton shrugged and followed him. 'You're the guv'nor. And who am I to deny a man's hunch? What do you want me to do?'

'See if you can find anything in the records about Radek's wife's death. She's supposed to have OD'd on sleeping pills. It was brought in accidental death at the inquest, but Fay thought it was suicide.'

'I'll see what I can do.' He sounded puzzled, not seeing where that was leading.

'Look up the newspapers, local and national. See if there was any speculation. Maybe it wasn't what it seemed.'

'Right, guv. You think it was Buster, then?'

'I don't know. But he ought to have told me Lev called. I can't get over that.'

Back in his room, Slider picked up the phone and dialled Coleraine's office. It was answered by a new secretary.

'I'm temporary,' she replied to Slider's query. 'Mrs Good-win's left.'

'That was sudden, wasn't it?'

'Yes, apparently,' she said with a determined lack of interest. 'Did you want to speak to Mr Coleraine?'

'Yes, please,' Slider said, rebuked.

Alec Coleraine was cool, and Slider wondered whether Helena had told him everything before she left. He didn't challenge Slider with it, however. 'I'm trying to catch up with things before tomorrow,' he said. 'It'll be another day off, for the funeral, and business doesn't look after itself. So I can't spare you much time.'

'I won't keep you long,' Slider said. 'I just wanted to ask you what you know about Lev Polowski.'

'What sort of thing do you want to know?' Coleraine asked cautiously.

'About his relationship with your father-in-law, partic-ularly.'

'Just a minute,' Coleraine said sharply, and the phone went dead. Slider waited in the black felt embrace of Hold, his mind out of gear. At least there was no electronic 'music' here. It was quite cosy really, and he was very tired. Then Coleraine came back. 'Just sending the temp away. I didn't want her overhearing.'

212

'About Polowski? Was it a secret, then?'

'Look here, don't play games with me,' Coleraine said with something between anger and apprehension. 'I know Lev's been arrested, and I've worked the rest out for myself. He and Marcus have been hanging around together, and Lev's as poor as a church mouse. Marcus put him up to it, didn't he? Offered him a share of the loot. I should have realised –'

'Should you?'

'The duffel coat for one thing. How many people do you see nowadays wearing a duffel coat?'

'You knew Lev had one?'

'It was Marcus's. I bought it for him, and it was damned expensive. From Burberry's. I was pretty annoyed when he casually gave it to Lev, just because Lev didn't have a coat. "Winter was coming on," he said. It was like something out of Tolstoy.'

'If you'd told us this before it would have saved a lot of trouble,' Slider said sternly.

'I didn't think about it,' Coleraine said, and there was a ring of truth to that. 'You don't think about overcoats when someone's been murdered.'

'All right,' Slider said, 'let's leave that. Tell me about Lev's relationship with Sir Stefan.'

'Well, Stefan found him in Poland, brought him back, gave him money for a time, promoted his career.'

'I know those things. I want to know about their personal relationship.'

'Look, Inspector, this mustn't go any further,' Coleraine said urgently.

'What mustn't?'

'About Lev being Stefan's – you know. About them having a – an affair.'

'You mean they were lovers?'

'Oh Christ, don't tell me you didn't know that? Isn't that what this is all about?'

'The question is not what I know, but what you know.'

'Well, they were – they went to bed together. But it's got to be kept secret. It mustn't get out.'

'I'm afraid it's bound to come out at the trial. It won't be up to me to prevent it.'

Coleraine almost groaned. 'Oh God, the scandal – the press – Fay mustn't know! It would kill her. Anything like that's anathema to her. She didn't really know what Stefan was like, and the idea that he could – that he did it with *boys* –

'You really think she doesn't know? She is his daughter, after all.'

'You don't understand. Fay is very innocent. Such a thing would never occur to her. Look here, I'd do anything to keep it from her – pay anything. Surely there's something you can do? I mean, does it matter *why* Lev shot Stefan? Everyone saw him do it. There can't be any doubt about that, can there?'

Slider passed over the suggestion of bribery, and said, 'Did Mr Keaton know about Sir Stefan and Lev Polowski?'

'Know? Oh, you mean that they –? Well, I don't know, but I should think he must have. He never said anything to me, of course, but then he wouldn't. He's as particular as Fay, more so if that's possible. It's not a thing he'd ever talk about.'

'You think he'd mind?'

'Oh, he'd mind like hell. He's a real puritan, and he saw himself as guardian of Stefan's reputation, you know. I remember a time when one of the papers gave him a less than perfect review for a concert, and Buster nearly had a fit. He wanted to sue, then he wanted to go round and beat the editor up. In the end he only wrote letters, but he went on writing them for weeks, because the paper wouldn't publish a retraction. If he knew about Lev he'd want to kill him.'

'Thanks. You've been very helpful,' Slider said.

This seemed to strike Coleraine as ominous. 'Inspector, you have charged Lev, haven't you?'

'Yes. Yes, he has been charged.'

'And – and Marcus?'

'No decision has yet been made about whether to charge Marcus on any count.'

'Whose decision is it?' Coleraine asked eagerly. Slider could almost hear him fingering his wallet. Of course, he'd have all of Radek's money to spend now.

'The Crown Prosecution Service,' Slider said. Mentally he added, do you want me to give you their number?

Norma came in, looking quietly triumphant. 'There was something. I don't know if there's any connection, but you guessed right, guv.'

'Sit down. Tell me,' Slider said. He was so eager he hardly noticed her long, beautiful legs as she crossed them at him. Besides, her finding Barrington sexy rather took the shine off it. He couldn't relish coming a poor second to the Man Mountain.

She put her notebook on her knee. 'Keaton joined Fitzpayne School in September 1948. He married Doreen Scoggins in September 1949. I got hold of a man on the local paper, the *Uckfield Gazette*, who was very helpful, and he faxed me through the report on the wedding. It mentioned that Doreen had previously been engaged to a local boy, Peter Hepplewhite, who had died tragically in April that year, of food poisoning. The *Gazette* bloke sent me the report on that, too. There'd been quite a fuss about it. Hepplewhite fell ill after eating at the local newly-opened Chinese restaurant –'

'In 1949? It must have been one of the first in the country.'

'It didn't last long, anyway. No-one else was taken ill that night, and health inspectors couldn't find anything wrong with it, but it closed down all the same. I suppose no-one wanted to risk eating there after popular local builder Hepplewhite, twenty-three, popped off in lethal chop suey horror mystery.'

'Who was with him on the night? Did it say?'

'Not by name. A group of friends, including his finacée Doreen. The paper was too busy milking the bride-to-be tragedy to mention any other friends. We could try the local police for the names?'

'If it comes to anything we may have to, but not yet. Was there anything else? What about Keaton's reason for leaving the school?'

'He gave his notice in in December 1952. They have to give a term's notice, so it wasn't a sudden thing. I spoke to the principal, who knew nothing about it – it was before his time – but he put me on to a retired master, name of Harris, who was on the staff then. I spoke to him, and he said that Keaton didn't leave under a cloud or anything of the sort. He gave his notice in due form, and should have finished in July, but he got permission to leave a few weeks early because he'd found another job which couldn't wait. Harris says Keaton's given reason for leaving was that he wanted to write a novel. They all thought it was very dashing of him, but Harris wondered why he couldn't write a novel where he was. If he had to take a job to support him while he wrote, Harris thought teaching was better than chauffeuring, especially given the long holidays.'

'So, no quarrels, scandals, feuds at the school?'

'No, sir. But there was another death.'

Slider almost rubbed his hands. 'At the school?'

'One of the masters, Simon Phelps. During the previous summer hols. Fell to his death down a chalk quarry.'

'Accident?'

'Apparently. Just lost his balance and fell. The interesting thing from our point of view was that Harris said he was a close friend of the Keatons, went around with them, ate out with them, visited their quarters at all hours. And he was a bachelor.'

'Ah. And this accident?'

'He and the Keatons were out on a picnic together when it happened.'

Atherton tapped and entered. He looked at Norma's legs, but only just, and only out of aesthetic appreciation. He might have answered that morning, if asked, that Sue had grey-blue eyes and a wide, beautiful mouth, but he had no idea what her legs looked like.

'Do you want my report now, guv?'

'Yes, come in. No, stay, Norma,' Slider said. 'He's been looking into Radek's wife's death.'

'There's not much to say about it. She was found dead in the morning by Doreen Keaton – Radek and his wife had separate bedrooms. The bottle of pills was open on the bedside table and half full, and they calculated by the number left that she must have taken a double dose. She'd been taking the sleeping pills for about six months – prescribed by the doctor, nothing funny about it. Doreen said that she had been nervous and irritable, but not particularly depressed, though she'd been drinking heavily that night after a quarrel with her

216

husband. The path report was unchallenged: she died of an overdose of narcotic. They brought it in accidental largely because there was no note and the dose, though lethal, was quite small. The thinking was if she'd meant to kill herself she'd have swallowed the whole bottle. As it was, they decided she'd been confused with drink and didn't know what she was doing.'

'And was there speculation?'

'Not in the press. It was very respectful – talked about Radek's genius and his war record, and what a terrible tragedy this was, and how it was to be hoped it wouldn't affect his work. Keaton was interviewed and gave them out a devoted couple, and Doreen said again that Lady Susan hadn't been depressed. The nearest thing to a hint was in a gossip column which said it was tragic when quarrels, which all married couples have, got out of hand, wondered why Lady Susan had been drinking so much, and mentioned apropos of nothing that Radek had recently conferred his patronage on a promising young female pianist who was as talented as she was beautiful.'

'So that makes three,' Norma said, looking at Slider.

'Three what?' Atherton asked.

'Bodies in Keaton's wake,' Norma said.

'Four,' Slider corrected. 'Don't forget Doreen, who died of gastroenteritis.'

'People do,' Atherton pointed out. 'And food poisoning. Hundreds every year.'

'Phelps fell down a quarry,' Norma said.

'Who's Phelps?' Atherton asked, and she told him. 'Staggered and fell?' he said when she'd finished. 'So you think he was poisoned at the picnic, do you?'

'I don't think anything,' Norma said. 'I leave that to my superiors. I'm just a humble footsoldier.'

Atherton, who had taken the other chair, leaned back in it, crossed his own long, lovely legs, and used his fingers to tick points off. 'So we have Buster wanting to marry Doreen and bumping off her fiancé to get him out of the way; then bumping off a master who – what was his crime? Hanging around Doreen? Was she that gorgeous?'

'Why not?' Slider asked. 'She looked pretty enough in the

photo I saw, and in a closed community like that she wouldn't have too much competition.'

'In any case,' Norma said, 'a man can be jealous without having anything to be jealous of.'

'Or a woman. Quite: it's an intransitive sin,' Atherton acknowledged. 'So, why Lady Susan? And Doreen?'

'I don't know.' Slider sat for a moment longer, staring at nothing. Then he pushed himself to his feet. 'I think I'll go and ask him.'

'Ask Buster?'

'He's the only one who knows,' Slider said.

'Then I'd better come with you.' Atherton said, with a sideways glance at Norma.

'Sir,' she said, 'if Mr Barrington comes in, what shall I say?'

'If he asks, tell him where I am,' said Slider. 'Don't tell him about my speculations if you can help it. I'll explain everything to him personally when I get back.'

They waited a long time at the door, and Atherton had given up and was ready to go, but Slider stood as though planted. Atherton had seen him in this mood before. In the grip of an idea, he became dogged but also oddly confident. It was a comforting trait in one's superior, especially when he seemed to be sprouting a wild hair.

At last there was a movement behind the door, and it opened slowly, to reveal Keaton blinking like an owl. His chin was unshaven, his eyes baggy and bloodshot, his trousers liberally creased across the lap as though he'd been sitting in them for days, which he probably had: they looked to Atherton's searching eye like the pair they'd interviewed him in on Thursday.

Keaton looked at Slider, not even sparing Atherton a glance. 'I thought you'd be back,' he said wearily.

'There's something I wanted to ask you,' Slider said, not like a policeman but like someone familiar, an old acquaintance or long-term neighbour. 'Can I come in?' Even a paranoiac would have had trouble finding him threatening. It was beautifully done, Atherton thought. Buster had stepped back almost before thinking, and by the time suspicion caught up with him Slider was over the doorstep and wiping his feet carefully and absently on the doormat.

'Can't you leave me alone? I've already told you everything I know,' Buster said, turning a look of dull resentment on Atherton.

'Oh, I know,' Slider said vaguely. 'I just wanted a chat about something.' He was ahead of Keaton now, and moving towards the stairs. 'The drawing-room, is it? Shall I go up?'

Keaton hesitated, looking doubtfully at Atherton, but Slider had started up the stairs. 'After you,' Atherton said, smiling; and thus bracketed, Keaton could only go up. It was plainly an effort for him, and Atherton felt guilty for a moment at putting the old man through the mill again.

In the drawing-room Slider went and sat down on the chaise longue and gestured to Keaton to take the armchair nearest him. Keaton sat nervously, placing his arms along the arm-rests and his hands over the ends as though he were about to be strapped in and acquainted with the National Grid. Atherton sat to his other side so that Keaton couldn't look at them both at once; but his attention was still fixed on Slider. Whatever his apprehensions, they were focused on Slider: Atherton barely existed for him.

'You see,' Slider said, as though merely continuing a conversation, 'I think I understand most of it. There are just one or two details I haven't worked out.'

'Details? Details of what?'

'Peter Hepplewhite – that's obvious, of course. And Simon Phelps – a little nudge and over he went. But Lady Susan, that's the puzzle. Not so much how you got her to swallow the pills, but *why?* I know it doesn't matter in the long run, but do I like to understand. It nags at my mind otherwise.'

Atherton had thought Keaton looked bad before, but during this speech his face seemed to grey, and he thought Keaton would either pass out or throw up.

'I don't know what you're talking about,' he whispered at last.

'I think you do,' Slider said unemphatically. 'Your wife Doreen – she'd begun to suspect, hadn't she? Or perhaps she'd suspected all along but you'd begun to be afraid she'd talk. Easiest thing in the world to get rid of her, I do see that. Opportunity is everything, isn't it? And then you had Stefan all to yourself – once you'd got rid of little Fay.'

'I never hurt her,' Keaton said faintly. 'I would never have hurt Fay.'

'No, but you got her sent away to school,' Slider agreed. 'Was Stefan hard to persuade?'

'It was him that wanted her to go. He said she couldn't stay at home with no-one to look after her.' His voice grew a little stronger. He seemed not to have noticed that he had not denied any of the other premises. 'Well, that was true, wasn't it? We didn't tour so much in those days, but there were still all the evenings we wouldn't be at home. Who'd have stayed with her then? But *I* didn't want her to go. It was Stefan's idea. She wanted to go, anyway. She hated her father.'

'Did she like you?'

'Of course she did. She knew I loved her. She still does. Who do you think persuaded him to do the concert at the church? I did that, for her.'

'And was it for her that you killed him?'

Keaton stared, his jaw loose. It trembled, but no sound came out.

'You killed him so that she could have his money, is that it? You knew Alec was in financial trouble, and you didn't want her to suffer, so you killed Stefan so that she'd inherit his estate.'

'No!' He found his voice at last. 'No! You've got it all wrong!'

'All right,' Slider said placidly, 'then you tell me. Why did you kill him?'

'I didn't! You're mad! You know I didn't! Lev shot him. Everyone saw!'

'Oh yes, Lev shot him,' Slider agreed, 'but that wasn't what killed him. You and I know what killed him, don't we?'

Still Buster stared, as though unable to remove his gaze. Atherton was afraid he might have a stroke. The shock of all this, at his age – and the horror of being accused, if he hadn't done it – and Atherton still had doubts about the guv's whole theory –

'You know?' Buster said faintly.

'Of course,' Slider said comfortably. 'But if it wasn't for the money, then why?'

Atherton actually saw the blood return to Keaton's face. His voice rose with indignation.

220

'For the money? What do you take me for? A common, vulgar criminal? I wouldn't kill anyone for money.'

Slider caught Atherton's eye and silenced him with the minutest flicker of his own. 'Tell me then. It was something to do with Lev, wasn't it? Why didn't you tell me that Lev had visited the house on Tuesday?'

Keaton turned his head away, his mouth puckering as though over a bad taste. 'I don't want to talk about it.'

'About Lev and Stefan? You didn't like that little arrangement at all, did you?'

Goaded, Keaton showed a flash of heat. 'You have to have it all out, don't you? You can't keep things decently hidden, any of you! It was bad enough with the women – sluts every one of them – but *boys*? And it was all so blatant! Even Marcus knew all about it. The next thing it was going to be in the press, and then where would we be? I told him it had to stop – the boy was the worst sort, loose morals, loose mind, loose tongue! He told me he'd get rid of him, and I thought he had. I thought it was all over. And then Marcus came round and tried to blackmail him with it.'

'That was his visit on the Tuesday?'

'We were just about to go out. I told Stefan not to see him, but he was always contrary. Well, it was his own fault if he didn't like what he heard. Marcus said he'd take the story to the press if Stefan didn't give him money.'

'You heard it all, did you?'

'There's an intercom in there, to the kitchen, so that he can call me when he's working, if he wants something. I fixed it years ago so that I can turn it on to listen when I want,' Buster said casually. 'I had to be able to look after him. He never knew about it, of course.'

'And what did he say to Marcus, when Marcus threatened him?' Slider asked.

'He told him to go to the devil. You couldn't bully him – no-one could. Stefan may have been many things, but he was no coward.'

'And then Lev turned up.'

'He insisted on seeing him. I could have told him how it would be.' Buster's mouth turned down. 'The filth that flowed out of that creature's mouth! I wouldn't soil myself with repeating it. Afterwards, when he'd gone, I told Stefan he'd been too soft with the boy, that he should have threatened him with the law if he didn't go away and stay away. It was obviously a put-up job between him and Marcus, that's what I thought. And then Stefan said he'd changed his mind, he was going to take the boy back.' He paused, contemplating something black and yawning in his memory. 'I thought he was saying it just to upset me, but the next morning he said it again. He said Lev was talented and ought to be helped and that he was thinking – thinking of bringing him to live with him. In our house.' He stopped. He had reached the heart of the horror as far as he was concerned.

'What did you say to that?' Slider prompted him gently.

'I said I wouldn't have it. He said it was none of my business. We quarrelled – the worst quarrel of our lives. I told him I wouldn't stay under the same roof as that creature, and he said in that case I could pack my bags and get out.'

'Surely he didn't mean it? He must have said that sort of thing to you before, but he didn't mean it.'

'He meant it all right,' Buster mourned. 'He said he was fed up with me trying to run his life. He said I'd turned into a nagging old woman, and he wanted young people around him. He said he'd give me a month's wages and I could leave at the end of the week. But where could I go?' He raised his eyes to Slider's. 'I've no family. I've never had any other home. I've a little bit saved, but not enough to keep me. And besides – I've been with him for forty years. He's my life.'

'So you thought if you had to live without him, it would be better to kill him?'

'Everything seemed to be falling apart,' Buster said with a dazed look. 'We'd been so happy. And I'd been looking forward to his retirement, doing things together, a peaceful old age. Now he was sending me away and taking that – that catamite into his home. And Marcus was going to tell the press – oh, he'd do it, out of spite, you know, because Stefan would never give him any money. We'd be all over the papers, everything pawed over and sullied, his reputation ruined for ever, our lives destroyed. I couldn't let that happen. Better a quiet, dignified end. I knew his heart was bad; all it needed was a little push over the edge.' He shook his head. 'I had no idea

Lev was going to do what he did. But then afterwards it seemed like a godsend. It was a way to get rid of him as well, and there'd be no more questions asked.'

'Yes,' Slider said sympathetically. 'You must have been afraid everything would come out – about Lady Susan and Doreen, and the others. It must have been a bad time for you.'

'I never thought about them. And I don't care about them now,' he said. 'How can you think it? It's Stefan: I gave my whole life to him, and he's gone. I just didn't realise before what it would be like to be without him. But there's nothing else I could have done. I couldn't let him destroy himself.'

'Why *did* you kill Lady Susan?' Slider asked.

'She was wearing him out. Her constant demands on him – physically, on his time, yes, but even more on his spirit. She wasted his vital forces. Music at his level takes everything a man has. I saw it every day. He was drained by her, and his music suffered. And she was jealous of me, of my influence with him. She was trying to turn him against me. He'd tired of her by then, anyway, but if they divorced he'd lose all her money, and he was terrified of poverty, after what he'd seen in Poland. So it was obvious what I had to do. She was an unhappy woman anyway, and I rid him of the burden of her, that's all.'

'How did you make her swallow the pills?'

He looked contemptuous. 'You can't make a person swallow pills – and if you could they'd throw them up again. It was in the brandy.'

'What was in the brandy?'

But the mood had been broken. Suddenly his focus sharpened. 'I thought you said you knew everything?' He remembered Atherton for the first time in ages and looked quickly at him, then back at Slider. 'You're trying to trick me, to make me tell you what you don't know.'

'No, no, not at all. I knew it all except that,' Slider said soothingly, but Keaton wasn't soothed. He seemed to shrink together on himself.

'I'll deny it,' he said. 'You can't prove I said anything to you – I know the law. You can't prove any of it.'

Slider looked at Atherton, and then stood up and walked across the room. 'There's a lot we can prove,' he said. 'For one thing, it was you who told everyone Stefan had a heart condition. But we know that wasn't true. His heart was as healthy as yours or mine.'

'What do you say?' Buster said faintly.

'Oh yes. That's a fact. The post mortem showed his heart was very strong. So why should you have put it about that he had heart disease, if not to pave the way for your plot to kill him?' He stood looking out of the window as he spoke, as though it were a matter so settled as to be unimportant. 'You thought that if he collapsed while he was actually conducting, everyone would assume it was heart and not look any further for a cause. That's why you gave him the stuff just before rehearsal, instead of letting him die at home, in bed.'

'But he told me! He told me he had a weak heart!' Buster seemed utterly bewildered.

'Well he was lying, I'm afraid. Which –' Slider stopped abruptly, his eyes fixed on the garden, things slotting into place with rapid, satisfying clicks. It was horrible, it was truly horrible, but it all fitted, and that was the only satisfaction one could ever have from investigating a murder – getting the answer right.

'Which makes you the prime suspect,' he finished. Atherton heard the difference in his voice and looked at him sharply; and Slider nodded to him, just perceptibly. 'Lev's bullet, you see, didn't do enough damage to kill a man with a sound heart. But Stefan was already dying when Lev pulled the trigger, from something that attacked the central nervous system. Something you'd given him.'

'No-one will believe that,' Buster said, but his voice was faint.

'All poisons are detectable, if you know what to look for,' Slider said. 'The pathologist told me that only this morning. Things have advanced no end since 1959 – they didn't have gas chromatography or atomic absorption spectroscopy then, did they? And of course, no-one was looking for poison in Lady Susan's case anyway. No-one thought of testing the brandy, or looking in your little shed at the bottom of the garden where you do your botanical research.'

Buster jerked in his seat at the last words, and Atherton began slowly to smile as he began to follow Slider's path.

'One is nearer to God in a garden than anywhere else on

earth,' Slider quoted softly. 'You made sure of that, didn't you, Mr Keaton? A very short route to God your pretty garden turned out to be. Tobacco plant, foxglove, deadly nightshade, henbane, laburnum – nature's a wonderfully deadly thing, if you know where to look. And you're a botanist. You'd know all about it.'

'I think,' Keaton said faintly but politely, 'I think I must ask you to excuse me for a moment. I have to go to the lavatory.'

He seemed hardly able to get out of the chair, but when Atherton made to help him, he shrank away. 'No, I can manage. Please – please don't touch me.'

Slider watched him walk to the door, and then flicked a nod at Atherton, who followed him out but came straight back in and said, 'It's just across the hall. We'll hear him come out.' Slider nodded and walked to the window again. 'At least it will get Lev Polowski off the hook,' Atherton said after a moment. 'Or will it? He'll have to be charged with something, I suppose. Attempted murder? Malicious wounding? But can you maliciously wound a dying man? And how close to dying was Radek, I wonder, when the bullet struck him? If it played any part in his death, if it only hastened it, Lev's guilty of something.'

'There's still Buster's little shed to examine,' Slider said, off on his own track. 'He may not have thought to clear it out yet, and even if he has, there might be enough traces to –' He stopped, frowning. 'What was that?' He listened, and then looked at Atherton.

'You don't think –?' Atherton said, and then they both ran.

The door was locked and there was no reply from within, but the hall was narrow there. Atherton hitched himself up onto the radiator, lifted both feet up against the door, and slammed it open. Buster was on the floor, his left sleeve pushed up. There was a medicine cabinet on the wall with its door open, and a hypodermic syringe on the floor by his right hand.

Slider crouched by the body. He wasn't dead yet. 'Call an ambulance,' he said.

Atherton hesitated. 'But they might save him.' Slider looked up. 'Just a little delay, guv,' he said urgently. 'He's killed five people, and they'll probably let him off.'

'Do it,' said Slider.

CHAPTER SIXTEEN

God wot?

The ambulance had been and gone, and the forensic team was taking the house and garden shed to pieces, and Slider and Atherton were standing in the drawing-room, waiting to go.

'I still think we should have let him die,' Atherton grumbled, but he didn't mean it now.

'You know we can't do that,' Slider said. 'And besides, we'll need his confession if we're going to get this one home.'

'It's going to be the devil to prove any of it.'

'I know. There's the trail of bodies following Keaton's career, and a few suspicious coincidences, but an awful lot of it's pure speculation. But Radek's still above ground, and Freddie said he'd find the poison if I could just tell him what to look for.'

'And can you?'

Slider grimaced. 'I think so. I think I know how he did it. It was the last thing left to work out, and I looked down from the window at his lovely border all full of blue flowers – including blue rocket, such a pretty, prolific plant. Also known as monkshood or wolfsbane.'

'Is it poisonous, then?' Atherton asked.

Slider rolled his eyes. 'Don't you know anything about plants?'

'I'm not a hayseed like you, guv,' Atherton protested. 'We didn't go about sucking hedges in Weybridge. None of this eye of newt business in the commuter belt.'

'The Latin name for blue rocket is aconite.'

'Oh, well, why didn't you say so?' Atherton said. 'Aconite is what Medea tried to poison Theseus with. The ancients called it the Queen of Poisons. So it comes from rocket, does it?'

'Aconitum to you. All parts of the plant are poisonous, and you can make a stiff brew from stewing the root as well. It attacks the CNS and paralyses the heart muscle –'

'*Et voilà*, syncope!'

'– sometimes before any other symptoms have had a chance to develop. It's extremely toxic, and it can act very, very quickly – in as little as eight minutes.'

'Well, that sounds promising from our point of view,' Atherton conceded generously, 'except that we have to prove Buster gave it to the old man, and I still can't see how. If he gave him something to eat or drink, he obviously took the evidence away with him, and it will have been destroyed by now.'

'No, he wouldn't have given it that way, because if there was any suspicion, that's the first place we would have looked. If he was going to do it, he'd work out a way that gave him a chance of getting away with it.' Slider turned away and looked out of the window again. 'The other thing about aconite,' he said slowly, 'is that it can be absorbed through the skin. They used to use it externally to treat rheumatic pain – it sets up a sort of tingling numbness. I came across it years ago, when I was a rookie – a case of accidental death, where an ointment containing aconite had been used on broken skin.'

'I don't get it,' Atherton said. 'Am I missing something?'

'You made a list of everything in the dressing-room,' Slider said, 'and in the bathroom. I looked at it this morning, and I realised that there was something missing, but I assumed Keaton must have taken it away in his pocket, and it didn't seem important.'

'Taken what away?'

'A tube of ointment. I just didn't make the connection until I looked out of the window here.'

'A tube of ointment? Did Radek suffer from rheumatism?' Atherton said, still puzzled.

227

Slider turned to him with unwilling eyes. 'Not rheumatism, you clunk.'

Atherton stared, and then enlightenment came. 'Ouch,' he said, screwing up his eyes in genuine sympathy. 'What a way to go. The poor old bastard!'

'At least it was a quick death,' Slider said.

Slider was not looking forward to having to explain the new developments to Barrington, even in his lately acquired pussy-cat mood. The shooting had at least been plain and unequivocal, a confession plus a gun plus a large assortment of witnesses, even if there had been unexplained and confusing shadows in the background. But this! As Atherton said on the way back to the station, in spite of anything Slider could do to stop him, this was just going to mean piles of work for everyone.

Barrington was still not in, however, when they got back, which meant a pleasant respite. Slider put the team to work on assembling the evidence of Keaton's past life, put Freddie on alert, and then went with one of the uniform boys to the hospital to see whether they were going to be able to drag Buster back from the brink. When at last it looked as though he was going to live, Slider left the constable there beside him and went back to the station. Barrington had not come in, nor called in, and was not answering the telephone at home. He was not responding to his bleep either.

'Gone out to play a nice round of golf and left it behind, I suppose,' McLaren grumbled. 'Bloody bosses. I know what kind of a row we'd get if we did something like that.'

The awkward thing as far as Slider was concerned was that he couldn't get Freddie onto the new autopsy until he had Barrington's cross on the dotted line.

'Necropsy, old thing,' Freddie said when he told him. 'Autopsy is an examination of oneself. Never mind, Radek isn't going anywhere. And Barrington will phone in before long feeling awfully silly about having left his bleep behind.'

'Well, if he's not back by close of play today, I'll have to get onto the Commander. We'll have to stop them taking the body away. You know they were going to bury him tomorrow.'

'Whoops,' said Cameron. 'I don't envy you that one. Grassing up your guv'nor to his guv'nor? Not very nice.'

'It's a bugger,' Slider said. 'And Wetherspoon thinks the sun shines out of Barrington's eyes, so the shower will be bound to fall on me.'

'From both directions,' Freddie agreed, with the relish even nice people usually display at the prospect of someone else facing an explosion.

'I wonder if there's anything wrong?' Slider said. 'It isn't like Barrington to be so vague. Weird, yes, but always punctual. Maybe he's ill.'

'He'd have phoned in,' Cameron said comfortably. 'Or his wife would.'

At half past five Slider and Atherton went upstairs to the canteen for lunch, which they'd had no chance to have before. While they were there, Joanna came in, sporting a plastic visitor's badge.

'So this is where you're skulking,' she said.

'Oh God, I forgot,' Slider said. 'I was supposed to phone you, wasn't I?'

'When you had something to tell me. Apparently you've nothing to tell me.'

'You know,' he said examining her closely. 'Who told you?'

'Norma. I rang asking to speak to you and she spilled the beans. So I thought I'd pop round, since I hadn't anything better to do.'

'You don't fool me. You were just longing to see me.'

'Dream on, sonny,' she rebuked him firmly. 'So your funny feelings were right after all?'

'I don't know if that's a good thing or a bad thing. It's going to mean a lot of work, just when we thought we were nearly finished.'

'Never mind, at least you'll be able to feel satisfied at the end of it. How is Mad Ivan taking the disappointment?'

'Mr Barrington,' Slider corrected sternly, 'has disappeared.'

'God, the excitement of your job! What do you mean, disappeared?' Slider told her. 'That doesn't sound too good,' she said. 'Has someone been round there?'

229

'That would be the police equivalent of poking a stick with an 'orse's 'ead 'andle in his ear,' Atherton said. 'Who's going to volunteer for that?'

'But he might have fallen down the stairs or something, and be lying helpless,' she said indignantly.

Slider sighed. 'I was just giving him a chance to turn up or phone in, that's all, in case he'd accidentally taken the day off. I was on the point of ringing his local nick and asking them to send someone round to see.'

'So I should think. Are you going to get off this evening? Because we've a lot to talk about and we still haven't got round to it yet.'

'I don't know when I'll be finished,' he said. 'Not until late, anyway.'

She smiled suddenly. Indeed, she positively grinned. 'Got anywhere else to sleep?'

He smiled slowly. 'Well, as it happens, I sort of haven't.'

As it happened, he didn't get to bed anywhere that night, because the local police, going round to Barrington's house and finding his car outside and no response from within, broke a pane in the front door and let themselves in. They found Barrington in the kitchen, sitting at the table, with the muzzle of his rifle in his mouth and his head – or quite a lot of it, anyway – on the wall behind him.

Joanna, in a brown furry sort of dressing-gown which made her look as if she ought to have a Sieff label sewn to the back of her neck, leaned her elbows to either side of her teacup and watched Slider eating a rather shapeless cheese omelette of her own hasty devising. It was a very late late breakfast and he felt as if he hadn't slept for years. Perhaps sleep was only a habit after all, and you could actually get out of it with practice.

'So it turns out he wasn't married?' she said.

'Never had been. It showed how little anyone knew about him. I feel so bad about him. He asked me to go and have dinner with him on Monday night. Think how lonely he must have been to unbend that far, and I turned him down.'

'It wasn't your fault. People don't commit suicide because

230

of what other people do or don't do, but because of what they are to themselves.'

'I didn't say I felt guilty, I said I felt bad. You should have seen that place! Men have no talent for home-making.'

'Some men. Look at Jim's little bijou nest.'

'True. But Barrington's house was so comfortless. Lots of dark, depressing wood and leather – did you ever see Lawrence of Arabia's house in Dorset? You could tell the man was mentally ill. He had a whole room lined with grey aluminium – walls and ceiling, the whole thing.'

'What, Barrington?'

'No, Lawrence. What Barrington had was a great ugly shelving unit taking up half his sitting-room, that looked as if he'd made it up himself out of old wardrobes. And all his shooting trophies were displayed on it. He was quite a crackshot in the army, and afterwards in his shooting club. Rows and rows of silver cups and shields and framed certificates, and he ends up with his brains all over the washable vinyl.' He looked up at her. 'It was a horrible kitchen, too. The wallpaper had a pattern of red tomatoes and green peppers in squares all over it, and the units were old and painted bright yellow. It must have been like that when he bought it. He'd never done anything to it. What a place to die.'

'Oh don't,' she said.

'And do you know what was in the fridge? Two steaks and a bag of ready-mixed salad. That's what he was going to give me if I went to dinner with him. And a frozen blackcurrant cheesecake in the ice compartment. That was the dinner I didn't join him for. What a lonely man.'

He saw Barrington's rock-like, acne-scarred face in his mind's eye, and the feral eyes looking out from the impassive façade. Year by year the granite must have built up, layer upon layer, separating him more absolutely from any contact, beyond hope of reversal. It must have been like being walled up alive, watching the last bright seed of daylight grow smaller, knowing that when it was gone all that would be left was the darkness and the cold.

Seeing he needed to go on talking about it, Joanna said, 'Why do you think he did it? He didn't leave a note, did he?'

Slider thought of Freddie saying 'They like to tell the tale, old boy.' Not Barrington, though. Too proud. And no-one, in any case, to tell. 'I don't know. I suppose everything just got too much for him. The toughest on the outside are often the most fragile inside.' He shrugged. 'It's the job. We all go through it – but he had no-one's shoulder to cry on. Maybe that made the difference.'

She touched his hand. 'You couldn't have helped, if he'd gone that far.'

'I know. But I could have given him a few moments of human contact, even if it didn't make any difference afterwards.' He sighed and reached for his tea. 'Then I had to go and tell the Coleraines they couldn't bury their dead after all.'

'God, yes, old Radek. I'd almost forgotten him in all the excitement. He's made a hole in our schedules, you know. I've got dates into next year that were with him. I suppose we'll keep the concerts and get a new conductor for them, but we'll lose all the recording sessions. That's a lot of money, and even for us work isn't that thick on the ground.'

'That's a good enough reason to go to his memorial service, then. They're going to hold it next week, whatever happens about the burial.'

'Will you be going?'

'Yes. I'll be the official presence. Want to come with me?'

'If you like.'

'She cried, you know,' he said, remembering. 'Mrs Coleraine. Whatever she said, she did care for her father. She cried on her husband's shoulder, and he patted her and looked as if he wanted to cry himself. He looked as if someone had shoved a stick in his head and given his brains a good stir. He'd been suspecting Marcus, we'd been suspecting him, then it turned out to be Lev. Now he just couldn't grasp the idea that it was Buster who did it after all; and sooner or later Mrs Coleraine is going to put two and two together about her mother. It'll come out at the trial, if not before.'

'There'll be a trial, then?'

'If Buster survives. He's pretty old, and he's got no good reason to live. If he gets pneumonia it'll probably be the end of him. It might be better all round if he didn't make it – it'll

232

be the devil of a case to put across, and it'll cause everyone misery. And how long's he going to survive in gaol anyway? Sometimes I don't like this job.' He hadn't told Joanna about Atherton's momentary lapse in Buster's bathroom. There were some things said that were better forgotten. 'Oh well, it won't be Barrington's problem anyway.'

'You'll have a new boss to get used to,' she said, pushing the toast-rack towards him. 'Won't that be fun?'

He gave her a tired smile. 'It couldn't be any worse than it was before.'

'Any idea who it might be?'

'None at all. I can think of some I'd like more than others, but in the long run it won't make much difference. The job is the job. Clearing up after other people's sin. The public refuse department.'

'In other words,' she said, 'everything's rotten. Life isn't worth living. Might as well end it all here and now.'

He smiled slowly. 'Oh no, I wouldn't say that.'

'I'm glad to hear it.'

'After all, I am going to be able to get rid of the house in Ruislip. The architect in me will rejoice at that.'

She grinned. 'If anyone will buy it.'

'Everyone isn't sensitive like me. And I'll have you know it's a much sought-after area.'

'That only means no-one can find it on the map.'

'There'll be a bit of money left over, after paying back the mortgage and giving Irene her half. Not much, but a bit. Enough for a deposit,' Slider said, and stopped. He felt too tired to start again. Lawyers, maintenance payments, removal men, custody agreements – a swarm of ants would have to pick over the bones of his old life before he could embark on a new one, and even then it would not be a clean start. You never shook free of your baggage, of course: failure and the consequences of it, responsibility, debt. That was why children could run up hills while adults always walked. Lucky Kate and Matthew. Lucky Joanna, for that matter, he thought, with nothing to be sorted out. She was just there, comfortably established, waiting for him to move in. And all he wanted to do now was curl up in her.

He had already forgotten his last sentence, but Joanna

heard it echoing on the following silence. They still hadn't talked about future plans – not even the practicalities of where they was going to live, assuming they were going to live together. But she could see the time wasn't yet, and she wasn't sorry to put it off a bit longer. It was still a bit of a nervous notion. She was used to her little ground-floor flat and her independence, and the second toothbrush on the window-sill would take some adjustment on both sides. She looked at his heavy eyes and grey skin, and said, 'I'll tell you one piece of good news, though.'

'Hmm?'

'I haven't got to go to work until this afternoon, so you can go to bed and get some sleep, and I'll still be here when you wake up.'

He pulled himself back across the chasm and reached over the table to take her hand. 'Sleep? Who needs sleep?' he said.

She grinned. 'You're an ambitious man, Bill Slider. You'll go far.'